THE
DANGERS
OF
THIS NIGHT

THE
DANGERS
OF
THIS NIGHT

An Everett Carr Mystery

Matthew Booth

To Jodi,
With all my love
And with thanks for the encouragement and patience

Praise for the Everett Carr Mysteries

"Everett Carr is…a marvellous protagonist. This is a descriptive, well-paced mystery…a very well-written first in series and a recommended read for mystery lovers."—Fiona Alison, The Historical Novel Society

"A slightly macabre but satisfyingly cosy crime. Booth handles the introduction of his quite significant cast with grace and ease…the opening scenes flow so beautifully together and the murder itself does not disappoint."—Mairi Chong, author of the Dr Cathy Moreland Mysteries, Amazon

"A classic locked room mystery in the finest tradition which will delight old and new readers alike."—Dr M Jones, Amazon

"A classic page-turner and must-read for all fans of Christie, Sayers, James and the country house murder mystery genre."—Ms M Powell, Amazon

"Enter the marvellous and enigmatic Everett Carr, who sees beyond the seemingly impossible… A wonderful homage to the Golden Age of crime."—intheamazone, Amazon reviewer

Chapter One

"I could kill the man and not feel the slightest pang of guilt about it," said Ronald Edgerton.

Everett Carr made no immediate reply. His dark eyes fixed themselves on Edgerton's florid features, on the small vein which throbbed in the man's right temple, and on the tiny droplets of whisky which glistened in the large, dark moustache. Carr took a sip from his glass of Montrachet and dabbed gently at his lips with his handkerchief. There was to be no excess wine on his own impeccable moustache and Imperial beard.

"It doesn't do to go around saying things like that, dear boy," said Carr. "People tend to misunderstand such things, especially when spoken by a respected barrister."

Edgerton smiled. "I doubt anybody would blame me for saying it, even if they did think I was serious. Don't tell me you like Erskine, because I shan't believe a man of your intelligence could be taken in by such a devil, Your Honour."

It was Edgerton's usual form of address, founded both on the legal profession's insistence on respect within its own hierarchy and from a misguided belief that it was amusing. Carr, as ever, smiled at it dismissively.

"I can understand why people find him difficult," he said, refusing to apologise for his evasion. "But it is still unwise to joke about murder."

"Erskine is more than difficult," replied Edgerton with genuine distaste. He smothered it with a dose of whisky.

Carr steepled his fingers and rested them gently against his lips. "What exactly do you have against him?"

"I just don't like the fellow," stated Edgerton gruffly. "Ill-mannered, brusque, opinionated, and far too over-familiar. Calls me Ronny, for Heaven's sake."

Carr smiled. "Yes, I have noted his fondness for shortening one's name."

"Downright insulting, if you ask me."

"But hardly a reason to dislike him."

Edgerton leaned forward. "I don't despise Jacob Erskine because of that. It's his insolence, his spite, his bullying attitude. Young George was serving him with a drink the other day, and he spilt it in Erskine's lap. Pure accident, you know, but Erskine reacted as if it was a deliberate act of malice. Thoroughly humiliated the lad and threatened to have him dismissed."

"Colonel Wharton would never allow such a thing to happen," said Carr.

Edgerton nodded. "Quite so, Your Honour, but George could never be sure of that, as Erskine well knew, so he was at liberty to embarrass the poor boy in front of half the club and make him fearful for his position. Totally uncalled for on Erskine's part but, like I say, the man is a bully. He acts exactly the same in Chambers. He treats our clerks and instructing solicitors with nothing less than contempt."

Carr had temporarily overlooked the fact that Erskine and Edgerton were barristers in the same set of Chambers, Darrow Square, but the memory now stirred in his mind. "Does nobody take issue with him over it?"

Edgerton scoffed. "Sir Julius Keane has never distinguished himself as Head of Chambers, Your Honour. You know him well enough. Keane is too weak, too afraid of confrontation, so you can imagine how a man like Erskine would deal with him."

Carr was not inclined to comment further. "I witnessed a rather disagreeable altercation between Erskine and Vincent Overdale the other day, too. Some quite ugly words were exchanged."

Edgerton snorted. "I suppose Overdale gave as good as he got. There's another one who is rather too sure of himself for my liking."

They were sitting in the principal bar of the Icarus Club, one of London's more exclusive gentlemen's clubs, situated in discreet mews a short distance from Grosvenor Square. The club had been established in the early days of the nineteenth century. Its founders had been a select group of academic, scientific, and literary notables, each one having achieved success in his chosen field with determination and perseverance. They were acutely aware, however, of both the need and the desire not to allow their success to smother their origins and they were determined that personal and professional hubris should not destroy them. They had shared a common belief that man must strive to greatness but, equally, he must not allow his success to blind him to his worldly status. It was this very doctrine which had prompted the founders of the club to name it after the son of Daedalus. Icarus had seemed to them to be a suitable symbol of this fundamental requirement of the human race not to misjudge its place or overreach its limits. As if the name itself was not sufficient proof of the founders' intentions, an imposing oil painting of the myth's tragic ending was commissioned and placed in a gilt frame over the main staircase of the club. It had hung there ever since, so that the slim, muscular form of the drowned Icarus, freshly pulled from the Icarian Sea, his ill-fated wings spread out behind him like a feathered shroud, remained the impressive if foreboding figurehead of the club's interior. The painting may have endured, but the original purpose of the club and its membership requirements had dwindled over the years. Some of the members had been known to complain that the exclusivity of the club had been permitted to lapse with the adoption of less stringent criteria for inclusion into it. Others counter-argued that the club had to move with the times if it was to persist into the future. Whichever side of the debate was correct depended on one's point of view, but any perceived lowering of standards was a complaint evident only to the more traditional members of the club. An outsider would never have detected any collapse in elitism in the club and, to those refused membership, its selectiveness appeared to be as rigid and as superior as ever.

The club was extensive as well as exclusive. It consisted of three floors, each with a winding staircase connecting it to the others, and each lined with luxuriant scarlet carpeting. The bow windows, glaring out over the gardens of the square below it, were latticed, with heavy velvet curtains draped decorously along the length of each of them. The corridors were long and wide, with rooms leading off to either side, the walls of which were either oak-panelled or lined with leather volumes of scientific studies, academic dissertations, and literary classics through the centuries. Each floor boasted a bar, identical to the one in which Carr and Edgerton were sitting, and a selection of reading and gaming rooms. The restaurant, renowned for its rare roast beef and French influences, was on the second floor and the bedrooms, all said to be the envy of any Mayfair hotel, were on the uppermost landing. Everything about the club suggested opulent privilege, its richness just as evident in its furnishings as it was in its food and wine.

"Overdale is a trifle impetuous, perhaps," Carr was saying. He sipped some of his wine and gently dabbed at his mouth once more.

Edgerton shook his head. "There's something funny about him. I don't know what, but he's not right somehow."

"The young are always a mystery to their elders," observed Carr.

Edgerton laughed. "I don't know why you insist on behaving as if you're older than you are."

Carr shrugged and began to nurse the shattered bones in his knee. "Perhaps because I feel old, my dear fellow."

Edgerton inclined his head. "I think it's because you miss the madness of the circus."

Carr smiled. "I have no desire to step foot inside the Old Bailey ever again, I assure you. My love affair with the place is over, and I am much more content in my retirement, thank you."

Edgerton drained his glass and waved an order to the barman for a second. "You can't keep away from crime entirely, though, can you?"

Carr lowered his head, fighting against the memory to which Edgerton referred. It had been several months since Carr had been instrumental in solving a violent murder at a country house owned by an old friend. It was not an episode in his life upon which he liked to reflect, but Carr was too polite to reprimand his companion for bringing it up. Nevertheless, he did not feel obliged to discuss the matter.

"That is all over and forgotten, my boy," he replied.

If Edgerton recognised Carr's veiled request to alter the topic of their conversation, he ignored it. "The newspapers seemed to suggest you had a hand in identifying the killer. Fancy yourself as a sleuth instead of a judge now, do we?"

"I have no such pretensions, and I would thank you not to think it of me."

Edgerton bowed his head in silent apology. He ordered another glass of the excellent wine for Carr and smiled back at him. "Let us stop all talk of murder."

Carr stroked his Imperial beard delicately. "I would be grateful if we did."

Even without Edgerton's relinquishment of the topic of violent death, they would have been prohibited from further discussion of it by the arrival of a tall, slim man of around fifty years of age. His hair was dark, swept back from a high forehead, and the features beneath it were both sensitive and intelligent. The eyes were blue, but so pale that they might be mistaken for grey, and they glittered from behind the lenses of a pair of horn-rimmed spectacles, balanced perfectly on the long, aquiline nose. He sat down in between Carr and Edgerton, nodding a welcome to both, and he ordered himself a whisky.

"Just a small one, George," Leonard Faraday said to the young waiter. He watched George walk away in order to complete the order, before turning back to face his fellow members of the club. "I suppose you heard about the incident with young George and Jacob Erskine."

Edgerton mumbled agreement. "We were just discussing it. Outrageous behaviour on Erskine's part. It was obviously an accident."

Faraday agreed. "But you know what Erskine is. He doesn't care what he says or who he hurts."

"We should have blackballed him when we had the chance," declared Edgerton.

"Wisdom in hindsight," agreed Faraday. His whisky arrived, and he toasted his companions before taking a long sip from the glass. "I needed that, I must say."

"Having a bad day, Faraday?" asked Edgerton with a smile.

"Trying to balance the club accounts. A monthly chore, don't you know."

"One of the perils of being secretary of this den of iniquity, no doubt."

Edgerton laughed along with Faraday. "You wanted the post, you know, so you must live with its drawbacks as well as its privileges."

The club secretary conceded the point by draining his glass and signalling to George that a second would be both welcome and necessary. The three members fell into companionable silence until the young waiter had delivered Faraday's second drink.

Carr began to stroke the silver handle of his walking stick. "It wasn't only George who crossed Erskine this week. I was just telling Edgerton that I witnessed a heated confrontation between him and young Mr Overdale."

Faraday paused for a moment, his glass lifted half-way to his lips, and his eyes shifted to Carr. "Really? About what?"

Faraday had been swift to appear nonchalant, but Carr had detected something close to fear in the pale, blue eyes of the club secretary. "I can't really say. I didn't eavesdrop, you understand. I only saw them from a distance, but it was undeniably a healthy quarrel."

"I can well believe it," said Edgerton. "Overdale is impetuous, and Erskine is argumentative. It naturally makes for a difficult combination."

"That is certainly true," said Faraday. "Still, I cannot think of any reason why Erskine and Overdale should argue. Did you not overhear any part of it, Carr?"

Carr stroked his injured knee. "Nothing definite, but I had the idea that Overdale owed Erskine some money."

"Money for what?" asked Faraday.

Carr shrugged his shoulders. "I couldn't say."

But Edgerton was not so reserved. "Gambling, no doubt. We all know Erskine is fond of the cards, and I daresay I am not the only one who suspects that his luck is not entirely natural."

"That is a very serious and offensive accusation to make without anything in support of it," cautioned Carr.

Edgerton was resolute. "Erskine is exactly the sort of man who would cheat at cards, and it's pointless to pretend otherwise. Have you seen him play? His luck is beyond credibility."

"He might simply be proficient," argued Carr. "You cannot malign a man in such a fashion just because you dislike him. To do so is to be as offensive as Erskine himself."

Edgerton was silenced not by the stark confrontation of Carr's words but by the calm and gentle manner in which the rebuke had been delivered. The barrister leaned back in his chair and cradled his glass in his lap, as chastened as a recalcitrant child who had made unpalatable remarks during a Sunday service.

"Vincent Overdale does not play cards," remarked Faraday after a moment's silence. "If he owed money to Erskine, it must have been for something else."

Carr glanced across to him. "Something else? Such as what?"

"I couldn't possibly say," replied Faraday with a smile.

Carr contemplated the club secretary for some moments, his instincts turning his bones to ice, but Faraday offered no more elucidation, and Carr made no further enquiry. It was only later, after death had struck at the Icarus Club, that the conversation recalled itself to his mind.

Chapter Two

On the following afternoon, Margaret Erskine poured a second glass of wine and glanced across at her husband. Jacob was sitting reading a newspaper, his lunch plate empty, but his own glass of wine barely touched. The delicate trickle against the crystal glass seemed to Margaret to sound like the roar of a waterfall in the toxic silence of the dining room. The meal had not been enjoyable, but they so seldom were that she had grown accustomed to their discomfort, to such an extent that she now barely registered either her anxiety at the anticipation of mealtimes or her relief at their conclusion. There was no reason why a meal should be any less unbearable than the rest of her marriage.

"Bit early for a second glass, wouldn't you say?" sniffed Erskine.

Margaret had expected the disapproval and, as if to counter it, she drank before she responded. "It is only a small glass, Jacob, and the wine is so very good."

He made no reply, and Margaret was not sure she had expected one. The rustle of his newspaper when he turned the pages was a substitute for any subsequent declaration of his dissatisfaction.

As she glared at him across the expanse of the dining table, Margaret wondered whether there was any trace left of the man with whom she had fallen in love three decades ago. Certainly, very little of the man she had known seemed to remain in the malevolent, corrupted figure with whom she now shared her life. Age had contorted his once radiant blond hair into the colour of untreated copper and, likewise, it had twisted the proud mouth into a coiled snake of displeasure and malice. The moustache, which once had burned so brightly, was now yellowed more by tobacco than sunlight, and the liver spots on his hands had replaced the tanned skin with which she had been entranced in their youth. His brown eyes, once so wide with eagerness for life, were now narrowed by bitterness and spite. It was not simply that he had aged. It was as if Jacob Erskine had allowed himself to be corrupted by his experiences, his excesses, and his weaknesses, so that they were all etched on his face, as if every scar, every crease of skin, and every greyed hair was an individual sin carved into his being.

Slowly, over the years, they had drifted away from family and friends and, in retrospect, Margaret felt sure that it had been because Jacob's personality had distanced and isolated them from others. Once, he had been enthusiastic; now, he was domineering. Where, in youth, he had been determined, he was now intimidating. He once talked about the survival of the fittest; now, he seemed only interested in destroying the weak. Over time, people had noticed this change in his nature long before realisation had dawned in Margaret's own mind. Social invitations were politely declined, reciprocal ones became less frequent and, finally, so rare as to be non-existent. Visits from family, letters, postcards from foreign travel all dwindled into nothing. By the time she had reached her fiftieth birthday, Margaret Erskine had become a lonely, abandoned woman whose world consisted primarily of a man she no longer loved.

She drank more wine and swallowed back tears. Across from her, Erskine himself raised his glass to his lips, and she watched his throat jump as he swallowed the wine, forcing herself not to interpret the gesture as a mockery of her. She knew she had begun to take solace in the stuff, and she was aware of his disapproval of her on account of it, but she refused to allow him to deprive her of what she saw as her only remaining pleasure. Still more, she refused to allow him to make her feel guilty for executing her own choices.

Executing...

That the word should have occurred to her startled her for a moment. She could not recall the first time she had contemplated murdering her husband, but she knew that it had not been an isolated incident. How often had she watched him take wine with a meal or guzzle whisky in his study and wished that she had placed something in the glass or the bottle beforehand? Was it as frequently as when she walked past his gun cupboard and thought about taking one of the shotguns out of there and turning it onto him? She could not calculate the number of times, but it would be no less and no more than the number of occasions when she had held a knife in her hand and wondered what it would be like to plunge it into the space in his chest where she knew a heart had beaten once and where, she must assume, it continued to beat. The vivid realism of her fantasies would always make her tremble and, in her private moments, she would buckle under their horror, and she would feel the cold tears against her flushed cheeks. Even now, almost automatically, she wiped her palm across her eyes but, for once, there were no tears there to be brushed away.

She became aware of his voice and the rustle of the newspaper as he cast it aside. "I'm going to the club after dinner this evening. Just so you know. I might well spend the night there."

Margaret felt a surge of relief swirl inside her, but it was tainted by an underlying fear. "Will you be gambling again?"

Erskine narrowed his eyes as if she was something unpleasant which he had to remove from the house by using a glass and a piece of card. "I don't see how whether I gamble or not has anything to do with you but, since you ask, I shall probably have a couple of hands, yes."

"I do wish you wouldn't."

"Why? In case I squander some of my own money, and I can't keep this roof over your head, I suppose. That would be a disaster for you, wouldn't it?"

"I just don't like you gambling, that's all."

Erskine laughed, but it had more of a ring of cruelty to it than humour. "Poor old Peg. She doesn't want to lose the life she's been given, but she hasn't got the ability to protect it herself."

The shortening of her name was as deliberate. She hated it, and Erskine knew as much, and his insistence on using the diminutive was a sneer of condescension rather than a term of endearment.

"Please don't be like this," Margaret whispered.

"The money we have is because of me," sneered Erskine, "so please be good enough to allow me to spend some of it how I see fit."

Margaret knew better than to argue, but there was something so malicious in his manner that she could not prevent herself. "I'm more than aware that you've made the money, Jacob, but that doesn't necessarily mean you can waste it. We are married, after all. What I say matters."

"To you, perhaps."

And he had smiled as he spoke. The words themselves, their implication, were hurtful enough, but the insolent and denigrating smile which had accompanied them intensified the pain. They smote her feelings with as much force as if he had struck her in the face with his powerful fists. More vividly than ever, the images of the poisoned glass, the shotgun, and the knife came into her mind, and the terrible, bloody consequences seemed to flood her brain with outrage and violence. So quickly did they assault her mind that she thought she let out a stifled, frightened gasp of air, but she couldn't be sure.

Slowly, as if uncertain that her legs would bear her, she rose from the table. He paid no attention to her, turning his glare back to his newspaper, but the mortifying smile remained fixed in place. She walked slowly along the length of the room, her mind fixed on her intentions, and when she looked down at her hands, she was surprised to see that they were still. It was as if they were the hands of someone else entirely, someone unafraid of the man sitting in the chair in front of her, someone to whom he was as insignificant as she was to him.

She was beside his chair now. The smell of him was suddenly prevalent in her senses. The cologne, too liberally applied to be anything other than oppressive, the stale cigar smoke, the faintest trace of the lunchtime wine. The glass was beside his plate, still barely touched, the crystal glittering in the afternoon light from outside. It was in her hand before she had time to register the action, and, with a similar detachment, the wine had landed in his face before she had the opportunity to process the thrust of her arm and the arc of the liquid.

For a moment, he remained motionless, his body paralysed by surprise and confusion. His lips lapped foolishly at the drops of wine which were scattered around his moustache and chin. His eyes blinked away the sting of the alcohol, and his nose twitched as the drink tickled its bridge and tip. His mouth moved in outrage, but no words came from it, although short, rasping breaths wheezed from between his teeth. He took the napkin from his lap and rubbed at his face vigorously. As the cloth was brought away from his face, Margaret saw that his cheeks were now flushed with anger, and those tobacco-stained teeth were visible through the furious snarl. With a growl and a curse, he hauled himself at her.

Here was the retribution.

He was in her face, his voice raging in her ears, although none of the words penetrated through to her. It was just the savage roar of a beast, spitting venom and bile at her with such viciousness that she had no choice but to cower from it, her eyes closed tightly against it. Spittle and excess wine flecked her cheeks and chin. He had pinned her arms to her side, his huge fingers clenching her upper arms so tightly that she knew, even in her subconscious, that there would be bruises at some point later in the day. She had the sensation of the world vibrating around her, although it took her some time to realise that he was shaking her. Helplessly, unable to fight against him, she felt herself go limp in that iron grip, like a rabbit once its neck has been broken.

And then there came the double fire in her cheeks, not unexpected, but fierce enough to make her catch her breath, the heat erupting on either cheek in quick succession. It had been so vicious, so aggressive, that she wondered whether the palm and back of his hand burned as deeply as her face from the impact. Her senses had barely registered the pain before her lungs exploded inside her, the breath within them exiting her mouth with a grunt of agony, as she crumpled against him in a bizarre embrace which was so intense that he had trouble extracting his fist from her stomach. She was aware suddenly of falling to the ground, the varnished floorboards soothingly cold against her reddened face. A trail of spittle stretched from her mouth, and she coughed it away. She could just about hear his guttural breathing above the rushing of blood in her own ears. Her eyes opened,

12

and she saw his polished shoes and the hems of his trousers, but when she tried to raise her gaze towards him, he was nothing more than a blurred image of himself. The feet moved, and she prepared herself for a further onslaught, but none came. Instead, he slammed his foot loudly on the floor, inches from her face, causing her to clamp shut her eyes and whimper in fear. She heard him snigger and, as the polished shoes turned on their heel to leave the room, she heard him begin to whistle before the door closed behind him.

She felt as if she could stay there for the remainder of the day, huddled on the floor, like a child balled in fear under the covers of the bed after a nightmare, but she knew she had to move. For a servant to find her in this state or, worse, for Jacob himself to return and witness it would be unbearable to her. She had to move, and she had to regain her poise. Her breath rasping in her throat, Margaret pushed herself onto her knees, her palms flat against the floor. She remained like that for a moment, her breathing becoming steadier and the nausea which had engulfed her finally beginning to subside. She got to her feet, steadying herself against the table, and she dropped into a chair. Grabbing the carafe of wine, she poured what was left of it into her glass and gulped it down, telling herself it was being drunk not for pleasure, but out of necessity and that, accordingly, there was no shame in having it.

Shame, the familiar emotion. This attack had been the latest of many. She could not recall the first time he had beaten her. Every blow, every stroke of his belt, and every pull of her hair seemed to have merged into a haze of continuous cruelty. There must have been a first time, but its details were now confused in her mind with those of each subsequent assault. Long after each one, she would feel still the pain of his fist or his foot on her face and stomach, she would feel the tenderness on the skin across the back of her legs and her buttocks from the leather of his belt or whichever length of cane he had chosen, and she would feel her hatred of him rise for supremacy over her own agony. But neither of those emotions would ever triumph over the shame which followed every incident.

Margaret knew it was irrational. She knew the shame should not be hers but his, but he showed no trace of it. She would always feel ashamed after he was done with her, and it was the greatest torment of all. Perhaps it was her inability to leave Jacob on account of the violence; perhaps it was her failure to fight back; perhaps it was her foolish habit of blaming herself for causing it to happen. Perhaps it was all of those things. Margaret doubted she would ever know for sure, suspecting that the truth of why he beat her and why she seemed to allow him was too complex ever to be fully understood. She shook her head. No, she did not permit this to happen. It was not that which haunted her; rather, it was the lack of courage to walk out of the door and never to return which she could not understand. It was the right thing to do, and she knew as much; but what she, and possibly nobody else in the world, would ever understand was why she felt unable to do so. All that was certain, she knew, was the pain and the shame of it all.

Her mind once more thought about a life without him, without his bullying, his violence, and his condescension. She thought about Hector Wharton, a man so different to Jacob. He seemed to be a protector rather than an assailant, a man in whose company she might feel safe instead of intimidated. He had sparked an impression in her of love, a suggestion that perhaps there was still goodness in the world, and she had allowed herself to begin to believe it whenever she was in his company. But, like an unprecedented raincloud in a summer afternoon sky, her mind would recall Jacob Erskine and the legal and moral bond of matrimony which tied her to him. Her dreams of a life with anyone else were futile, no matter how thrilled she might be in someone else's company, or how strongly another man might be attracted to her. None of it mattered; she could never be with Wharton or anyone else, not now. When she had made her vows, in happier and less brutal times, she had meant them. Now, no matter how much she might regret them and wish them nullified forever, she knew that she had to abide by them. Margaret Erskine did not believe in divorce.

For better or worse, regardless of any of the beatings. For richer or poorer, no matter how much of their money he gambled away and spent on his own pleasures. Till death did them part, no matter how it came about.

Margaret Erskine's mind began to fantasise again about the murder of her husband and, as the imaginings became more vivid, she began silently to sob.

Chapter Three

In his office at the Icarus Club, Colonel Hector Wharton took the Mark VI Webley from the drawer of his desk and wondered whether he might be compelled to use it for one last time.

The gun had been at his side throughout his service during the war, and Wharton had used it on more occasions than he liked to admit. How many men he had killed personally, he could not say, but he suspected it was numerous. However, Wharton tried not to feel unduly guilty about the lives he had taken with the weapon which he now held in his hands. When he had killed, it had been his duty to his country, as an act of war, and to feel anything to the contrary was futile. And yet, he suspected that each of the men he had seen die at his hand had taken something of his own soul to the grave with them. Wharton was conscious of his duty, but that did not mean that he was without heart or emotion, and the dreams about his experiences in Passchendaele, and of the men he had killed there, were no less vivid or troublesome simply because they could be justified by the honour of serving his country or by the official alibi of war. But the thoughts of death which had passed through his mind over the past few weeks had no such alibi to excuse them. They were not sanctioned by a stamped paper from Whitehall, and nor were they excused by the subsequent placing of gold and ribbon on one's breast. They were private thoughts of the murder of a man for personal reasons.

Wharton may not have been able to recall the faces of all the men he had killed, but the details of his first meeting with Margaret Erskine were as vivid in his mind as if they had happened that morning. He could still remember the velvet Grecian evening gown, as deeply coloured as the claret which had accompanied the grilled beef at dinner, and the gentle elegance with which she had accepted his offer of a cigarette and sipped at her Martini. She had listened to his conversation with a genuine interest, not with the forced fascination which Wharton had noticed some society women had feigned in order to speak to him. There was no trace of sycophancy in Margaret Erskine, only the sense of an honest intelligence.

"You belong to the same club as my husband, I believe, Colonel Wharton," she had said as he handed her a drink from the tray which was being passed around.

"The Icarus Club, yes. I am the Chairman, as a matter of fact." Had he expected her to be impressed by this almost childish announcement of hierarchical superiority? If he had, he had been rewarded with little more than a raise of the eyebrows and a bow of the head. Perhaps that had been enough for him.

"I'm afraid my husband spends more time there than is good for either of us," she had replied. "He gambles rather too much for my liking."

Wharton had not considered it politic to enter into a debate on the subject. "We all have our vices, surely?"

Margaret had looked at him, her eyes squinting through the smoke of her cigarette. "Have we, colonel? What vices could you possibly have?"

He had not replied, except to smile widely at her. They had drunk their cocktails innocently, but neither one of them had allowed their eyes to deviate for long from the other for the remainder of the pre-prandial conversation.

Looking back, Wharton wondered what might have happened if he had told her the truth at that dinner party. That he despised her husband, that Erskine was a disgrace to the club and to himself, and that of all the injustices Wharton had experienced in his half-century of life, the fact that Jacob Erskine had married Margaret instead of him was the cruellest of all. Wharton had experienced love only in terms of his affinity for the army and his patriotism. The love of a woman, given and reciprocated, was an unknown quantity to him and an affair, not to mention marriage, had never been foremost in his mind. There had been experiences, of course, but they had been fleeting and nothing short of functional, the repercussions of too many drinks on leave from service, when no consequences of the dalliances had been entertained either by Wharton himself or the girls concerned. But serious romantic entanglement, the sort of relationship he had experienced in literature and music only, had never formed part of his ambition or his nature.

Margaret Erskine had changed all that.

It had all occurred too late, of course, and it was the inevitability of that fact which seemed to Wharton to be the cruellest thing of all. It would not be so unbearable if he did not feel sure that Margaret reciprocated his feelings. He was convinced of it and, if it were not too arrogant to say so, he thought she had done so since that first meeting, just as he had done. Love had waited decades to strike him but, when it had, it had done so without hesitation or uncertainty and Wharton felt sure that Margaret had been similarly afflicted. But she was married and, social requirements aside, Wharton felt unable to act on his desires. He was proud of his sense of honour and duty, and they had been a credit to him in his professional and private life to date; but, where Margaret was concerned, they were nothing less than a curse.

How differently it might all have been if he had met her first, if she had been unmarried when she walked into that room in her claret dress and sipped Martinis with him, before sitting opposite him over the grilled beef. How much happier they would be if Jacob Erskine did not stand between them. Wharton had hated Erskine on sight, long before his feelings for Margaret had developed, but that hatred had intensified because of this adulterous, but unrequited love.

How much easier it would be if Erskine just died.

As soon as the thought entered his head, the revolver began to grow heavy in Wharton's hands. He placed it down on the desk and stared at it for a long moment. He was now no longer sure why he had taken it out of the drawer. As a reminiscence of days gone by or as a contemplation of a time to come? It stared back at him, the chamber and barrel seeming to dare him to use it to bring his dark fantasies to life. Wharton shook his head, as if to banish the temptation back into the wilderness, but, without a use for it, either as a memory or as a weapon, it seemed to Wharton to be ridiculous in its idleness.

He began to clean it, if only to convince himself that he had taken it out for a reason and not simply to contemplate the death of a man he reviled, the same man who was, however unwittingly, preventing the happiness both of Wharton and the woman he knew he loved. He had dismantled the weapon and was cleaning the cylinders with a solvent and brush when there was a knock at the door. Wharton put down the gun and the brush, and dropped the cloth he had used to handle the revolver onto the desk.

"Come in."

The door opened, and a large, heavily built man stepped inside. He was dressed in an opulent, green doorman's coat, double-breasted, with ornamental buttons and gold, braided epaulets. He carried a glossed top hat, and his trousers were the striped variety of a mourning suit. The elegance and formality of the uniform were at odds with the build and features of the man. His skin was coarse, scarred by the usual adolescent skin complaints of years ago, and his nose was bulbous and misshapen, speaking of more than one injury both inside and outside of a boxing ring. The lips were thin, turned downwards, giving the impression of a caricature of a Victorian miser. The head itself, free from any hair, was a dome whose whiteness seemed more prominent because of the crimson of the cheeks and the deepening purple of the broken nose.

"You wanted to see me, colonel," said Cyril Parsons, standing to attention in front of Wharton, as if he was reporting for duty in the barracks, twenty years previously.

"I did, Parsons. Thank you for coming."

Wharton leaned back in his chair. He watched Parsons' eyes fall on the revolver and take in the open drawer of the desk where it was kept. Parsons frowned slightly, almost imperceptibly, but a subtle clearing of the colonel's throat brought the doorman's attention back to him. Parsons looked into the hard, brown eyes of his superior and held their gaze. He knew that Wharton considered him to be an uncouth, gruff stain on the carpets of the

Icarus Club, but Parsons cared as little about that as he did about almost everything else. Wharton's smooth, closely shaved cheeks and the precise moustache with its own clipped authority, which mirrored those of its wearer, were as distasteful to Parsons as his own appearance was to Wharton. The luxuriance of the colonel's dark hair, only slightly flecked with grey and swept back from its intelligent forehead, prompted in Parsons a similar repugnance that his own baldness fuelled in Wharton. As the colonel thrived on the formality of dressing properly, of ensuring that one's appearance was immaculate, so Parsons detested the confinements of his uniform. He liked nothing more than shedding himself of the stiff collar and the suffocating tunic and coat he was compelled to wear, like a snake ridding itself of its dead, scaly, useless skin.

Parsons' eyes flickered to the revolver. "Souvenir of the madness?"

Wharton grunted, placing the rag he used to clean the gun over the weapon's components. Parsons watched him, his eyes lingering on the mechanics of the revolver. Slowly, dimly, the sounds of war returned to his memory. The roar of guns, the explosions, the shouts of agonised determination blending with the cries of anguish, all of them seemed to come from a distant part of his consciousness, swelling until they threatened to burst his temples. Parsons felt the familiar prickle of sweat on the sides of his head and at the nape of his neck.

He was brought back to reality by the gruff noise of Wharton's voice. "Parsons, I don't want to have to warn you about this again, do you understand?"

"Warn me about what?"

"You know full well about what."

And, perhaps, that was true. There were only two reasons Parsons was ever called in to see the club chairman. If it wasn't one, it was the other. "Don't tell me someone has claimed to witness me drunk on duty again, colonel, because I won't believe you. It isn't true. I wouldn't do that, not after last time."

"Have you taken the pledge, Parsons?" There was no attempt to disguise the mockery in Wharton's voice.

"Only in this place, colonel. On my own time, it's my business." Parsons glared, daring the colonel to contradict him. "If it isn't the bottle, it must be the cards."

Wharton rose from the desk with a curse. "Must you be so damned cavalier about it all? This club has standards, Parsons, and gambling is not amongst them."

Parsons sniggered. "I must have mistaken the gaming rooms for something else, then."

"You know perfectly well what I mean, man. Members are at liberty to indulge in a few hands with each other, of course, but you are an employee, not a member. Your gambling on the premises is a breach of the rules and of your contract of employment."

Parsons was sneering now. "I'm not good enough to touch your cards, is that it, colonel? You'd do better to speak to the organ grinder, not the monkey. Have a word with Mr Erskine, why don't you?"

Wharton started, his recent thoughts about Jacob Erskine chiming in his mind. "What about Erskine?"

Parsons frowned. "The poker nights are his idea, colonel. I'm only ever there at his invitation. Ask anyone who plays. We're only there because of Erskine."

Wharton's fists had clenched, an almost instinctive reaction to the mention of Erskine's name, and his breathing had shortened. Parsons, for his part, remained belligerently obstinate, his eyes hardened with confrontation and his lips twisted in defiance. A moment passed between the two men, although neither of them acknowledged it. Wharton placed his balled fists into the pockets of his trousers and walked slowly from behind his desk.

"I shall take it up with Erskine, rest assured," he said. If Parsons believed him on the point, he did not show it. "Be that as it may, however, the fact remains that you are not permitted to gamble on the club premises. I'm sorry, Parsons, but you leave me with no choice."

Parsons stiffened, balancing his weight evenly on his feet, as if about to prepare for a boxing bout. "Are you throwing me out, colonel?"

Wharton shook his head. "If I hear that you have participated in any gambling sessions with Erskine or anyone else whilst in the club, on duty or not, I shall have no option other than to dismiss you. Are we clear?"

"Crystal," hissed Erskine, leaning into Wharton's face. "Is that all?"

Wharton held his glare for a moment, before nodding his head. Parsons smiled malevolently, turned on his heel, and left the room. He had not been intimidated by Wharton, even if the colonel had intended it, but what had been said was necessary. Whether Parsons would take heed of it, however, was a different matter entirely. Nevertheless, Wharton would not hesitate to carry out his threat if he was compelled to do so. It was not only a matter of duty but one of honour, both his own and that of the Icarus Club itself.

The revelation that Jacob Erskine had been the instigator of these illicit poker games had jolted Wharton but, in retrospect, it should not have surprised him. Erskine was exactly the type to arrange such things, without giving any consideration to the rules and reputation of the club. There would have to be some discussion about Erskine's continued membership because of it, and Wharton made a mental memorandum to speak to Leonard Faraday about it. Erskine's conduct was yet another reason for Wharton to despise the man. Taken in conjunction with his feelings for Margaret, it might be said that Wharton had more than sufficient reason to wish Erskine dead.

Slowly, Wharton returned to his desk and sat down. With deliberate and careful fingers, he resumed the cleaning of his old service revolver, wondering once again whether he would have cause to fire it and, if so, whether he would be able to find the courage to do so.

Chapter Four

I t was early evening when Jacob Erskine arrived at the Icarus Club. The air was chilled but not unbearable, the dark skies above showing no sign of any impending rainfall, so that Erskine had not brought his umbrella with him. Otherwise, he was dressed formally, as the club required him to be after the hour of six o'clock, although there had been the usual frustrations at tying his bow tie. Erskine advocated formal dressing for dinner, at home and at the club, but the intricacies of his tie were a daily challenge for him. He resolutely refused to indulge in a made-up affair, insisting that he would not be championed by a piece of decorative silk, but the ritual of tying the thing irritated and confounded him. How people like Everett Carr were able to produce knots which were so refined, so perfectly imperfect as to be the sign of a true gentleman, was beyond him. But, after fifteen minutes, he had succeeded in accomplishing an acceptable effect, although it meant that he had left home for the club in an ill temper.

It was not only the tie which had vexed him. The lunchtime incident with Margaret remained in his mind, and his anger began to flare once more as his mind recalled her insolence in throwing the wine into his face. It was a momentary rage, however, swiftly replaced by a sense of satisfaction at his customary gratification of bringing Margaret to her knees, of forcing tears to her eyes, of humiliating and terrifying her. He had never understood why she goaded him in such a fashion, thereby prompting the reprisals which she knew must come. He could only assume that, in some sickening and perverse way, she enjoyed what she compelled him to do. Some women were like that, Erskine thought, and he had experienced some of them in his youth. Erskine smiled, recalling his pleasure at seeing them all, including Margaret, broken, humbled, and submissive.

By the time he arrived at the club, his mood had lightened. As he crossed the square, he whistled to himself, his mind now reaching forward in time to the cards and their own, unique thrill. Erskine was feeling lucky, as if the red and black sparks of chance would fall in his favour all evening, bringing with them their own taste of temptation and greed. Not that it was all a matter of luck, he thought. There was skill and intelligence behind every successful gamble, and he knew that he was blessed with both. It was people like Cyril Parsons, blessed with neither, who would be no worse off after every hand than if they put a match to their money in the first instance. Erskine's smile faded, and his brow creased in anger, as he recalled how much Parsons owed him in outstanding debts. Not a king's ransom by any means, but enough for Parsons to struggle to pay, and a figure high enough for Erskine never to consider allowing it to pass by unpaid.

He could see now that Parsons was on duty. Even dressed in the finery of the regulation gabardine coat, with its golden braids, and the glossed top hat contrasting with the flawless white of the chamois gloves, Parsons looked like a thug. The man was too large to convey any sense of elegance; his coarse skin, the narrow eyes, and the voice which belonged in the vilest pub in the East End all made a mockery not only of the garments he was compelled to wear but also the club in whose name he wore them. Erskine wondered, not for the first time, why Wharton and the club bothered to employ the man. If and when Erskine ever found himself in Wharton's place, a possibility which was not so remote as some people might think, one of his first changes to the club would be to replace Parsons.

Erskine was ascending the steps to the entrance to the club now, and Parsons had opened the door for him. Erskine glared at the doorman who, in turn, returned the stare without any pretence of respect for or fear of the man.

"I want what you owe me, Parsons," declared Erskine. "You've had more than enough time to pay."

"I'll get you the money," murmured the doorman.

"Some men would not have been as patient as me. Remember that." Erskine leaned forward, his voice lowering. "There is such a thing as honour, Parsons. I doubt a bruiser like you knows much about a gentleman's word, but it counts for something. Your word counts for nothing. I want the money. By the end of the week."

"I told you I'd get it."

Erskine grunted. "You told me that last week too. Perhaps you don't realise what a scandal not paying your debts is. You don't mix in polite company, I daresay, but even in the grubby holes you inhabit, not paying your debts must be a cause for disowning a man."

Parsons pointed a finger into Erskine's breast. "What will your opinion of me matter if they throw us both out of this place? What will your debt mean then, Mr Erskine?"

If the doorman had hoped to unsettle the member, he had failed. Instead of alarm, it was sneering derision which crept across Erskine's face. "What are you talking about?"

"Wharton knows what you've been up to." Parsons was smiling as he spoke, a crooked twist of his lips which was only one beat away from being a snarl. "Against club rules, these little frolics of yours, Mr Erskine. Members only, see? You're not supposed to gamble with me and my sort."

"I gamble with whomever I choose."

"Not here." Parsons pointed through the open door, towards the foyer of the club. "Had me in his office in there, Wharton did. Gave me a proper warning, no room for doubt."

"And you told him I was responsible for our little get-togethers?"

"Damned right, I did."

Erskine contemplated the doorman for a moment, although the expression of amused disdain did not leave his face. "Do you think that scares me, Parsons? Do you think I'm intimidated either by you or Wharton? I've seen off better men than both of you, believe me."

Parsons smiled. "I don't know whether you're frightened of anyone, Mr Erskine, and I don't much care. I'm just telling you what's what, that's all."

"Wharton only has power over either of us for as long as he is chairman of this place. And he won't be forever."

"But he's the gaffer for now, and that's what matters. Watch your step, Mr Erskine, that's all I'm saying. A friendly warning, like," he added with a cold smile.

Erskine let out a low, cruel laugh. "What makes you think Wharton and the club would take your word over mine, in any case? People know what you are, Parsons. A drunkard, an unstable and worthless wreck. Do you think they'd believe you over one of their own?"

"From what I've seen of you, sir, you're more like me than any of them." Parsons could see that the words had stung, however much Erskine had tried to conceal the fact.

Erskine pushed his finger into Parsons' chest. "I want my money. If I don't get it, you're done."

Parsons allowed the member to push past him and into the foyer of the club. He watched as Erskine removed his coat and hung it in his usual place in the cloakroom. Erskine checked his appearance in the large mirror on the opposite wall of the foyer and assured himself of its suitability. It was as he walked up the few steps from the foyer into the main corridor that Parsons called his name.

"Maybe people aren't as afraid of you as you imagine, sir," said the doorman. "I may not wear my decorations on my sleeve like Colonel Wharton, but that doesn't mean I wasn't awarded them. I've shot better and more dangerous men than you, Erskine. Crack-shot, me, you know. One good thing to come out of the war." He raised an outstretched index finger towards the member. "I could get you between the eyes from here without blinking, given the chance."

Erskine did not reply. Despite the distance between them, Parsons could see the smile flicker across the man's face. It was not a question of mockery or of disguising any sense of fear. Parsons doubted he had frightened Erskine, any more than the reverse had been true. The smile seemed to be nothing more than an acknowledgment of a statement of fact, one which Erskine accepted as the truth and in spite of its barely concealed threat. Slowly, deliberately, Erskine took out his cigarette case and lit one of its bespoke contents.

"My money, Parsons, by the end of the week," he said. "There's a good chap."

Parsons watched as Erskine skipped up the remainder of the steps and disappeared to the left, down the corridor towards one of the club's bars. The doorman remained rooted to the spot, as if the hatred and violence which were rising within him were so heavy that his legs could not support them. His fingers had curled in on themselves, the big fists whitening with the tension, and the urge to plough them into the walls suddenly seemed to overwhelm him. His breath rasped through his nose and his eyes narrowed as he fought with his urge to follow Erskine and release this repressed and violent tension on the man.

It was only when a slight movement of black appeared on his peripheral vision that Parsons' trance was broken. Now, he could see the foyer stretching out before him, the black and white squares of the chequered floor suddenly vibrant in their mutual contrast; he could see the few marble steps up which Erskine had walked and the crimson carpets of the corridors which stretched out on either side of them. They were framed by the ornate, baroque marble archway which framed the entrance to the inner sanctum of the club and beyond which was the large staircase which stretched up into the higher echelons of the place.

It was into the frame of this archway that the movement of black which had interrupted Parsons' transfixed gaze appeared. With the sudden clarity of sight which follows such a state of self-hypnosis, Parsons recognised the black as a dress suit, contrasting the same ebony and ivory as the chessboard of the floor which separated Parsons from the archway. A set of cold fingers seemed to tap their way up his spine as he watched Everett Carr step into the corridor ahead of him.

Carr stood motionless for a moment, leaning on his silver-handled cane and thoughtfully stroking the moustache and Imperial beard. He was watching Parsons intently and he did so for a long moment, before turning his gaze in the direction in which Erskine had walked. He looked back at Parsons and gave a small bow of the head, before walking away.

Until that moment, Parsons had not felt anything approaching fear. Now, unsure of how much of the confrontation with Erskine had been overheard by Carr, the doorman had an oppressive sense of foreboding. It might not have been fear, not of the type which almost broke Parsons in the trenches, but it was close enough to induce prickles of sweat on the big man's neck.

Cursing, he pulled open the front doors of the club and returned to his post.

Chapter Five

L eonard Faraday, seated at his desk in his office at the Icarus Club,
opened the envelope in front of him and counted the money which
it contained. It was the third time he had done so that day, not out
of any necessity or pleasure, but because he liked to be certain about matters
of finance. It was perhaps a symptom of being a banker by profession which
had caused him to be cautious about money. Certainly, his skill with finance
meant that his own income, stemming from his professional salary and
private investments, was not unhealthy. He would not be a member of the
club at all if matters were otherwise.

And yet, his skill came with a certain degree of paranoia. Fifty pounds
was not a trifling amount, he told himself, and it did no harm to be sure
that the entire sum remained intact. He had taken it out of the bank
earlier that morning and placed it in the safe in his office at the Icarus
Club. It was as safe a place as any, he thought, and it would only be there
temporarily. On the following day, he would take it to his stockbroker,
together with instructions to invest the fifty pounds in the stocks and shares
of the Duellona Conglomerate. The investment, Faraday had been assured,
was a sound one, and Faraday's financial instincts seemed to confirm it.
Within the year, this initial fifty-pound investment was expected to provide
Faraday with a suitably impressive return. The prospect exhilarated Faraday,
and this third counting of the notes seemed suddenly to be more sensual
than practical, as if they were the contours and curves of a lover's body.
Faraday seemed to pass into a reverie of fiscal bliss.

Without warning, the door opened. Faraday shoved the money back into the envelope and, with an anxious urgency, he tossed the package into a drawer in his desk. He was not sure that he had done so swiftly enough to prevent Vincent Overdale from seeing it, but the younger man gave no indication that he had noticed anything. Faraday swallowed a sigh of relief and leaned forward in his seat, as if to create a physical barrier between Overdale and the contents of Faraday's desk drawer.

"I wondered if you were ready for dinner," said the younger man.

Vincent Overdale was almost thirty years of age, although his complexion and softness of skin suggested that he was a decade younger. His hair was fair, almost golden, swept back from a high forehead, but rather too unruly to be entirely respectable. His eyes were a deep blue, almost electrifying in their intensity, and the eyebrows were permanently arched. The combination gave the impression of an insistent and supercilious audacity. The smirk on the thin lips, almost as permanent as the curve of the brows, gave his expression a constant suggestion of implied wickedness, a mischief bubbling below the surface of his exterior. He was dressed formally, the white dinner jacket flawless in its brilliance, so that the black of his trousers and tie seemed like a moonless night and the crimson of the carnation in the lapel strikingly vivid. Not for the first time, Faraday found himself captivated by the younger man, his nerves prickling to attention and his senses trembling with anticipation.

"I have some things to do first," replied Faraday. "Club business."

Overdale perched himself on the corner of the desk. "I'm hungry, Leonard."

"I will only be a few minutes. Please, Vincent. Go and have a drink, and I will be with you in a short while."

Overdale sniffed. "You always put club business before me."

Faraday closed his eyes. So, the petulance was to be employed. Vincent Overdale might have been beautiful, but he was not without his own brand of ugliness. Faraday supposed that it was impossible to have beauty without ugliness, just as it was impossible to define goodness without evil, or sunlight without nightfall. In Overdale, it was manifested in his selfish peevishness. Faraday had witnessed numerous occasions, in public and in private, where Overdale's mood had darkened when his will had not been granted, when an opinion of his had been challenged, or when his jokes had not found favour. To Faraday, it was a disagreeable, even hateful trait, but he was compelled to suffer it. To live with it was, after all, better than surviving without it.

"Don't say things you know are not true, Vincent," he said softly.

"But it is true." Overdale leaned forward. "All I want is dinner."

"And we will have it, but not right away." Faraday placed his hand on the younger man's own and, when it was sharply removed, he tried hard to disguise his hurt. A change of subject was in order. "What have you been doing today?"

Overdale shrugged and rose from the desk. "This and that. Nothing exciting."

"Were you alone in doing nothing?"

Those deep blue eyes hardened. "I don't like being interrogated, Leonard."

Faraday ignored the protestation. "Have you seen Jacob Erskine today?"

Overdale sneered. "No, thankfully. Why do you ask?"

"I thought he might want his money back."

When Overdale spoke, there was a blade in the tone. "What do you mean?"

"I heard that you were in debt to him."

"Who told you that?"

Faraday smiled faintly. "Is it true?"

"No."

"Why would anybody say it, then?"

Overdale shrugged with contempt. "You tell me, because I don't know. Better still, ask whichever little bird told you the lie in the first place."

"I doubt the person concerned is a liar," replied Faraday, his mind drifting back to Everett Carr.

"Meaning that I am, yes?"

Faraday did not reply. In truth, he was not sure what answer he could give. "So, who were you with today?"

"Friends." The tone of Overdale's voice had now turned bitter. "I would have been with you if you weren't always so preoccupied here."

"Which friends?" Faraday refused to engage with the childish sullenness.

"You don't know them."

A moment of silence passed between them. They both knew that Overdale had lied twice during the exchange, so neither of them needed to acknowledge it. Instead, Faraday leaned back in his chair and latticed his fingers in his lap. Overdale turned his back on him and began to pace the room, his head lowered so that he could not catch the glare of the older man's eyes.

"You know I hate it when you do it," said Faraday at last.

Overdale shrugged. "I enjoy it. It passes the time."

"It'll kill you."

Overdale smiled. "We must all die of something."

It was a typical response. Faraday tried to conceal his irritation at the dismissive tone and the flippant treatment of a subject which he wished Overdale would take as seriously as he did himself. Perhaps it was not simply the frivolous attitude which Faraday despised, but because the tone itself emphasised a deeper, more fundamental concern which plagued him. Perhaps it was because Overdale's nonchalance demonstrated the difference in their points of view of life and, furthermore, the gap in their ages.

It was a familiar anxiety, one which had settled in Faraday's consciousness from the moment their affair had begun. Up until meeting Overdale, Faraday had believed that his major concern about his nature was society's attitude towards it. He knew that any love affair in which he became engaged would exist in the shadow of the threat of hard labour. He had been reticent in matters of the heart for that reason alone, consciously choosing to be lonely and free, than in love and imprisoned. Even then, when he thought about it, he wondered whether or not the consequences of the law were nothing more than an excuse. Was it not the reaction of his peers, the disgust of society, which he feared most? Whatever the reason, Faraday had convinced himself that he would forever be alone, his nature and desires suppressed, but his liberty his own. It was only when he met Vincent Overdale that his emotions were released.

They had met when Overdale was admitted to the club. His father was a distinguished member, although he was now no longer a regular feature of the place. The death of his wife had driven old Hamish Overdale into seclusion, so that his only son was the only representative of the family at the Icarus Club. And yet, it had been on his father's reputation and account that Vincent Overdale had been permitted to join the club. Nobody dissented, but Faraday knew that there were some hypocrites in the club who considered young Overdale to be inferior to them and, consequently, unsuitable for membership. Nothing was ever said, but Faraday was not fooled by the silence. For himself, privately, he had been overjoyed at the decision to admit Overdale and, from his first evening in the club, Faraday had ensured that the young man had been welcomed. Publicly, he had been the accommodating club secretary; privately, he had been the smitten schoolboy, who experiences love and desire for the first time.

Faraday was not a conceited man, but he had known almost immediately that Overdale had reacted to him in a similar, if not identical, fashion. They had become friends swiftly, but it was not until Overdale turned to Faraday for comfort in the wake of his mother's death that the relationship deepened. Faraday could recall the tears of grief against his cheeks as he held the boy in his arms, just as he could hear his quiet words of assurance whispered in the pale and delicately formed ears. How the kiss had happened was a hazier memory, but what followed was so sharply defined that it might have happened only a few hours ago rather than two years previously. But, even then, in the first dawn of their affair, Faraday had been uncertain about it. So many aspects seemed to him to be immoral: that he had taken advantage of a young boy in mourning, that his previous discretion about his private life had begun to lapse, and that he was closer in years to Overdale's deceased mother and estranged father than the boy himself.

Overdale had shown no such reservation. His own discretion was uncertain, his brash nature a potential danger to both of them, and his appetites were as lavish as they were insatiable. The speed with which he lived his life emphasised Faraday's concerns about his age and, after some months of attempting to match Overdale in his enthusiasm for life, Faraday had refused to allow himself to be seduced further by the endless glasses of champagne and the incessant noises of music and dancing. Overdale, with the energy of youth, had refused to acknowledge any restraint. If anything,

Faraday suspected that his appetites had intensified.

When Faraday looked back to the young man, Overdale was smiling. The petulance had evaporated, having been replaced entirely by a youthful vigour, and the surly expression had been swapped for one of careless happiness. The pouting lips had stretched into a grin, exposing the regular and immaculate teeth, and the eyes had softened into a blue shimmer. Another spell was being cast, one which Faraday found as infuriating as the changes in mood. To Faraday, the genuine smile which Overdale now deployed was infectious, capable of dissolving any argument between them, and Faraday could never fail to succumb to it. He did not know what was more irritating: his inability to resist it or Overdale's knowledge of the effect it would have.

Faraday rose from his desk. "All right, Vincent, you win. Let's go into dinner."

"We have time for a drink first, of course?"

"Of course."

Overdale pointed to the desk. "Shouldn't you put that envelope of money back in the safe?"

So, he had seen it after all, and Faraday's efforts to conceal it had not been swift enough. His stomach lurched at the words, and he felt his cheeks begin to burn with a sensation which was not quite embarrassment but more of guilt, as if Overdale had caught him in some sort of illicit act. He mumbled a response and took the envelope out of the drawer. Once more, out of habit, he checked its contents before opening the safe and placing it inside. He walked slowly to Overdale's side.

"What's it for?" asked the young man.

"Nothing for you to worry about." Faraday let his eyes linger on Overdale's face. "Are you lying to me about owing money to Erskine?"

There was a roll of the eyes before the answer came. "No. Now, don't mention that vulgar little man again. He'll sour the taste of the champagne and the oysters."

Faraday said no more, but his mind was in turmoil. He had felt the glare of Overdale's eyes on the back of his neck as he turned to the safe, and now, standing at the door of his office, Faraday could feel it still, just as he could seem to taste the bitter twist of deceit on Overdale's lips as they gently kissed his own.

Chapter Six

It was a little before their half past seven reservation that Marcus and Sonia Trevelyan arrived at the restaurant, *Bianchi's*. The early arrival had no adverse effect, as their table was ready for them, but they declined the *maître d*'s invitation of a drink at the bar, preferring to be shown immediately to their seats. As was customary for an establishment of such quality, the restaurant was busy and the reservation had been necessary, although Trevelyan doubted that he would have struggled to be accommodated, even in the absence of a prior booking. He was sufficiently recognised by the front of house and chefs alike to be afforded preferential, if not exclusively special, treatment.

Some would have said that Sonia Trevelyan was beautiful; others would have preferred to say that she was striking. Nobody would have denied she was attractive. Her features were angular, but not to the extent that their effect was unappealing. The cheekbones were high and prominent, the nose long but patrician, and the rosebud lips were pursed, as if in a permanent invitation to be kissed. Her eyes were as dark as her luxuriant hair, cut short and finger waved, and her porcelain skin contrasted elegantly with its darkness. She moved with an easy allure, although she seemed entirely unaware of the eyes which followed her as she walked through the dining room. Whatever assessment was made of her, be it beautiful or striking, she seemed to have no inclination of being possessed of either attribute, a quality which, in itself, only increased her sensuality.

Marcus was no less impressive. Like Sonia, his features were pale and smooth, the similarly dark hair swept back from his narrow brow. His eyes were brown, but so light as to be almost hazel, and one of the heavy eyebrows was raised slightly in a sardonic, upward curl. His mouth was long and thin, and it seemed always to have the flicker of a smile about it. His cheeks were gaunt, but they were defined by two long creases on either side of the mouth, which intensified the suggestion of permanent humour in his expression. He was tall and athletic in build, the shoulders broad and powerful, so that he swayed as he walked through the restaurant, his movements sleek and feline, like a panther stalking prey in the jungle. If the husbands in the room watched Sonia take her seat, their wives were watching Marcus take his, but neither of the Trevelyans took any notice of any respective display of admiration.

They ordered drinks: a Manhattan for him, a dry Martini for her. They were provided with menus, but they did not look over those immediately. Trevelyan lit a cigarette and leaned over the table to oblige Sonia. She accepted with a smile and placed the cigarette in a small, black holder, the long fingers, gloved in black velvet, manipulating both items with ease. She looked around the restaurant, taking in the crystal chandeliers in the domed ceiling, the light from them glinting and refracting in the champagne flutes and wine glasses on the pristinely covered tables. The furnishings were brass, set in oak, but they were polished to such an extent that they might have been gold. The ambience of luxury was enhanced by expertly placed and well-groomed aspidistras scattered throughout the dining room. From somewhere, someone was playing a mixture of classical and popular pieces on a piano, accompanied by a single violin, but Sonia could not see from where the melody came. Somehow, the idea that the music was coming from nowhere made it seem even more enchanting, casting it with a curiously ethereal quality.

"This place is beautiful," Sonia said. "I can see why you like it."

"I'm pleased it doesn't disappoint," he said. "I can recommend the chicken liver pâté to start, although you may prefer the soup."

Sonia looked at the menu, as if seeing it for the first time. "And for the main course?"

"The beef. Once tasted, always ordered again."

Their drinks arrived and, this time, they placed the order for food. Trevelyan ordered a bottle of Bordeaux to accompany the meal and, in anticipation of the wine, he sipped his cocktail. Sonia did likewise, her dark eyes glancing round the room once more.

"Who was it who recommended here to you?" she asked.

"As a matter of fact, it wasn't a recommendation," answered Trevelyan. "I was invited here to dine one evening by Everett Carr. It's one of his regular haunts. The man has impeccable taste, as you can see."

Sonia let out a small laugh. "I like Mr Carr. He's a darling."

"He'll be at the club now, I suppose. He usually is at this time."

"Are you going there after dinner, too?"

Trevelyan shook his head. "You know I don't like leaving you alone."

"I don't mind," she assured him.

Trevelyan bowed his head in concession. "Well, I might nip in for a nightcap, then. But no more. You shouldn't be on your own."

"Don't smother me, Marcus, please." She took a long sip of the Martini. The drink was strong, and it took hold of her senses at once, as if it had been a cold, sharp slap across her face. "It makes it all come back."

Trevelyan's eyes froze. "I saved you from all that."

"Please, don't let us spoil the evening." Sonia squeezed his fingers, a gesture not only of solidarity between them but of entreaty. "Let's have another drink, Marcus. Dare we wash away the past with Martinis and Manhattans?"

Now, at last, he smiled. "You better believe we dare, my girl."

The new cocktails had only just been delivered when Trevelyan saw the man with the spectacles. Patrick Crane, a fellow member of the Icarus Club, was being shown to a table, his head bowed, as if he was anxious not to be seen. His hair was fine and blond, neatly brushed and trimmed, and the eyes behind the tortoiseshell spectacles were so diffident that their sense of shyness might also have explained the scarlet of his cheeks. He was thin but, unlike Trevelyan's litheness, Crane's slight build conveyed an impression of frailty. His limbs were like sticks, oddly cumbersome in their length, and he walked with something of a shamble, as if his feet were too large for him. Trevelyan knew that Crane was ineffectual, but he was no less affable for it, and Trevelyan rather liked the man, in spite of his hesitant and withdrawn attitude. Crane would only contribute to discussions or debates when invited and, once he had stuttered through his opinion, he would invariably apologise for it. It was a tiresome habit but, Trevelyan suspected he would like Crane less if he abandoned it.

"I say," he said now, "there's Patrick Crane. I didn't know he came in here."

Sonia glanced over her shoulder at the man in question. "He looks familiar. Where might I have met him before?"

Trevelyan smiled. "Several places, but I am not surprised you don't remember. He isn't a man to leave a lasting impression. You met him when we went to dinner at Lord Balcon's place in Mayfair last month."

A memory stirred in Sonia's mind. The dinner had been excellent, and she had talked easily to a nervous, reticent man, for whom she had felt a certain degree of sympathy. He had been talking to her with difficulty, as if being in the presence of a girl flummoxed him and instilled in him a need to overcompensate for his timidity. And yet, he had listened attentively to her and had given no indication that he expected anything from her beyond the conversation itself. Time had passed since the Balcon dinner and, in the interval, Sonia had given the man no more thought, until now, when he was sitting across the room from her.

"I do remember him, yes," she said. "He was extremely kind. Nervous, perhaps, but kind. And with beautiful manners."

"Nervous is the word," scoffed Trevelyan. "Hard to imagine him fighting battles in the Courts."

"A barrister?"

"Solicitor." Trevelyan sipped the second Manhattan. "If rumours are to be believed, he's got himself into a bit of trouble."

Sonia looked back at Crane, as if trying to imagine him in any form of distress. It was almost impossible to envisage him coping or surviving it. "What sort of trouble?"

"Apparently, he gave bad advice to one of his clients and cost the man a small fortune. The client is suing for negligence."

Sonia frowned in sympathy. "How awful, the poor man."

"Yes, but he did make the error of judgment in the first place." Trevelyan sipped more of the drink. "It's made even worse because Crane and the client are both members of the Icarus Club, so they see quite a bit of each other."

"So, you know the man concerned as well?"

"As do you, although I think we would both prefer not to."

"Who is it?"

"Just someone you've seen at some dinners and social gatherings. Forget it." Trevelyan shook his head. "It doesn't matter. Finish your cocktail."

"Marcus, tell me."

He allowed a moment to pass before he responded. "Very well. Crane was acting for Jacob Erskine."

Her pouting lips tightened, as if a sudden and bitter taste had come into her mouth, and her nostrils flared. Her skin seemed to prickle with malignant expectation, and she became aware of a sudden chill on her bones. To counter it, regardless of whether it was imagined or not, she took a long drink from the cocktail glass. Trevelyan watched her. "Are you all right?"

She smiled, despite herself. "Yes, I'm fine. Mention of that hideous man makes me feel sick, that's all. Have you never seen the way he leers at me? Every time he looks at me, I know what he's thinking. I hate him."

Trevelyan now understood not only what she was thinking but why it would occur to her. He began to play with his wedding ring. "He reminds you of what happened."

"Every time, whenever I see him." Tears had welled in her eyes now. "And it makes me think about everything since."

Trevelyan watched her take another drink, and he heard the ice tinkle against the glass, a delicate noise caused by the trembling of her hand. "Has he ever touched you?"

"No." The repudiation, honest though it was, came with a splutter of laughter which was as nervous as it was relieved.

"Has he ever tried to?" Trevelyan watched her shake her head. "If he has, I'll kill him. You know that, don't you?"

Sonia stared him, as if her determined glare of the dark eyes could convince him more than her vocal denials. "He hasn't tried to touch me, I promise you, Marcus. But I can see that he'd like to. And that's enough."

Inappropriately, almost absurdly so, a smiling waiter delivered their appetisers. The pâté and the soup were excellent but, to be enjoyed entirely, they required an appetite which was dwindling too quickly. Marcus poured Sonia a glass of water from the iced jug which had been provided with the Bordeaux, and she drank it down swiftly and gratefully. It seemed to calm her almost immediately, and Marcus felt that no similarly soothing words would be required or effective. After a moment, Sonia looked back at him. Her eyes were less saddened, and the pout on her lips had stretched into a smile. She nodded a promise that she was eased, that the moment of unpleasantness had passed.

"Do you want to go?" he asked.

"Absolutely not. I won't have our evening ruined by Jacob Erskine." After the briefest of moments, and in a voice which suggested that she felt obliged to qualify her statement of intention, she added: "Or by anything else."

Marcus smiled. "That's my girl."

Sonia looked down at the soup. Taking her spoon, she tasted it and Marcus was pleased to notice that the trembling in her hand had largely dissipated. She placed the spoon in her mouth and swallowed down the soup.

"It's delicious," she said with a smile, but she suspected he knew that she could taste nothing, not now. "Thank you, Marcus."

He smiled at her, but his eyes were serious. "We need only worry about ourselves, Sonia. Nobody else matters."

"I know," she replied. "And that's how I want it."

"I will always be there for you. Never think otherwise."

She conceded her acceptance of his affirmation by tasting the soup once more. Now, it had flavour and she felt she could enjoy it. Marcus began to talk about unrelated matters, deflecting her attention and diverting her thoughts. He was a master of it. He had been blessed with the ability to turn her mind from her nightmares. What she would have done if he had not possessed it, or if he had abandoned her to the darkness, she did not know. She refused to allow herself to think of it, because she was sure that the thoughts would culminate in a certainty that she would have taken her own life long before now. She was alive, and as happy as she felt able to be, only because Marcus had saved her. From the violent past, as well as from herself.

By the time the meal was over, Sonia Trevelyan had buried her nightmares back from where they had surfaced, and she promised herself that she would never allow them to rise again. It was a noble intention, but there was no way she could have known how swiftly they would rise again in all their terrifying and vibrant intensity.

Chapter Seven

Patrick Crane sipped the glass of champagne which he had ordered and continued to watch the Trevelyans from over the rims of his spectacles. He knew that they had both seen and recognised him when he arrived at the restaurant, but he had no intention of engaging them in conversation. He felt neither the inclination nor the desire to do so in the present moment, and yet, for a few uncomfortable minutes, he had anticipated an invitation to join them, one which he feared he would have to summon the courage to refuse, no matter how much he might long to accept it.

With an honesty and clarity of thought, as cold and sharp as the champagne itself, Crane wondered about his reluctance. Dinner with Sonia Trevelyan would be so captivating that to call it a pleasure would have been to underestimate its effect. On the contrary, it would be an honour as exciting as it was intoxicating, but to be forced to share it with Marcus would be to ruin it. It was not that Crane disliked Marcus Trevelyan, but his presence would be an intrusion into the paradise of Sonia's company.

And yet, even if Marcus had not been there, Crane wondered whether he would have been able to dine alone with Sonia, no matter how much his heart might burn with exhilaration at the prospect. Last month, at the Balcons' dinner, their conversation had been without hindrance, but it had been protected not only by the presence of other people able to fuel the fire of the discussion, but also by the natural politeness of strangers. If she were to speak to him now, she would have preconceptions and opinions of him, which might be so favourable that he feared he could not uphold them or, conversely, ones which would be so adverse as to render him unable to defend himself. His certainty of his own futility and the danger that she might herself recognise it in him were just as much a reason to refuse to join them as the mere presence of Marcus himself. Crane's fears were to come to nothing, however, as sufficient time had passed since he had taken his seat that any such invitation would now be inappropriate.

The Trevelyans paid him no more attention, but Crane found that he was unable to take his eyes from them. He watched Marcus only to ensure that he did not detect Crane's concentration on Sonia. To be caught in the act of staring would have been offensive as well as embarrassing. Once or twice, he noticed a change in Sonia's demeanour. He saw a freezing of her movements, an abrupt tension in her body, as if she had become aware of a sudden horror. On each occasion, her hackles had risen, as though she had felt the presence, without warning, of a spider on her skin, and Crane found himself wondering what course their conversation had taken to cause such a change in her demeanour. The incidents had lasted no longer than a few moments and, in due course, she had relaxed sufficiently to seem to begin to enjoy her soup, but these subtle displays of fear had been as unmistakable as their cause was inexplicable.

Patrick Crane tried to force his mind away from Sonia Trevelyan. It was not the first time he had attempted to do so in the past month. His sleep had been interrupted regularly on account of her intrusion into his already fevered dreams. During the day, his mind would ramble aimlessly into consideration of what she might be doing, how she filled her days, and what places she might visit. Walking through London parks and down its vibrant streets, he would see black, waved hairstyles, smell familiar perfumes, and he would experience a storm in his senses, that curious mixture of trepidation and anticipation which nervous love inspires, and his disappointment that the hair and perfume did not belong to Sonia was as intense as his relief. Seldom did he permit himself to fantasise further about her, and yet ideas about how her lips might feel against his, how her hand might fit into his, and how her breath might brush against his cheek persisted in gnawing at the perimeters of his imagination and he was afraid that it was only a matter of time before his internal defences were breached by those rising emotions.

The pressure in his head was not solely due to them, however, but rather more to the futility of it all. He was not a courageous or confident man, but he was an honest one, especially with himself and he knew that his life would never contain Sonia Trevelyan within it. How could he expect otherwise? Even without her relationship with Marcus, it was a foolishly childish dream to entertain.

These doubts came to him, as they so often did, in the voice of his mother. Her voice was vivid in his mind. Strident but forceful, the words coming with a declaration of their own virtue and their own insistence that what they said was the truth. He had been exposed extensively to its smiling malice, disguised as maternal concern, that he ought to have developed some degree of immunity to it, but the voice never failed to insinuate itself into his conscience. Whether Delilah Crane had any notion of the effect she had on her son, Crane was unable to say. In his darker moments, he suspected that she knew precisely how she treated him and revelled in it. In a more charitable frame of mind, he could convince himself that she had become oblivious to her conduct, just as he had failed always to come to terms with it. He had fluctuated between the two conflicting conclusions too frequently to know for certain which was true.

It was his father's fault, of course. From the moment Archibald Crane had walked out of the marital home, refusing to accept that the child was his, Delilah had never been able to forgive her son. Since his birth, Patrick Crane had been a nuisance to his mother, the cause of her own unhappiness, and he could never be permitted to forget it. The reminders of his guilt were not necessarily stated directly; they could manifest themselves in veiled threats, spiteful asides, and mocking statements of derision.

"You will never know true love, Patrick," she would say. "Not the love I knew from your father. That was the sort of love you read about, the kind of passion which you never believe you truly deserve. You ended it for me, of course, but I hope Archie is happy now. I always wanted him to be happy. He deserved it."

Patrick would never dare to ask whether he deserved happiness too. It would be like goading a snake with a stick. It was far easier simply to accept what she said as truth and, over time, he would find himself apologising for it.

"I am sorry I am a burden to you, mother."

She would smile at him, rueful as well as malicious. "You're not a burden, my dear boy. You are a reminder. A memento of a life I could have had."

"I don't understand."

"Your father didn't want you, and, as a result, he no longer wanted me. You're a reminder of that, Patrick, but you do not have sufficient purpose to be a burden."

She may not have wanted him, but his mother was likewise not prepared to share him. He had never been blessed with a surfeit of friends, but those he had made were seldom permitted to visit or, if they were, the experience was never repeated. Whatever bond he formed with boys of his own age, they were never to last.

"I don't like that McKenzie child, Patrick," Delilah would tell him. "He is very likely to end up in prison, or worse. We do not want you to go the same way. You should avoid him. I daresay you would not survive a sentence behind bars. Best to sever ties with him now, I think."

On one occasion, an invitation to stay at a friend's family's country estate for the weekend had met with Delilah's particular brand of resistance.

"Why would you think of leaving me alone in this house for the entire weekend, Patrick, darling? Do you think that is fair? You spend two days playing and laughing, whilst I sit alone here wondering if you are alive or dead? Besides, those people are not our sort. You will hardly fit in with them. They will laugh at you because you don't know which knife and fork to use for which course at dinner, and you will be unable to stand up to their mockery. You will be entirely miserable, and I can't have that. So, no. Better you stay here and avoid any unpleasantness, don't you think?"

The threats would always be stated as a suggestion, but they were never less than a command. The conflict between her contrasting attitudes towards him could only ever have isolated him. Whether he had ever truly hated her, he could not say, but he knew that he did not love her. Age had not withered her. If anything, her advancing years and her increasing dependence on gin had deepened her manipulation. He had suspected as much but it was not until he stumbled hesitantly into his first attempt at a love affair that he had become certain of it.

"I am planning on getting married, mother," he had said. She had not replied, but her glare was no less eloquent for it. "I've qualified as a solicitor, and I have found a position, so I think it is only right that I marry."

"To that girl with the large eyes and indecent skirts, I suppose."

He had lowered his gaze to the floor, his cheeks burning with rage. "Please don't talk about Felicity like that."

"Felicity, is it? Lilith, more like, or Jezebel."

"You have no right to speak about her like that. I love her."

Delilah had laughed with scorn. "What do you know of love, my boy? Only what you have learned from me, and that is not the same as the love a man must have for his wife. You are ill-equipped in so many ways to deal with marriage, Patrick. Don't be ridiculous about it."

"I am going to marry her, mother."

His resilience had not angered her. Crane might have been surprised, had he not understood that she would hardly consider any rebellion on his part to be worthy of anger, scorn, or similar emotion. She had shaken her head. "You shall do no such thing. Your father walked out on me because of you and, God knows, that gave me reason to abandon you, but I didn't. I stayed with you, and I devoted myself to you."

"I won't abandon you, mother."

"You say that, but you will. You won't be able to avoid it, not once this girl of yours starts making demands on you for a family. And what then? Where will that leave me, once you have no time to visit me or remember me? I never thought you capable of being selfish, Patrick. I suppose I don't know you as well as I thought. It is such a shame, to find out one doesn't know one's own son at all."

There had been no marriage, and there had been no further love affairs.

Crane looked down at his plate to find that his starter course had gone cold without being touched. He called for the plate to be taken away and ordered a second glass of champagne. It would be his last, he assured himself.

He had not thought about the broken engagement with Felicity for some time. She had never quite passed from his memory, but she did not figure prominently in it either. He supposed that she was married now, living somewhere far away with a family of her own. No doubt she was happy. Felicity had been different to Sonia Trevelyan. She had been far less alluring, not so mysterious or exotic in her beauty, and, in retrospect, Crane wondered whether he had ever loved her at all. Certainly, what he thought he felt for Sonia was far more intense than the feelings he had experienced for Felicity. Perhaps, after all, his mother had been right, and he knew nothing at all about love.

A sudden nausea, tinged with champagne, passed over him. Delilah Crane had considered Felicity to be a biblical whore. What, Crane wondered, would she make of Sonia Trevelyan? He dared not think of it, the speculations too offensive to be given consideration, but there was no doubt that his mother would consider a relationship between her son and Sonia Trevelyan to be inappropriate, even if it were possible at all. Her imagined objections came to him in her mocking, peevish voice.

"Why do you imagine she could possibly be attracted to you?" Delilah would say. "She is far too beautiful to take you seriously, Patrick. You should grow up and see the world as it is. This girl is not for you, and you could never hope to maintain her or keep her happy. She could never be satisfied with a mediocre, not to say negligent, solicitor."

His mind, driven by spite and hatred, turned inexorably to Jacob Erskine. As if the recollection of the dispute between them was a physical burden on him, Crane's shoulders slumped, and he sank slightly into his seat. The consequence of Crane's professional mistake had not been insignificant, he was the first to admit it. A legal deadline had been missed resulting in the striking out of a piece of litigation which Crane's firm was handling for Erskine concerning a boundary dispute. Erskine's response had been typically volatile.

"That land was mine, and old Peterson was trespassing on it," he had barked. "The whole point of the case was to prove him wrong and get him off what was rightfully mine. As a barrister, I knew that I had a case, a provable case, and you knew it too. But because of your bloody incompetence, the case is lost, and I cannot resurrect it. Old Peterson can stay on the land, and I cannot extend my own property across it. The value of that property has been irrevocably diminished, and it's cost me a damned fortune. Do you understand that, Crane?"

He had understood it, of course. There was no possibility of failing to comprehend either what had happened or what the consequence of it would be. What was more difficult to appreciate was why Erskine was taking the action he was. Crane could not doubt that Erskine would be aware that the debt he felt Crane owed him was beyond the latter's means. Crane's firm was successful, but it was small. Erskine would know that even Crane's complete bankruptcy, both professional and personal, would still leave the major part of the debt unpaid. The litigation against Crane would never result in a monetary award sufficient to reimburse Erskine for the money he had lost.

But perhaps the money was not the point. Despite his knowledge of Crane's financial status, Erskine himself did not need the additional income which the litigation would generate. Erskine was rich enough without any supplement. If it was not the money which drove him, the much more frightening alternative was that Erskine's determination to ruin Crane was personal. Perhaps it was the shame, the ruin, and the scandal which would undoubtably follow the final hearing of the claim against Crane which appealed to Erskine. If so, it was surely a much crueller and sadistic motivation, one which horrified Crane far more than the litigation itself. Was it possible for someone to despise him so intensely? He knew that he was not a man whom it was easy to befriend, but he had hoped that he was not so disliked to warrant such treatment. And yet, Erskine was launching this campaign against him and doing so with impunity.

Caught between the scorn of his mother and the loathing of Erskine, like some sort of emotional Scylla and Charybdis, Crane had never felt so helpless. If only one of them would die, the pain would be halved. He had not wished his mother dead for some time now, but the dream was not entirely new. Somehow, his hatred and fear of Erskine seemed to intensify those similar feelings in him towards his mother. Crane felt the ice crystals of sweat forming on the fire in his temples as the fantasy of removing one of the monsters from his life took root in his imagination.

He doubted he could ever bring himself to kill his mother. The bond between them was profound, even if it was not loving, and the thought of matricide seemed too horrible to mould into reality. With a sickened smile, Crane thought about the unbearable mockery if he made the attempt and failed. What would Delilah Crane say to that? The snide and contemptible ridicule would be too oppressive to survive. Any attempt to murder his mother might well end with his own self-destruction.

But Erskine was a different matter.

There was no bond there to be afraid of, no consideration of emotions beyond those macabre ones which had taken hold of him. Erskine was no better than an animal, barely human, so that if Crane did put a bullet in the man's heart it would mean as much to him as shooting grouse in the Highlands. Delilah Crane hated and, likewise, was despised only by her own son. Erskine was disliked by many others, even to Crane's limited knowledge. At the club, for instance, in those opulent surroundings of the Icarus Club, Crane knew that Erskine was no more than a pariah. Perhaps Crane was no less of a leper in the community but, surely, he was preferable to Erskine. Might the club not thank him for disposing of the parasite?

His thoughts were interrupted by the waiter bringing his first course. Crane began to eat, but the bitterness in his mouth was too overpowering to allow the subtle blends of flavours and textures of the food to impress themselves on his palate. His senses finally conceded defeat and allowed themselves to be consumed by the thoughts of murder which were searing themselves into his mind. He could do nothing about his mother, perhaps, but she was only one of his torments, and Crane felt sure that if the other source of misery disappeared entirely, he might have a rejuvenated vigour to tolerate her. And so, his mind began to concentrate on Jacob Erskine, on the litigation, and on that bullet which he had imagined piercing the malignant old grouse's cruel heart.

Chapter Eight

Colonel Hector Wharton had waited until he was certain that Erskine was settled in the club before leaving himself. It was a little after nine o'clock, which meant that the meeting he had planned would only be a short one. To complain about it would be pointless: no amount of time he was able to spend with the woman he loved was ever enough, but it meant that every moment was precious.

He walked down the steps to the foyer and pushed open the front door. Parsons was on duty, but he did not speak to him, nor did the doorman engage in any attempt at conversation with Wharton. There was little more to be said after their earlier confrontation, so it was no surprise that no words were uttered. There was simply a nod of acknowledgment from both men, and Wharton stepped into the mews and made his way to Grosvenor Square. During the short walk to the square itself, Wharton could feel the sharp and lethal blades of Parsons' eyes on the space between his shoulder blades. They did not trouble him. Let Parsons indulge himself in his own spiteful petulance, it was no concern of Wharton's. What had been said was necessary, and Wharton made no apology for it.

The walk to his destination occupied no more than a quarter of an hour. When he arrived at the house, he saw that there was a single light on in one of the downstairs windows. Save for that single point of illumination, the house was in darkness, so that the light seemed all the brighter against the blackness of its surroundings. Wharton ran up the steps which led from the street to the front door and pulled at the bell. He checked the street at either end and the small park opposite the house, but he saw nobody. It was deserted, and the stillness was somehow disconcerting, so oppressive that the distant sound of traffic seemed to be an illusion. Wharton turned his attention back to the door, ignoring the impressions which were being forced upon him by the quiet evening and, very possibly, by his conscience.

Margaret Erskine opened the door, and he rushed inside, closing it behind him. In a moment, he was holding her in his arms, his lips brushing her hair, her cheeks, and, finally, her lips.

"Have you seen Jacob?" she whispered.

"He's at the club," Wharton replied. "He'll stay there for long enough."

Wharton ran his hand down her cheek and, as if seeing her for the first time, he took in the dark shadow of violence which stained one side of her face. It was a livid purple, the edges blurred with yellow, the colours so vibrant that in any other circumstances, they might have been beautiful. Margaret turned away from him and raised her palm to the bruise, as if by doing so she could obliterate it or hide it forever from Wharton's penetrating glare.

"How the devil did that happen?" he asked.

"It's nothing. Please, don't make a fuss."

"Don't make a fuss? Look at your face."

"It was my fault."

"How did it happen?" he insisted. "Tell me."

"I fell, that's all."

But the reply had been so hesitant, so unconvincing, that the lie was easily detected. "You can't expect me to believe that."

"Please, Hector, just leave it."

"Did Jacob do it?"

The question came after a moment's pause on Wharton's part, and it was asked without emotion. It contained no suppressed rage, no anger, and no degree of concern. It was a request for information and nothing more, but it was all the more terrifying for it.

"I threw wine in his face at lunchtime," she said, as if that was sufficient explanation. "It was my fault, Hector. I deserved it."

"I suppose he told you that."

"It's true."

"We both know that it isn't." Wharton touched the damaged cheek tenderly. "Nobody deserves this. The fault is entirely his."

Margaret held his hand for a moment and then turned away. He followed her into the drawing room and, with her consent, poured them both a whisky. He watched her sip at the drink, grimacing slightly at its fire, making every effort to avoid looking into his eyes. Slowly, he drank his own whisky and began to pace around the room.

"Has he done anything like this before?"

When she did not reply, he knew the answer. As if to confirm a suspicion, she lowered her head, and a gentle, repressed sobbing began to come from her. Wharton swallowed back an urge to curse and, as he did so, he realised that he was suppressing a need to sob himself. He drained his glass and placed it on the mantelpiece before walking to the settee where she was sitting and lowering himself beside her. He took the glass from her trembling fingers and placed it at his feet on the floor. Gently, he put his arms around her, and she allowed herself to buckle into his embrace, the sobbing increasing in pace and volume until they came with such force that her whole body quivered with the effort and emotion. At last, she pulled away from him and dabbed the remnants of tears away from her eyes with the handkerchief which he had offered her.

"How long has it been going on?" asked Wharton.

"Longer than I dare admit. It has got worse over the years."

Years? Wharton realised as soon as she said it that he had been unprepared for the reply. He had expected her to reply in terms of days, weeks, just possibly months, but the truth of the matter shocked and appalled him.

"The bloody coward," he hissed. "Wouldn't be able to stand up to a man, I dare say."

"I wouldn't be too sure about that," Margaret replied. "I don't think he has any fear. He thinks he can do what he likes, and he expects people to allow him."

"I've a good mind to put that idea to the test and confront him."

Margaret was horrified by the idea. "For God's sake, don't do that. It would only make matters worse."

Wharton inhaled deeply. He knew that she was correct, that his interference would cause more harm than it prevented, but his acceptance of the fact left him with a profound feeling of impotence. He was silent for a long moment, his mind not concentrating on anything in particular, until a thought occurred to him which prompted a change in his demeanour. His cheeks paled, the fire of disgust in his eyes extinguished by a sudden wave of panic.

"Has he ever attacked you in other ways?" he stammered, the words coming with difficulty.

She knew what he meant, and she could understand his reluctance to put the monstrous idea into words. Perhaps she was grateful to him for refusing to do so. Knowing his meaning and hearing it spoken out loud were two entirely different concepts, and Margaret knew that her reaction to one would be more volatile than the other.

"No, never." She took hold of his hand, as if to assure him. "He hasn't been near me in months."

"That's something, I suppose," said Wharton, instantly regretting the foolishness of it, as if any goodness could be salvaged from the toxic blackness of the situation. "I'm sorry," he added. "Damned stupid thing to say."

If Margaret Erskine agreed with him, she did not say so. She began to feel a dilapidating exhaustion come over her, as if Wharton discovering how truly unhappy her marriage was had lifted a burden from her conscience, which was so heavy that its release sapped all energy from her soul. She sank back on the settee, sighing heavily, and her eyes rolled upwards towards the ceiling. Wharton was silent and motionless, but the hard and determined glare of his eyes, transfixed on an uncertain point in the distance, suggested that his stillness was external only.

"You must try not to worry about me, Hector," said Margaret.

"How can I not? I used to worry about you before I knew how he treated you. Now that I know about his brutality, how can you possibly expect me not to worry even more?"

"I can manage him." It was spoken with less certainty than the words suggested.

"Can you?" Wharton turned his glare onto her. "How long before he puts you into a hospital? Or worse?"

"He only retaliates, Hector," she replied. "I told you that I threw a glass of wine in his face at lunch. If I don't do things like that -"

He cut her off with a snarl. "How many times will you excuse him? You can't live your life not daring to speak in case your husband considers what you say to be a personal attack against which he must defend himself with his fists. Don't forget, I know Erskine too. He's the sort of man who would find offence in anything said or done to him if he saw fit to do so."

"It isn't like that."

"Are you sure? I think it is entirely possible that he would manufacture a confrontation between you, just so that he could have his sick pleasure of beating you when he feels like it."

"I have to believe that isn't true, Hector. Otherwise, I would be trapped in a nightmare."

"You're already trapped, Margaret," Wharton insisted, his voice rising with frustration.

"I must have hope," she countered. "I have to believe that this was the last time."

"It won't be. Surely you can see that? Why would Erskine suddenly stop acting like he has been for so long? He won't, that's the truth - and you can't bank on this never happening again."

"What choice do I have?"

"Leave him!"

He shouted the words with such force that it seemed as if they had been inevitable. It was as if the entire discussion had been engineered to produce this effect, to drive the conversation towards this final, inexorable conclusion. It was an old argument, one which Margaret was tired of having, but one which she knew she would never be able to avoid entirely.

"I don't want to go over all that again, Hector."

Wharton was insistent. "I don't understand you, Margaret. How can you possibly want to stay with him when he treats you this way? Divorce him, walk away, and we can be together."

She was shaking her head long before he had finished speaking. "He would not grant a divorce, even if I asked for one. But I've explained all this to you, Hector. I don't believe in divorce. I took vows, and I meant them, so I must abide by them."

"Things can change, Margaret. You do not have to abide by vows which you no longer believe, surely."

"I was brought up to believe in the sanctity of marriage, Hector."

He was raging now, his past frustrations which he had buried for her sake now breaking the banks of his restraint and flowing freely. "And what good will these morals of yours be if you're dead? What if the next blow to your face knocks you into the corner of a table and smashes your skull? What will your morality matter then?"

As his voice rose, her tears fell with a contrasting and sombre silence. "Please, don't speak like that, Hector."

"I'm speaking the truth," he said. "A possible version of it, at any rate. I love you, Margaret, and I cannot bear to see you hurt. I try to urge you to leave Erskine for selfish reasons, of course, but also because I know that you want to be with me, but you insist on putting this obstacle in our way. Maybe I could have lived with things being as they have been, but now that I know what Erskine is, I cannot remain passive any longer."

"What do you mean?"

He tempered his anger, but she could see that not all the fury had dissolved within him. "You must divorce him. You cannot stay here and risk your life."

Now, she found her own sense of outrage. "You cannot order me to leave him, Hector. Yes, I hate Jacob, I wish he was out of my life, of course, I do. I wish I had met you first, that I had never set eyes on him at all. But I did meet him, and I did marry him. He is still my husband, even if I hate him."

"If you hate him, why can't you divorce him?" Wharton found circular arguments bewildering.

"Because I would hate myself for doing it far more than I hate him." She looked up into his eyes. "What price would I pay for leaving him? I would be free, yes, but it would be at the cost of my own conscience. Can't you understand that? I would be spared his violence, but I would no longer be myself."

It was said with an almost naïve candour, without any pretence of pleading or insistence, so that it was a plain statement of unquestionable honesty. Wharton was struck immediately by its sincerity, so much so that he perhaps overlooked the courage which had been necessary to say it. For the first time, her reluctance to divorce Erskine seemed to begin to become clear to him, its blurred edges of confusion sharpening with clarification.

"Perhaps I can understand that," he confessed. "No doubt I should have done so much earlier than this."

"I'm sorry if I seem contradictory," Margaret said. "It is easier to feel the way I do than to explain it."

Wharton shook his head. "No, I understand well enough. But none of what you said changes the fact that you might be in great danger if you stay with Erskine."

"I have no choice," Margaret repeated.

Wharton walked over to her and took her in his arms once more. He gently stroked her hair, kissing her head softly, and he felt the tension of emotion release itself from her body, as if being in his embrace provided a measure of safety and comfort, a protection from the anxiety which must dominate her life.

"We will think of something," whispered Wharton. "We will solve the problem somehow, I promise. I love you, Margaret."

She did not reply, but her arms tightened around his waist. She wondered how he imagined they might solve the dilemma in which they had found themselves. He could not know that earlier in the day, she had fantasised about murdering Jacob Erskine, however idly, and nor could she know that he had indulged in similar thoughts, or that the idea of murder had already infiltrated the mind of Colonel Hector Wharton. It seemed to him to be a plot which was so easily executed that it might have been entirely trivial. Margaret might not wish to break her marital vows but, to Wharton, who had never taken those vows personally, they seemed to provide an answer to their troubles. The sanctity of marriage, which Margaret seemed incapable of breaching, need not be broken as long as Wharton had the courage to invoke the familiar vow that the marriage would persist until death intervened.

As he held the woman he loved, Wharton thought back to the old Webley revolver which, only a few hours previously, he had cleaned carefully and wondered whether he would ever fire again.

Chapter Nine

L ooking back on matters, it was apparent to Carr that the first steps towards murder were taken on the following afternoon. It was not his custom to visit the Icarus Club before the evening but, as coincidence would have it, it was one of the rare occasions when he had nothing else to occupy his time and a glass of the club's excellent chilled Burgundy seemed to be a pleasurable way to pass an hour or so. The temperature had dropped noticeably during the morning and, as so often happened, the increasing coolness had caused his shattered knee to ache, so that he was compelled to take a taxi.

He arrived at the club a little after half past twelve. Jacob Erskine was in the bar when Carr entered. There was nobody else around, and Carr did not relish the prospect of Erskine's sole company. There was no obligation to engage him in conversation, aside from a polite nod of greeting and acknowledgment, but Carr had hoped for some companionship. Too much of his time, he reflected, was spent alone. It was no doubt a natural consequence of the murder of his wife, Miranda, killed in an assassination attempt on Carr himself by gangsters whose leader Carr had condemned to death. It had remained the pioneering tragedy of his life, crystallised by the permanent reminder of it in the form of the bullet in his knee. Time had healed the psychological wounds to an extent, but the physical reminder of the incident ensured that he would never truly recover from it. Loneliness was, perhaps, a foregone conclusion in the circumstances. Nevertheless, Carr preferred to think of himself as alone rather than lonely, a distinction he thought it was important to make, although he was inclined to believe that the old poet was correct and that man was not meant to be his own island. There were times when Carr, as much as any other man, desired company and conversation, but Jacob Erskine was not the well from which he would have chosen to draw it.

Fortunately, Carr's fears were not to be realised. After he and Erskine had acknowledged the other's presence with a bow of the head and a mumbled greeting, Marcus Trevelyan stepped into the room. Any antipathy which Carr might have felt towards Jacob Erskine was not reflected in his opinion of Trevelyan. He was everything which Erskine was not. Where the older man was belligerent, coarse, and vindictive, the younger man was polite, affable, and relaxed. If Erskine's face was bloated and enflamed by excess, Trevelyan's was lean and handsome, with the vigour and charm which only youth can inspire. He was a man of business, as Carr recalled, something connected with financial trading, but the precise details had always been hazy to Carr, a man not entirely at ease or enthusiastic about numbers and figures. Whatever Trevelyan's work was, it had served him well. His lithe figure was clothed in the very best suit, set off by the most expensive of silk ties. The cuff links were impressive, the watch-chain across the waistcoat so subtly delicate as to be almost priceless, and the shoes might well have been handmade. Trevelyan might be a wealthy man, but he lacked the arrogant desire to declare it at any opportunity.

"Trevelyan, my dear boy, how nice to see you," said Carr, shaking the young man's hand. "A drink?"

"A glass of sherry, if I may, Mr Carr. Very kind of you."

"Order me a large whisky, would you, Carr? There's a good fellow." Erskine had settled himself in a leather armchair in the corner of the room. He had a full measure of whisky in a crystal glass on the small table beside him, Carr noticed, but it had not prevented the demand for another.

Carr's grimace of distaste was hidden by the moustache and Imperial beard. He nodded agreement politely and placed the order with the attendant behind the bar. Trevelyan had been less successful in disguising his hostility towards Erskine, however, as Carr noticed when he turned to face him and saw the hardened glare of hatred behind his eyes.

"This place would be a much brighter one without that snake," hissed Trevelyan.

Carr smiled gently, recalling to his mind Ronald Edgerton's similar comments two days previously. "Mr Erskine is a difficult man to like, certainly."

"I should think anybody you speak to in the club would say as much."

Carr disliked this kind of private assassination of character. Irrespective of his own views about Erskine, he found it unpalatable to deride or slander a man behind his back. To Carr, it was more preferable simply to refuse to engage the man, to ignore his presence, at least until such time as politeness made it impossible; thereafter, civility was more desirable than conflict, however deeply a prejudice must be buried to achieve it. Trevelyan seemed content to continue this surreptitious slaying of Jacob Erskine, but Carr was not about to permit himself to become an accomplice in it.

"And how is your charming wife, Trevelyan?" The steering of the conversation's direction was successful, if not entirely refined.

The change of subject immediately brightened Trevelyan's handsome features. The creases in his thin cheeks broadened as he smiled. "Sonia is very well, Mr Carr, thank you for asking. I took her out to dinner last night, as a matter of fact. To *Bianchi's*."

Carr's cheeks flushed with pride and gratitude. It was not so much that Trevelyan had taken Sonia out for dinner than that he had taken her to Carr's preferred restaurant in London. It meant that Trevelyan had enjoyed his own visits there, in Carr's company, enough to continue the recommendation by taking her. It was a vindication, a way of showing Carr that his own taste and hospitality had been recognised and appreciated.

"My boy, I am delighted," he said. "I trust she enjoyed it."

"How could she not?" grinned Trevelyan.

"Then her taste is as delightful as she is." Carr sipped his Burgundy.

Trevelyan's smile broadened. "She sends her best wishes, sir."

"And you must return them." Carr gave a small, courteous bow. "If I had been blessed with a daughter, I would like to think she would be as much of a credit to me as Sonia must be to her father."

"I wouldn't know." Trevelyan's eyes had dimmed. "Unfortunately, Sonia's father is dead."

Carr was visibly embarrassed. "I had no idea. I'm sorry."

Trevelyan shook his head, as if to dismiss the awkwardness. "It was a long time ago. She was only a child, back when she lived in the village of Church Benham. She grew up there, you see."

"To lose a parent at such a young age is one of life's cruellest tricks," observed Carr, with genuine sadness in both his voice and eyes.

"It's something she and I have in common, of course," said Trevelyan.

"Your father is dead too?"

"When I was twelve."

"I am sorry to hear it."

"One must play the cards one is given, Mr Carr. Sonia's father drank himself to death, I'm sorry to say. I can at least be consoled by the fact that my father wasn't as selfish as that, since his death was entirely accidental." He gave a grim, saddened smile. "A severed artery, with a pair of shears."

"So much pain," said Carr softly, stroking his broken knee as he did so.

"Doesn't do to dwell on it," said Trevelyan, washing away the taste of the memory with the remains of his sherry.

Carr sipped again at the chilled Burgundy, and Trevelyan ordered a second glass for himself. Erskine's whisky remained on the bar, untouched, and Carr turned to draw its recipient's attention to it. There was no need for him to do so. Erskine was standing at Carr's elbow, his eyes glinting under the heavy brows. He slammed down his empty glass and took up its replacement. It seemed to Carr as if Erskine was about to say something, but he was prevented from doing so by the sound of his name being barked from the doorway. The three men at the bar turned to find Hector Wharton striding towards them.

"I thought I'd find you here, Erskine," roared Wharton. "I want a word with you."

Erskine was instantly defensive. "You're interrupting a private conversation, colonel. I would have thought, as chairman of the club, you would have more manners."

"Don't you dare preach to me about manners," snarled Wharton. "A man like you hasn't the first idea how to behave like a decent human being."

Carr felt it necessary to intervene. "Must we have insults immediately before lunch? Young Trevelyan and I simply wanted a quiet drink together."

Wharton replied, but his eyes did not deviate from Erskine's face. "What I have to say won't take long, Carr."

"That does not mean you should say it here."

Erskine was equally belligerent. "It won't take long to say because you won't be saying it at all, Wharton. You have no words which I could possibly want to hear."

Wharton laughed, a burst of air from his mouth which was laced with malice. "Is that your attempt to bully me, Erskine?"

"Take it as you please."

Now Wharton was up close to his adversary, so that he could smell the same stench of excessive cologne, stale tobacco, and fresh whisky which Margaret must have smelt when he was striking her face. "Not as good at bullying men as you are women, eh? Harder to dominate someone who is likely to fight back, isn't it?"

Erskine stiffened, but he maintained his resolve. "No idea what you're talking about."

"You're a liar," spat Wharton. "And, worse, you're a dirty, bloody coward."

Everett Carr brought his hand down forcefully onto the bar. "Enough of this. Wharton, what has got into you? I don't know what all this is about, and I don't want to, but this conduct is deplorable."

"So it is," said Erskine, sententiously.

"I meant the conduct of both of you," snapped Carr. "A plague on both your houses, gentlemen. If you can't keep civil tongues in your heads, I'd politely ask you both to leave and allow Trevelyan and me some peace."

Wharton fumed for a moment, his cheeks brightened by hatred and his eyes burning with rage. "I know about you, Erskine, and I know about your wife. Believe me, things are going to change, you bloody coward. Mark my words, I will see to it."

"Are you threatening me, Wharton?"

"Take it as you please." The command was delivered with a smile.

Erskine did not react to his own words being thrown back at him. "I don't know what you think you know about my wife and me, but I would ask you to keep your nose out of my personal affairs."

"I know everything about you and her," whispered Wharton, "and, because of it, I want you out of this club. Have your resignation ready for the committee by noon tomorrow."

Erskine laughed. Of all the responses he could have given to Wharton's ultimatum, laughter was the most insulting. It was a brief rumble of genuine but malicious humour and it was more of an affront than any coarse word or act of minor violence.

"If you think I'm leaving this club, Wharton, you've got another thing coming," sneered Erskine. "Since you've brought up the matter of membership, I may as well tell you that I've been thinking about something for a long time, and now is as good a time as any to announce it. You see, you're not as popular here as you think you are, Wharton. There are some who think you're past your best. Time for new blood, they say."

Wharton was momentarily confused by the words but, in a bolt of inspiration, Erskine's meaning registered itself in his head like a kick to the temples. His eyes widened in abhorrence. "You're not suggesting that you might take over from me, surely? You think you can vote me out and replace me, is that it?"

"Exactly."

"It'll never happen," insisted Wharton. "The members won't allow a devil like you to run this place, and I doubt you could do it efficiently, in any case."

"Don't be so sure."

"I swear to you, it will never happen." Wharton was sneering now, his anger emitting from his clenched teeth like the steam from a long-forgotten kettle.

Erskine pressed the tip of his finger into Wharton's breast. "Every dog, colonel. Remember that. Every tired, old dog."

He allowed his implication to settle into the silence which followed the confrontation, and then, with a broad smile and another grim growl of malicious laughter, he threw his whisky down his throat and slammed the empty glass on the bar. Erskine looked around them, smiling impertinently, and he bade them farewell, before excusing himself and ambling out of the room, his swagger driven not so much by indifference as arrogance.

At the door, he turned on his heel. "I think I'll nip along to the other bar. The company in here has become rather tedious."

Wharton watched him leave, and, for some moments after, he remained silent. Neither Carr nor Trevelyan interrupted it, both realising that it was more prudent to sip their drinks than to offer any unsolicited verbal encouragement to Wharton. The colonel, his face still flushed from the altercation, turned slowly from the direction in which Erskine had left and faced them both.

"I think I'll have a drink myself," he said.

It was Carr who placed the order. Nothing was said until Wharton had taken a deep drink from the glass of whisky which Carr had handed to him, and it was the colonel who spoke.

"I'll be damned if I'm going to allow that serpent to oust me from my position in this club," he said. "Whoever takes over from me will be a man of standing, not an obnoxious bully like Erskine."

Carr coughed diplomatically. "Do I take it that there is a problem with his wife?"

Wharton seemed not to have heard initially, not until his eyes flickered, and he looked strangely at Carr. "He won't get away with it. Not with any of it. I'll make sure he doesn't."

"Be careful what you say," cautioned Carr, his instincts at once alert and the ends of his nerves prickling with foreboding.

Wharton ignored him, his mind fixated on something else entirely. "Everything has gone too far."

With that, the colonel finished his drink and left the bar. Trevelyan glared after him, his eyes narrowed and his brows creased. He looked across at Carr and lowered his voice. "What do you suppose all that was about?"

Carr shook his head. "I would not like to say."

"An ugly scene. No surprise that Erskine caused it, of course."

Carr's expression was troubled, his lips pursed, and his eyes hardened with concern. "Very ugly indeed. It leaves a very bitter taste in one's mouth."

Trevelyan frowned. "Are you all right, sir?"

"I am fine, my boy," replied Carr, almost to himself. "I just have a premonition, that is all. A sense of something threatening."

"I wouldn't let it worry you, Mr Carr. I doubt the club will elect Erskine as chair even if he does stand."

"You misunderstand me, my friend. It is something much more worrying which troubles me."

Everett Carr dismissed Trevelyan's subsequent enquiries with a smile and drank some of his wine. He had no desire to express his concerns, especially when he had nothing but his own instincts to support them, but he felt certain in his own mind that there were events taking place around him which could only lead relentlessly to a single, terrible conclusion. He could not know when it would come to pass, any more than he could predict who might be responsible for it, but Carr was sure in his own mind that something dreadful was about to happen in the Icarus Club, and he knew that it was something far more serious than a squabble about the chairmanship of the place.

As Trevelyan ordered another round of drinks, Everett Carr tried to cleanse his thoughts of the inexorable threat of violence and the grim expectation of violent death.

Chapter Ten

O n that same afternoon, Vincent Overdale had expected to find
Leonard Faraday in his office at the Icarus Club, so, when he
received no response to his knocking and had opened the door,
he was surprised to find the room empty. For a moment, he wondered where
Faraday might be. He had not mentioned any specific plans to Overdale,
which was unusual in itself, and Overdale could not think of any place where
Faraday might want to go without him.

If his initial reaction to the empty office had been surprise, it was swiftly
replaced by a bitter and darkly sinister peevishness that Faraday had not
confided in him about his intentions. It was not that Faraday's movements
were of particular interest to Overdale, quite the opposite, but he did not,
and perhaps could not, accept that this was a reason for Faraday not to
advise him of his intentions. The injustice of the situation was all the more
severe when Overdale took into account how often Faraday questioned him
about where he himself had been and with whom. It was indicative of the
imbalance in their relationship, one which perhaps had been permitted to
endure for too long. Sniffing with contempt, Overdale turned his back on
the empty office and slammed the door shut.

He took a moment to calm his thoughts. They were unhelpful and
counterproductive, especially if he was to ask Faraday to help him out of the
current predicament in which he found himself. Perhaps part of his anger
at Faraday's absence was that it had robbed Overdale of the opportunity
to speak to the older man, a denial made all the more devastating because
of the mental fortification required to summon the courage to approach

Faraday at all. This resilience had been necessary not only because Overdale would have to admit to breaking once more that same promise which he always seemed to breach, but also because each time he was forced to ask for money from the man who had shown him such kindness, Overdale felt a small part of his soul dissolve. It was one thing to take a kind and generous man for granted, but it was quite another to be aware that one was doing so with impunity.

Overdale was aware of what sort of man it made him to act in this fashion, but there seemed little point in changing the fact of it when Faraday permitted it to continue. Would he change his conduct if Faraday even once refused him? Might that be the spark of resistance which Overdale needed to alter his ways? If there were definitive answers to those questions, they were beyond Overdale's reach. And, as the sadness of the eyes turned into a sneer of malice, he wondered if they ever needed to be. Why should he be the one to change? Faraday was perfectly capable of refusing him; if he did not wish to indulge Overdale's wishes, he was not obliged to do so. For as long as he did, however, what did it matter if Overdale continued to accept whatever was offered? It was not as if Faraday did not receive some repayment in kind.

Overdale was suddenly aware that his mouth was parched, the familiar wage of his previous night's sins. A glass of water would be appropriate, but Overdale had no taste for such prosaic remedies. A cold champagne or a fierce glass of whisky would serve just as well and invigorate him all the more. As the decision was made, a rapid succession of memories seemed to flash across his mind like bullets from a Vickers machine gun. None of them were particularly lucid or well-defined, but each had an impact on Overdale's recollections. There was, suddenly, the spectral taste of champagne on his tongue, the ghostly fingers of hands on his knees and thighs, the cold memory of warmer lips on his cheeks and neck, and the sound of echoing laughter ringing in his ears. In the middle of these wisps of remembrance, there seemed always to be his own face, reddened and damp with excess, his features distorted by intemperance, and his hair wild with revelry. And, as ever, there was the burning in his nose, the familiar sensation of the habit whose initial allure was intoxicating but whose aftermath was nothing less than painful. His realisation of it brought him back to his present, the memories of his raucous past now swallowed by his jaded present.

Overdale took a moment to compose himself, leaning back against the door of Faraday's office. His temples and the back of his neck had beaded with sweat, and the dryness of his tongue now seemed worse than ever. With an effort, he brought his breathing under control and dabbed at his face with his handkerchief, moving his jaw to make sure that it would function if he became compelled to speak to anybody. At last, satisfied that he looked acceptable, if not flawless, he made his way to the nearest of the club's bars. He was relieved to find that it was empty, save for the handsome George tending the bar, and Overdale took relish in ordering a glass of the very best champagne. If George had any opinions on the suitability of the hour for such indulgences, he did not express them, although Overdale thought that there was the slightest tremor of amusement in the boy's eyes as he handed over the chilled flute. In other circumstances, Overdale might have amused himself for a while and thrown discretion and fidelity to the wind, but it seemed neither wise nor appropriate to do so.

He took a seat in the far corner, his back turned to the bar, so that he would not be distracted. He held the flute to his lips, pausing to prepare himself for the onslaught, and then he arched his neck and gulped down most of the drink. He resisted the temptation to retch, instead forcing it down his throat and allowing the chill of it to hit his stomach. He lurched, but he instantly felt better for it, and the second mouthful, following swiftly on the heels of the first, was even more soothing in its effect. Overdale sank back in the chair and found that he was breathing heavily, his skin prickled by the intoxication of the alcohol.

"Burning candles at both ends, Overdale?"

The voice had seemed to come from the pit of his own consciousness, so much so that he did not acknowledge it immediately as being real. It was only as the familiarity of the mocking and spiteful tone of it settled into his mind that Overdale stirred to greet it. He shifted in his chair and looked towards the door. The bulk of the silhouette which stood there was blurred, and it took a moment for Overdale's eyes to recognise it, the dimmed edges coming into focus as the man approached. There was the familiar snigger, both contemptuous and threatening, and what Overdale took to be a click of fingers, followed by a barked order for a whisky.

"Bit early for champagne, I'd have thought," whispered Jacob Erskine, taking the seat opposite Overdale.

"Leave me alone." The voice was coarse, so weak that it barely seemed to be his own.

"Hair of the dog, is it?"

"I just wanted a drink."

"Needed one, by the look of you." Erskine accepted his own glass of whisky from the waiter and drank deeply from it. "You shouldn't touch the stuff if you can't handle it."

Overdale sneered. "I can take my drink as well as the next man."

Erskine grinned. "And I bet you know the next man intimately."

The words were spoken with such malice that they belied the amusement in his eyes. Overdale was struck immediately by a sense of fear. Erskine's meaning was surely unambiguous but, likewise, it was not clear enough for Overdale to risk taking offence at it or to launch a defensive argument against it.

"Leave me alone, Erskine," he hissed, with as much malevolence as he could muster within himself.

"Perhaps it wasn't just the drink," said Erskine, his voice once again heavy with implied threat.

Overdale finished his champagne and signalled for a second. His senses were returning to him now, his youthful arrogance beginning to reassert itself within him. "I take it you have something to say to me, Erskine, or else you wouldn't be here."

"Nothing to say other than what you're expecting. Have you got it?"

"Got what?"

"Payment."

"I've already paid you."

"That was for last month."

"It certainly was not."

Erskine leaned forward. "You should start taking better care of yourself, lad. All this drinking and—shall we say?—*socialising* is starting to distort whatever goes on in your head. You're losing track of time."

"Rubbish."

Erskine leaned forward. "You owe me, boy, and you will pay."

"Not now."

"I decide when you pay, lad." Erskine's voice was so low that its menace seemed even more acute. "You give me what I ask for when I ask for it, because I own you."

"Don't be ridiculous."

Erskine's eyes were fierce, but his voice was disconcertingly calm. "I know everything about you, boy, you remember that. I could ruin you in a moment, and I wouldn't blink whilst doing it."

Overdale swallowed, but his mouth was dry. "I can't just give you money, Erskine, and nor will I."

"Do I need to have words elsewhere about your filthy little games? Remember, boys like you have got a lot more to lose than men like me. Having one dirty secret is bad enough, but you've got two of them, haven't you?"

The conversation was interrupted by the arrival of the drinks. Overdale found that he was shivering, and the condensation on the glass, the shimmering evidence of the coldness of the champagne, seemed to make him quiver even more. Erskine picked up the whisky and threw it down in one arrogant toss of the head. He let out a sigh of satisfaction and rose to his feet, fastening his jacket as he did so.

"The usual amount, Overdale," he declared. "By nine o'clock tomorrow night. Don't let me down."

Overdale glared up at him. "Do your worst, you bastard."

The challenge suggested courage, a refusal to buckle under the threat of a bully, but Overdale felt more afraid than brave, and he suspected that his stubborn retort was a symptom of fear rather than daring. The smile which crept across Erskine's lips suggested that he had realised as much, and the gentle shrug of the shoulders demonstrated that the matter was of little concern to him. He repeated the deadline and then took his leave, whistling a low and mournful tune as he went.

Overdale picked up the glass of champagne and drank, his hand shaking as he lifted the glass to his lips. He was as furious as he was frightened. His defiance of Erskine might have appeared resolute, but Overdale knew that it was only compensation for his inability to summon a similar boldness against the far darker spectre which lurked in the shadows of his daily existence. He could summon courage against Erskine, however foolish or misplaced, but the other malign influence in his life was more difficult to confront. Erskine's demand for money was almost petulant by comparison with the far more sinister debt which Overdale knew would have to be paid if his life was to continue. And yet, it seemed to Overdale that he could do himself no harm by ridding himself of at least one of his torments. A wicked idea seemed to boil inside him, just as the familiar sense of paranoia began to close in on him.

He rose from his seat and made for the door. He glanced back to George and, through the distortions of his fear, it seemed to him that those handsome features were now dangerously inquisitive and, for the first time, Overdale realised that the conversation with Erskine might have been less than discreet. A wave of panic almost drowned his senses as the idea of being the centre of gossip amongst the staff of the club flooded his mind and he had an image of a possible future for him, disgraced and imprisoned for a variety of criminal offences, one of them being a caprice of nature and another the product of his own decadent debauchery.

And, all the while, he could imagine Jacob Erskine grinning and whistling in the wings.

Overdale walked out of the bar and into the corridor. Almost blindly, he raced up a flight of stairs, barely noticing any of the people he passed or any of the well-known furnishings. His pace quickened, his brow suddenly dampened with sweat, and when he finally stopped running, he found that he was breathless. He was surprised to find that he was back at Leonard Faraday's office door. Perhaps he had always planned to come back here, but he had no memory of deciding it.

He knocked on the door but opened it before allowing any time for a response. The office was still empty, and it showed no signs of Faraday having returned in the interval. Overdale, earlier annoyed by the absence, was now devastated by it. He had wanted assurance, comfort, arms around his shoulders, which would show him that the future was secure and that he had no cause to fear it. As it was, there was only the abandoned desk, its notepads, and pens neatly stored away, and the chair pushed under it. The size of the desk and the long back of the empty chair seemed to emphasise not only Faraday's absence but also Overdale's isolation. As if realising it with a sudden and stark clarity which was beyond his control, Overdale sank to the floor under the weight of his loneliness. He heard himself whimper, and he felt the damp of tears, but both sensations seemed to come to him from a distance, as if they were declarations of the anguish of someone else entirely. In the moment, Overdale could not remember the last time he had wept. He was not prone to tears, considering himself too assured of himself to be given to such displays of weakness, and he was filled with a sudden self-loathing, a disgust at his loss of control both of his situation and of himself.

Wiping his eyes with the balls of his hands, Overdale fought back any further tears. His eyes hardened, and his breathing became small, sharp explosions through his nose, almost feral and animalistic expulsions of breath. He looked around the room but saw nothing, his mind racing with confused ideas and haphazard decisions about how he could escape the trap into which he had fallen. Something had to be done, he knew that, and he had to act promptly if he was not to be lost forever. His mind continued to run with itself, and the final thought which seemed to crystallise from the fog of Overdale's mind was one whose darkness he had not anticipated. He was surprised, but somehow not shocked, to note that the idea came to him without compunction, without guilt, and, perhaps most horrific of all, without any degree of fear.

Chapter Eleven

That evening, Jacob Erskine dined early, and by half past eight, he was sitting in the silence of the reading room at the Icarus Club.

He had brought with him a large brandy, and this he placed on a small table beside one of the red velvet armchairs which were scattered throughout the room. The reading room was the one spot in the club where privacy was assured. It was treated by the members as a form of library, pursuant to a well-established but unwritten rule, so that conversation was kept to a minimum and personal solitude was both encouraged and respected. In a similar vein, the walls of the room were lined with fitted bookcases, each filled with leather-bound volumes, periodicals, and reference books. Their topics were diverse: scientific tomes, literary dramatic works, volumes of poetry, detective stories, and humorous magazines. The shelves boasted a variety of recognised names, from Shakespeare to Shelley, Doyle to Christie and Sayers and their like, to *Punch*, all interspersed with convoluted theories surrounding the history of medicine, electro-microscopes, and the expansion of the universe. God Himself was represented both by copies of the King James Bible and several theological dissertations arising from its doctrines.

None of these were the focus of Erskine's attention on that evening. He was consumed only by the contents of the note which had been delivered to him whilst he dined. It had been an unexpected communication, and the handwriting on the envelope, so familiar to him, suggested that it might be prudent to delay opening and digesting its contents until he was alone. Now, sitting in the reading room, his eyes racing over the words on the half sheet of paper, Erskine realised that his discretion had been not only sensible but necessary.

He read the note twice, as if the first reading of it was impossible to credit. After the second, Erskine let out a low growl of outrage and swore bitterly. For a long moment, he ruminated on the consequences of what he had read, on its presumption and arrogant assumption of his compliance with its demands, before screwing it into a ball and throwing it onto the flames of the fire in the marbled fireplace. He took a long sip of the brandy, but it failed to placate him. The feeling that he was being played for a fool refused to stop gnawing at his pride, and his frustration began to burn in a furious rage. The brandy seemed to fuel the flames of that rage, just as the flames of the fire in the grate flickered on the periphery of his vision. For a moment, it seemed to Erskine that he was surrounded by fire, as if his life had finally caught up with him and he had been plunged finally into Hell.

The clock had begun to strike nine when the door opened. Erskine had been counting the roll of banknotes, delivered to him only a few moments ago after a heated exchange with the person concerned. The sound of the door opening broke the silence in which Erskine had been sitting in contemplation. He looked up to greet the visitor, ready to bark an insulting dismissal at whoever it was, but when he saw who stepped into the room, he swallowed the rebuke and allowed it to subside within him. The only noise for a moment was the crackling of the fire and the chimes of the clock on the mantelpiece above.

"This isn't a good time," said Erskine.

"It's the perfect time."

Erskine shifted in his chair, but he did not rise. "I know we've got a lot to discuss, but right now, other things are on my mind."

"None of it matters. Not now."

There was something in the tone of voice which alerted Erskine to the sudden possibility of danger. It seemed incongruous to think that there could be any threat. The luxury and comfort of the club seemed somehow not to permit the idea, and yet Erskine's instincts were alive to the possibility, arched like a cat's back in the advent of distress. His thoughts had consumed him, so that he had not noticed that his visitor had moved away from the door momentarily and was now moving back into Erskine's line of sight. The dark figure remained silent, silhouetted by the lights which shone behind it, so that any trace of the features was masked by shadow.

It was only when Erskine saw the gun that he realised that the threat was altogether more real than any optical illusion. He saw the barrel level itself at him, and the single black eye of the revolver seemed to rob him of the capability to cry out. Time seemed to slow down, as if the seconds had become hours, so that Erskine seemed able to see everything with a cruel clarity. The muzzle of the gun seemed to increase in size, intensifying the darkness of its evil purpose, and the figure behind it seemed to blur out of recognition, except for the sharp, determined hatred of the eyes. When the shot came, Erskine's mind interpreted it as the clamour and uproar of the battlefield. Screams of men seemed to crash through his mind, wails of agony and regret following on their heels, accompanied by the roar of guns and the booming of exploding grenades. Almost simultaneously, he seemed to know that there had been only one shot and that the single scream of fear and agony had been his alone.

Erskine seemed to experience it all from afar. He saw himself recoil into the back of the chair, his vision misting with tears and the smoke of the gun. He saw the crimson spread over the front of his dress shirt and erupt in a sickening arc out of his breast, flecking his face, and he saw his legs and arms spread out limply as a result of the violent shaking of his body. He saw the banknotes rise and fall in the air before him, before settling softly around him. In that particular moment of life when a man knows he is being embraced by death, Erskine became aware of who and what he had been. He saw now how his attitudes had made enemies, how his cruelty had destroyed others, and how it was now destroying him. He was not a man to repent, but a sudden uncertainty of what it had all been for seemed to strike him, even as the blood and life drained out of him. His last thought, one which barely registered in his mind, was that nothing he had done in his life, none of his achievements and none of his realised ambitions, had been enough. He seemed to be aware only of what he would now never achieve, what he would never see, feel, or experience. Now, there was nothing for him but emptiness and a lonely existence only in the bitter memories of others. As if in protest at the realisation, his body gave a final lurch of movement and then fell motionless and limp in the red, velvet chair.

The revolver, still smoking, lay inert at his feet.

Chapter Twelve

I t was Everett Carr who discovered the crime.

He had been on his way to the bar for his final drink of the evening when he passed the reading room. The corridor down which he walked was empty and heavy with silence and, for a moment, Carr indulged himself in the stillness, a calming contrast to the bustle of the club restaurant. Carr smiled gently, his eyes closed, and the quiet of the passageway seemed so soothing as to be recuperative. His state of mind was so peaceful that when he passed the reading room, the horror of what he discovered seemed all the more intrusive and chaotic. The door being open did little more than stir his interest, not least because the club doors were kept closed as a matter of custom, but there was no reason for Carr to suspect anything macabre. It was only when he peered into the room that the full extent of the violence gripped him by the throat and caused him to gasp.

Jacob Erskine was sitting in one of the armchairs, his legs splayed out in front of him and his arms hanging uselessly over those of the chair, his eyes gazing at Carr with the startled stare of death. He was dressed formally, the white of his stiff shirtfront made all the more brilliant by the dark stain of scarlet which was spread across it. A revolver, which so obviously had inflicted the wound, was lying at the dead man's feet. Pathetically, almost stupidly, Carr noticed that one of Erskine's patent evening slippers had become partly dislodged from his foot. Covering the body, scattered across it like large, random snowflakes, was a number of banknotes. They looked as if they had been thrown at Erskine, some of the stray notes coming to rest foolishly on the dome of his forehead and in his gaping lap. Carr lowered his head sadly. The location of the wound was sufficient proof that suicide was out of the question, and the scattered banknotes seemed to suggest likewise. There could be no doubt about the facts of the matter.

Murder had come to the Icarus Club.

Carr turned on his heel. Moving as quickly as his shattered leg would permit, he made his way down the corridor to the bar. Almost at once, he saw Leonard Faraday step into the corridor and make his way towards his office. Carr hissed his name, loudly enough to be heard, but without risking drawing any unwanted attention. Faraday smiled at him, and he was about to speak, when Carr thrust his finger to his lips and beckoned him to approach in silence. Faraday complied, frowning, and he spoke only when he was by Carr's side.

"What's the matter?"

Carr gestured to the reading room. "We need the police, immediately."

"The police?"

Without waiting for further invitation, Faraday leaned forward and peered into the room. Carr watched as the man's eyes widened and the colour of his skin turned to that unnatural white, like the belly of a fish, which only the sight of violent death can produce. Faraday's throat fluctuated swiftly, and Carr suspected that he was resisting the urge to vomit. His lips moved uselessly and at such speed that any words he might have spoken would have been unintelligible. Softly, Carr placed a steadying hand on Faraday's shoulders. Faraday flinched and pointed wildly into the room, before clasping a hand to his mouth.

"My God, the money," he stammered, his voice barely more than a croaking whisper.

Carr seemed to ignore the words. "We must get the police. Go and telephone them from your office."

"What am I going to do?" hissed Faraday, and then, with more urgency, he growled, "How could this happen?"

But Carr shook his head. "Now is not the time for conjecture, Faraday. We must telephone for the police, and we must do it now."

Faraday nodded dumbly. "My office. I'll go and phone from my office."

Carr nodded with an encouraging smile. "Where's Colonel Wharton?"

"In the bar. I've just left him."

Carr saw at once that Faraday was too shaken to be discreet enough to summon Wharton without creating a scene. The man's eyes were wild with confusion and shock, so that they were incapable of concealing the existence of disaster. Again, Carr patted the secretary's shoulder and gently removed him from the doorway, steering him away from the horror.

"I shall fetch Wharton whilst you summon the police," Carr said. "This is the time for action and discretion, Faraday. Now, go."

The secretary complied, and Carr made his way to the bar. He found Wharton sitting in a corner, a glass of whisky in his hand, and an expression of suppressed rage on his face. As Carr approached, Wharton glared up at him, as if the intrusion was both unwelcome and unnecessary.

"I must have a quiet word in private, colonel," declared Carr in a hushed voice. There was no trace of urgency or panic in his tone, but there was a determination about it which suggested that he would not be easily swayed from his course.

Wharton seemed to recognise as much, but he maintained that any conversation would be an irritant to him. "I just need to be left alone for a while, Carr. Say what you must and leave me in peace."

Carr, his eyes narrowed with concern, was adamant. "It must be in private, colonel, and it must be this instant."

Wharton drained his glass and rose. He did not speak further, but he followed Carr out of the room and into the corridor. Carr led the way to the reading room and halted at the entrance. He prevented Wharton from moving further into the room by placing the silver handle of his cane on the man's breast.

"Prepare yourself," he said. "For the present, discretion is vital."

Carr stepped to one side, watching as Wharton took in the details of the terror which was set out before him. There was a harsh rasping of air, as the breath which Wharton must have been suppressing spat itself from between his clenched teeth. The eyes, glazed with whisky, drifted over the body, over its wound, over the money which covered it, and finally to the gun on the floor. As his attention fixed upon the weapon, Wharton's lips creased back over his teeth, and an ugly snarl escaped from his throat.

"My gun," he hissed, fear and confusion contorting his features and his voice. "It's my Webley. By Heaven, it's my revolver, Carr."

Wharton began to remonstrate, protesting his innocence despite the absence of any accusation. It became a brief but ludicrous pantomime of conflicting views, fuelled perhaps by the quantity of alcohol which Wharton seemed to have consumed, and Carr was aware of its impropriety. He clamped his hand over Wharton's flapping mouth and asserted his own authority.

"This is shocking and terrible," he said, removing his hands from Wharton's lips, "and it will mean a long period of discomfort for the club, but we must retain our control. It is far too early for any conclusions to be drawn, and it is not, in any event, for us to draw them. The police are on their way, and we must wait for them to arrive. For now, it is our duty to make sure that nobody enters this room and that nobody leaves the club, but we must do it without giving any cause for panic."

His words seemed to have a magical effect on Wharton. The eyes lost some of their ferocity, and the mouth stopped its futile attempts to form words. His breathing, previously so erratic that it must have starved his lungs, now became regulated, if not entirely normal. His hands still trembled, but they showed no more propensity for unfocused rage, and the fists uncurled themselves and hid their shame in his pockets.

"Thank you, Carr," he said. "The shock, you see. I hated Erskine, God knows, but I never wished for this. And with my gun," he added, as this specific cause for fear reasserted itself in his consciousness.

"When did you last see it?" asked Carr.

"Yesterday, when I cleaned it. Cyril Parsons saw me doing so."

"How was that?"

"I'd summoned him to my office." Wharton shrugged. "Just a coincidence that he arrived as I was cleaning the gun."

"Did Parsons know you owned it?"

Wharton saw the question in Carr's eyes and, for a moment, it was as if he could read the other man's thoughts. "It was no secret, Carr. I should say everybody knew I had it."

"Where do you keep it?"

"In my desk."

"Was that common knowledge too?"

"I suppose so." Wharton frowned. "That money. Where has it come from?"

Carr did not reply, his eyes narrowing as he recalled Faraday's reaction to the bank notes. A number of ideas formed in Carr's brain, nothing more than idle speculations whose substance was no less fragile than the silk threads of a spider's web. If Carr had wanted to make any form of response, he was prevented from doing so by the return of Faraday himself.

"The police are coming," announced the secretary. He allowed himself one final glance into the reading room, as if to assure himself that the horror was real.

"Excellent," said Carr. "I shall wait here for them. I think you two should begin to explain matters to the members present."

"Is that wise?" asked Wharton.

"The news will come out as soon as the police arrive," replied Carr. "We may as well have it out on our own terms."

Wharton nodded his agreement, and he and Faraday went about their grim business. Carr, left alone, leaned against the wall and closed his eyes, allowing his mind to drift back over those delicate ideas which had occurred to him, although none of them were inclined to blossom into definite lines of enquiry.

How long he had remained there in silent thought, Carr could not say, but it was long enough for him to be startled by the voice which broke suddenly through his thoughts like a siren in the darkness. It was a familiar and welcome voice, one which addressed him by name and with a note of efficiency and tact. The man who approached was large, his heft not entirely the result of bad diet and lack of exercise, but in equal part a naturally muscular bulk. His hair was the colour of human bone, almost white but slightly jaundiced from the effects of endless exposure to cigarette smoke. The cheeks were flushed pink and the clear blue of his eyes suggested a cheerful honesty, a combination which gave the man something of the appearance of a country farmer, an impression encouraged by the tweed suit which he wore as a matter of course. As he approached, he offered a huge flipper of a hand which Carr shook warmly.

"Haven't seen you in a long while, Mr Carr," said Inspector Mason.

"A few weeks, perhaps, inspector. I'm sorry we must meet again under such terrible circumstances."

Mason laughed darkly. "Can a police detective and a judge ever meet under pleasant circumstances?"

"A retired judge," Carr qualified, as if by doing so, he could dilute Mason's implied cynicism. "And I would like to think that our acquaintance is not based solely on our professional roles."

"A fair point, well made. Forgive me, Mr Carr, it's been a long day, and it looks as though it won't be over any time soon." His eyes were dancing around the corridor, not so much in appreciation of the opulence of the Icarus Club as with an impatience to see inside the reading room. "Shall we have a look, then?"

Carr nodded slowly and took a stiff step backwards to allow the inspector to pass by him into the room. As he stepped forward, Mason pointed to the other man's shattered knee. When he spoke, the jovial tone had darkened with concern. "It still gives you trouble?"

"It always will."

"You had Doyle Cullearn hanged," Mason said. "We got him at last between us. Is that any consolation for what happened afterwards?"

Carr's dark eyes met the clear blue of Mason's and held them for a long moment. "Not much of one, inspector."

"Perhaps not. But we got him, Mr Carr, and thank God we did."

Carr did not reply. Mason looked into those dark, saddened eyes for a long moment before smiling gently and giving a small nod of his massive head. He said nothing more on the subject of Doyle Cullearn's death or, by implication, the murder of Miranda Carr. Instead, he touched Carr on the forearm, a small but welcome gesture of supportive compassion, and stepped into the room where the effect of deliberate murder awaited his attention.

Chapter Thirteen

Mason did not approach the body immediately. He stood some distance from it, his hands in his pockets. Carr remained to one side of the detective, leaning on his cane, wishing that he could sit down even for a brief moment to relieve his damaged leg of some pressure. It would not be appropriate to sit in one of the unoccupied chairs in the room, and Carr was aware of the fact. His own discomfort, he acknowledged, would have to be endured in the wake of the initial stages of a criminal investigation.

"You knew the deceased, Mr Carr?" Mason asked.

"Jacob Erskine."

"A member of this club, of course."

Carr nodded. "Not a particularly well-liked one, inspector."

Mason raised an eyebrow. "Indeed? Had some enemies, did he?"

"He had one particular enemy, certainly," replied Carr without humour, staring sadly at the corpse. "As to anything else, it would be little more than gossip, which you will agree is unhelpful."

"Quite right, Mr Carr," replied Mason. "Always best to stick to facts. If the dead man did have enemies, no doubt I'll find out soon enough."

Carr smiled gently. "No doubt, inspector."

"What time was it when you discovered the body, sir?"

"A little before ten o'clock."

Mason consulted his own watch. It was now a few minutes past the half hour. "Do you know when Erskine was last seen alive?"

"I cannot say for certain, but I saw him go into dinner at seven o'clock or thereabouts."

"That would be at the club restaurant?" Mason watched Carr give the obligatory nod of the head in confirmation. "That will serve as a serviceable time of death until the quacks get a look at him. And the cause of death seems obvious but, again, we shall have to allow the pathologist to verify it. I suppose this is the weapon used?" Mason pointed with the toe of his shoe to Wharton's revolver.

"I have not examined it," said Carr, "but it would seem to be the case."

Mason glanced at him, smiling impishly. "Is there a reason why you'd examine the gun, Mr Carr?"

Carr returned the smile. "Curiosity only, inspector."

"I know about your curiosity, sir. Are you having thoughts about satisfying it on your own terms, by any chance?"

"I would not dream of hindering the police in their enquiries, I assure you."

Mason sniffed. "Being a member of this club yourself, sir, you will know how things operate here. You'll know the people concerned. That might be of some help rather than any hindrance."

Carr bowed his head. "I am happy to assist in any way I can."

Mason chuckled, but nothing more was said for the moment. The inspector now moved further into the room and, taking a handkerchief from his pocket, he picked up the gun and checked the chamber. "A single shot fired. Have you ever seen this gun before, Mr Carr?"

"No, but I hope I am not telling tales out of school when I say that it belongs to the club chairman, Colonel Hector Wharton."

"Does it indeed?" It was evident that the inspector thought the point to be of some significance.

"So he told me just before you arrived. He says it was common knowledge that he owned a gun and where he kept it."

"Which was where?"

"In his desk drawer."

Mason grunted, handing the weapon to one of his subordinates. "What about this money?"

Carr frowned, and his reply seemed to be spoken to himself rather than to the inspector. "That is an altogether more fascinating mystery."

"Any ideas about it?" Mason waited for a reply, but he was to be disappointed. "It'll have to be collected together and counted."

"All in good time," murmured Carr.

He was staring at the body and the money, his dark eyes narrowed and the moustache and Imperial twitching with curiosity. Mason had seen this level of concentration before, most frequently when Carr had been sitting on the Bench presiding over a case which Mason himself had compiled. The inspector had not appreciated initially how keenly the judge's mind had been sifting over the evidence presented to him. It was only over time, over the numerous cases Mason had investigated which had resulted in trials before Carr, in his judicial capacity, that the detective had come to realise that those dark eyes and the keen brain were seeing and inferring things which he, Mason, had overlooked entirely.

Carr had moved towards the body, and he was now circling the chair in which the wreck of Jacob Erskine sat. Mason watched Carr lean forward slowly, a slight wince of pain twisting his face as the damaged leg was stretched out to one side. The dark eyes hovered on the scarlet stain and the blackened edges of the damage done by the bullet, but only the briefest of movement from the eyes and lips showed Carr's repugnance and outrage at the crime. Mason wondered whether it was Carr's personal knowledge of the victim or the more general fact of murder itself which sickened the former judge. The answer, supposed Mason, was obvious.

Carr had straightened his back now and was gently pushing one of the many scattered bank notes to one side with the ferrule of his cane. Mason watched as Carr carefully picked up what the banknote had been concealing. Carr turned to the inspector, the object held tightly between his forefinger and thumb, and Mason stepped forward to examine more closely the piece of evidence between them. It was a small, curled, white feather.

"What do you make of that?" he asked.

Carr's eyes had widened with fascination. "A very telling little item, I would say."

"Would you?"

"Undoubtedly. Especially when you consider the type of gun used to commit the murder." Carr placed the feather into the envelope which Mason had offered him. "Do you not see the significance?"

Mason placed the envelope in the pocket of his coat. "I can't say it strikes me as particularly important, I must confess."

"Where do you suppose it came from?" asked Carr, now walking slowly around the chair towards the fireplace.

"No doubt you'll think me very stupid, Mr Carr, but I'd say it could have come from almost anywhere."

Carr clicked his tongue in disappointment. "Hardly from anywhere, inspector. I would suggest that it came from a very specific place. Look around you, and my meaning will become clear."

Mason glanced around the room, but Carr's promise of explanation did not come to fruition. He looked back to Carr, his expression now hardening with frustration and annoyance. Carr, sensing that the detective's patience was dissolving, smiled warmly and, when he spoke, his tone was conciliatory.

"Forgive me, inspector," he said, "I did not intend to cause any offence, I assure you. This feather leads me to a conclusion which seems so obvious to me that I take it for granted it will be so for everybody."

"Perhaps you would just explain, Mr Carr."

Carr pointed with his cane. "You will see that every chair in this room, save one, has a single velvet cushion on it. Only the chair beside the door has not. How does that strike you?"

Mason's eyes widened with comprehension and, when he spoke, his voice was trembling with excitement. "Somebody used one of the cushions to silence the sound of the shot."

"Precisely. And the weapon was a Webley, you will note."

Mason was nodding. "Revolvers don't take silencers."

Carr bowed with dignity. "My point exactly, inspector. The killer had to improvise. Now, the question which we must answer is why he should wish to deaden the sound of the shot."

Mason shrugged his shoulders. "So that nobody heard it, naturally."

"You miss my point."

Carr's voice had grown distant, as if his attention had been caught by something of equal, if not more importance. He was staring into the ashes in the grate of the fireplace beside which Erskine had been sitting. He probed them with the tip of his cane, seemingly without purpose, although Mason doubted it was an aimless gesture. Slowly, with a grunt of uncomfortable effort, Carr lowered himself to the floor and allowed his long fingers to dance around in the remains of the fire. The grey flakes were curiously soft to the touch, somehow seeming too delicate to be connected to the power of the flames which had created them. Carr's fingers scrabbled around in them, his lips tightened in frustration beneath the moustache and beard. Finally, with a low chuckle of triumph, he retrieved from the black and grey ruins of the fire a charred and brittle fragment of what had once been paper. He forced himself to his feet, hissing with discomfort.

"It seems as if Erskine burned something before he was killed," said Carr.

Mason was cautious. "That could have been thrown in the fire at any time."

But Carr shook his head. "Not so, inspector. It must have been today. The grates are cleared each morning, you see."

"But it might not be connected with the murder," insisted Mason.

Carr conceded the point with a bow of the head. "Perhaps not, but I would say it is better to assume a connection until we prove otherwise." He turned over the burnt paper, sniffed at it, and passed it over to Mason.

"The fragment of a note or a letter, by the look of it," said the inspector. "Not enough words still visible to make much sense of it."

"It tells us very little, it is true," murmured Carr. "We can discern the words, *'forced my hand'* and *'hate you,'* but very little else."

Mason nodded. "And what looks to be the letter P at the bottom of the page. Mind you, it could just about be the top half of a capital letter R, too. Part of a signature, no doubt. Do you know anybody with either of those initials?"

Carr's lips were pursed in thought. "Patrick Crane, a member here. Or possibly the doorman, Cyril Parsons. If it is, as you suggest, the letter R then it might be Ronald Edgerton, another member."

"Do you recognise the handwriting at all?"

Carr shook his head. "In any case, the scorching has distorted it to some extent."

Mason was staring at the note. "It certainly isn't a friendly communication - mention of forcing someone's hand, hatred of the dead man. We must find out who sent it and why, of course."

Carr was smiling. "I think there is no great mystery about that, inspector."

"You know?"

"I have an idea, but it would hardly be prudent to say so without evidence." Carr pulled his watch from his waistcoat pocket. "It is late. Might I ask what your next move will be?"

Mason sighed. "I must wait for the pathologist, and then I will make some preliminary enquiries with the members. Formal interviews will begin in earnest tomorrow."

Carr nodded his agreement. "Excellent. A sensible course of action. I shall, of course, be available for an interview whenever you say."

With a final bow of farewell, and a shake of hands, Carr left the room. Mason watched him leave, his brows furrowed, his mind alert to the fact that Everett Carr seemed to have learned more from the scene of the murder than he had himself. It was not a sensation which Mason welcomed but nor was it one which he felt able to ignore. He watched Carr descend the stairs from the corridor of death and, almost against his will, Mason felt something which, he was forced to confess, might have been relief that the retired judge was involved in the matter.

On the lower landing of the Icarus Club, Everett Carr had paused in reflection. He thought back to the body of Jacob Erskine, at the lifeless eyes which had glared back at him, as if pleading for some indication that his death would not go unpunished, that it would not be permitted to pass either unnoticed or without meaning. Carr's lips tightened, and he began to feel an overwhelming determination take hold of him, an almost religious compulsion to discover the identity of the killer. It was true to say, as he had stated to Mason, that Erskine had been disliked, but that was no reason to deprive him of his right to live his life to its natural end. The presumption of someone, as yet unknown, that they were entitled to deprive even the worst of men of his life was as disgusting as it was conceited. Carr's throat tightened with outrage, and his dark eyes hardened with resolve.

The sound of voices resurrected him from his private thoughts, and Carr saw two men approaching him. He stepped to one side to allow them to pass, noting that one was a uniformed officer and the other was a nondescript man carrying a medical bag. The pathologist had been expected, and now he had arrived. Carr continued to descend the stairs as, on the landing above him, the process of murder commenced.

Chapter Fourteen

When he arrived at the Icarus Club on the following morning, it seemed to Carr that the atmosphere of the club had altered. It struck Carr that the mood of the place had darkened, a sombre melancholy having replaced the usual polite amiability. It was as if the intrusion of murder had been able somehow to alter the fabric of the surroundings, leaving behind it a tangible trace of its macabre effects. The club was eerily quiet. As Carr walked up the main staircase from the entrance hall, he was struck by how abandoned the place seemed. There was none of the usual activity, no raised and boisterous voices, no laughter, no tinkling of glasses, and no clatter of cutlery. He passed nobody on the stairs, and the rooms into which he looked were empty. He became aware suddenly of his own solitude and, irrationally, he had the queer sensation that he was somehow intruding into some private mourning, a tragedy of which he should not be part, as if his very presence in the club was an offence. He supposed that many of the members would not wish to come to the club in the aftermath of murder, as if the crime might somehow taint them if they returned too soon to its midst. He could understand such reluctance, perhaps, but the absence of human life seemed only to emphasise the grim existence of death.

He found Mason in the reading room. The body of Jacob Erskine had been removed but its memory was so vivid in Carr's mind that he almost seemed to see it sitting in the velvet armchair which remained in place. It was as if he could still see the splayed limbs, the futile patent slipper hanging off one foot, the crimson patch of death on his breast. Their memory was so clearly defined that it seemed somehow worse than the reality. It was as much of a trick of the mind as the shift in atmosphere, but Carr found that he could not discard it, however hard he tried to reassert his sense of logic and rationality.

Mason smiled as Carr approached him. "You were right about that feather coming from a cushion, Mr Carr. We found the item itself thrown over one of the bannisters into the foyer below, a bullet hole in the centre of it. The killer must have just thrown it away once he fled the scene. No risk there, of course, since any member of the club could have thrown it away."

"No doubt, inspector," said Carr. "And yet, why use the cushion to silence the shot at all?"

To Mason, the answer seemed so obvious that any further comment was unnecessary. "I've had the money found on the body counted too. Thirty pounds."

"Not an insignificant amount."

Mason nodded his agreement. "We've narrowed the time of death to between half past eight and ten o'clock. Erskine was seen leaving the restaurant a little before half past eight, and you discovered the body at ten. The doctor sees no reason to disagree."

"And the gun?"

"It was the weapon used, no doubt about it."

"Did you speak to Colonel Wharton last night?"

Mason shook his head slowly. "We took only provisional statements. By the time the doctor had done his work, it was too late to do anything particularly constructive."

"But I presume you will want to interview him as a priority?"

Mason nodded. "Would you care to join me?"

If Carr had expected the invitation, he did not show it, and nor did he demonstrate any gratitude for it. He simply bowed his head in consent and followed Mason out of the room, where the smell of death still hung heavily in the air.

Wharton had made it known that he would be in his office, and he was as good as his word. As Carr and Mason entered, Wharton rose from his seat, as if such formality was not only expected of him but was of some assistance in aiding him to confront the horror which had disturbed his routine. He had expected Mason but, as Carr stepped humbly into the room behind the bulk of the detective, Wharton started, his eyes initially widening in alarm and then, disturbingly, narrowing with concern.

"What are you doing here, Carr?" he asked. The voice was polite, but its suspicion was unmistakable. "This is a confidential interview, surely."

"It can remain so," replied Carr.

"How can it if you are party to it?"

Mason felt it was necessary to intervene. "If I may, sir, I have asked Mr Carr to be present. He and I are old acquaintances, you see, and he knows the workings of the club and the people concerned."

Wharton was deflated by this official sanction of Carr's presence. It was evident that he had expected Mason to dismiss Carr, and the inspector's approval of the situation unsettled him. He glanced back at Carr, as if to reassert his own disapproval of his involvement, and shook his head. He invited both Carr and Mason to sit down.

Wharton sat down once his guests had settled themselves on the two wooden chairs on the opposite side of the desk. "If you think it is appropriate and necessary to have Carr here, inspector, I shall respect your judgment."

"I'm honoured, thank you, sir," said Mason, making no effort to disguise the sarcasm in his voice.

Wharton seemed not to be offended by the remark. He seemed barely to have heard it. "I'm still trying to make sense of it all, to be honest. None of it seems real. I keep expecting to hear Erskine at any moment or to see him barking an order for another drink. It seems impossible to accept that one will never see him again."

Carr stroked his wounded knee. "It is shock, colonel, an impulsive refusal to acknowledge the truth. Sudden death distorts one's mind, especially when it is death by violence."

Wharton's eyes were fixed on his agitated fingers, which drummed on the edge of the desk, and his bottom lip was curled back between the teeth. Carr watched him closely, fascinated by the nervous anxiety, which was so evident in Wharton's distracted glare, and the small beads of sweat which gathered on his temples. It was naïve to expect Wharton to be unaffected by the death of Erskine simply because he did not like the man, but Carr had not anticipated such a profound reaction to it. The use of Wharton's own revolver would have added a further frisson of unease, perhaps, but Carr had an inescapable premonition that there was something altogether more troubling which had seized Wharton's conscience.

Mason must have detected this suppressed anxiety as keenly as Carr, but he made no reference to it and, when he spoke, his voice was without emotion, the dull and practical tone of an official interrogation. "It was your gun which was used, I believe, colonel. I understand that most members of the club knew about the gun."

"I made no secret of it."

"Nor of where you kept it?"

"No." The word was spoken as if it was some sort of admission that Wharton ought to have been able to predict the gun's use and that he had failed somehow to prevent the crime.

Carr cleared his throat softly. "I think you said Cyril Parsons saw you cleaning it."

"That's right."

"You had summoned him to this office, as I understand it?" Carr smiled cordially. "Why had you done that, colonel?"

Wharton clasped his hands together, as if in some futile attempt to create a barrier between him and Carr. "It was a piece of private club business."

The prevarication was destined to fail, and Carr's smile seemed to say so. "I'm afraid murder destroys any sort of privacy, colonel. The inspector will tell you as much."

But Mason had no opportunity to confirm, if he had any intention of doing so at all, as Wharton responded immediately. "I don't suppose it is of any relevance to what has happened."

"That is for the police to decide," cautioned Mason.

Wharton leaned back in his chair and considered his words carefully. "Parsons was gambling on the club premises. As Carr knows, it is against club rules for members of staff to engage in drinking or gambling within the confines of the club."

Carr frowned. "Gambling with whom?"

And now, Wharton seemed to understand the importance. His eyes widened, and his lips parted in realisation. "With Jacob Erskine, amongst others."

Mason leaned forward in his chair. "Did you confront Erskine about it?"

Wharton shook his head. "I assured Parsons I hadn't yet done so. I felt that it was Parsons who needed reprimanding first and foremost."

"Perhaps you were afraid of any confrontation with Erskine on what is essentially a trivial matter," said Carr.

"You know as well as I do that Erskine was capable of generating an argument out of nothing."

Mason felt it appropriate to move the conversation forward. "The time of death has been fixed as being between half past eight and ten o'clock last night, sir. Where were you during that time?"

Wharton responded mechanically, but his eyes betrayed a sense of antipathy at his obligation to explain his movements. "I was in here going over some club business, of no relevance to the murder, and then I went to the bar. I felt I deserved a drink."

"What time did you go to the bar?"

"I didn't check my watch, but it must have been a little after nine."

"Was there anybody in the bar when you got there?"

"Several people."

Carr raised his hand in a discreet request to be heard. "Who was tending to the bar?"

"George."

"An admirable chap," Carr said.

Wharton concurred. "He will confirm my statement, inspector. As will Leonard Faraday, the club secretary. He came in a few minutes after me, and we had a drink together. A short while later, Carr broke the news about the murder."

Carr nodded. "I saw Faraday leaving the bar and called him for assistance, inspector."

Mason digested the information in a brief moment of silence. "I wonder if we could go back to the question of your revolver, colonel. It was kept in your desk drawer, you say. Was that drawer locked?"

"Of course. If you care to look, inspector, you will see that the lock has been forced." Wharton rose from his chair and stepped to one side, so as to facilitate the examination.

Mason moved round the desk and kneeled down in front of the drawer. Slowly, at his own troubled pace, Carr rose and did likewise, standing behind the official detective. There was no doubt that the lock had been prised open. The gold handle hung slackly by one of its screws, forced loose by the impact of the snapping of the lock, and the wood around the bolt of the lock itself was splintered beyond repair. Mason checked the other drawers, but found that they were all secured.

"When did you notice this?" he asked.

"Last night." Wharton held the inspector's glare. "I came into this office to do some paperwork, as I told you, and I noticed it then. I made a cursory search of the office for the weapon, of course, but I could find no trace of it."

Carr smiled with sympathy. "No wonder you felt deserving of a drink, colonel."

If Wharton appreciated or was soothed by Carr's apparent compassion, he did not show it. "The last time I can say for certain that the gun was in the desk was when I last cleaned it the day before yesterday."

"You didn't check on the gun in the intervening period?" asked Mason.

Wharton shook his head. "I had no need to."

Carr had resumed his seat, his brows furrowed and the dark eyes heavy with concentration. He allowed Mason to ask a number of routine questions, none of which seemed to him to be either vital or pertinent, but they permitted a period of time for Carr to gather his thoughts. A silence had fallen on the room before he spoke again.

"I wonder if I might be permitted to ask a very difficult question," he said.

"If you must," replied Wharton.

Carr was untroubled by the brusque reply. "Yesterday afternoon, there was something of a scene between you and Erskine."

Wharton's attitude was dismissive. "That has nothing to do with what has happened, Carr."

"If my memory serves me well, you made a threat to Erskine. About things being about to change for him. What did you mean by that?"

Wharton's forced indifference intensified. "I meant nothing by it. Heat of the moment and all that."

Carr was far from satisfied, and his dark eyes expressed as much, but his lips stretched beneath the impressive moustache into a wry smile, which left Wharton in no doubt that his assurances were not accepted. The colonel, perhaps to his credit, maintained his resolve.

Mason, for his part, was not so willing to compromise. "I would still like to hear about it, colonel."

Wharton flashed him a glare, as if to plead the inspector not to waste his own time, as well as that of the colonel himself. "I assure you that it is a blind alley. Carr overstates its importance."

"Indulge me," demanded Mason.

Wharton's composure was retained, but there was no doubt of his disgust at this ambush against him. Mason might have been expected to pry into private affairs, but the same did not apply to Carr, and Wharton's sneering expression towards his fellow club member left the matter in no doubt.

"Erskine suggested that he might be plotting to take over my position as chairman of the club. It was an empty threat. He would never have been able to secure sufficient support."

"Could you afford to take that chance, colonel?" asked Mason with a mocking innocence.

"Yes," stressed Wharton. "Besides, even if he had succeeded in ousting me from my position in the club, it is hardly a motive for murder. It would cause me some mild embarrassment, no doubt, and it would not be in the club's best interests, but it would hardly justify killing the man."

"That might depend on how well you handle public embarrassment," said Mason. "And how strongly you feel about the welfare of the club."

Wharton stiffened, as insulted as he was sickened by the inspector's implication. "However strongly I feel about either issue is nothing compared to how strongly I value my own neck."

Carr had continued to smile softly to himself throughout this exchange, amused by Wharton's half-truths and his steadfast evasion. Gently, he raised himself out of his chair and gave a small, polite bow.

"If you will excuse me, gentlemen," he said, "I have other matters to attend to. I am sorry if my presence here has caused any discomfort or offence. I meant neither, and I certainly have no wish to prolong such ill will."

"Please, Carr, don't leave on my account," said Wharton, as if the graciousness of Carr's apology had somehow shamed him into capitulation. "The shock of this terrible mess made me overreact, no doubt."

Carr waved his hand in a dismissive but calming gesture. "Not at all, Colonel. You were quite right to protest. I have nothing more to add to this interview in any case. I think it would be much better if I left you both alone."

Mason watched as Carr left the room, bowing once more before he did so. The inspector turned back to face Wharton and, with a gruff and authoritative clearing of his throat, he began to ask several more questions. They were, in turn, repetitive, routine, and irrelevant, but Mason had no intention of giving the impression either that he felt compelled to follow Carr, as if the amateur were the senior officer and the inspector a subordinate, or that the driving force of this investigation into murder was, in fact, Everett Carr.

Chapter Fifteen

George was polishing glasses in the bar when Carr tracked him down. He was a slim, eager youth, his features regular and handsome, despite his slightly protruding teeth, but his manner was both respectful and effusive. He did not hesitate when Carr beckoned him over. He liked Carr, who seemed to George to be less pompous and condescending than many members of the Icarus Club. If George considered that the older man's beard and moustache were overstated, or if he thought that the gaudy necktie and handkerchief were so extravagant as to be ridiculous when set against the customary black suit, he was not imprudent enough to say so.

George refused the offer of a seat and, feeling obliged to reciprocate, Carr remained standing too. George's eyes were active, fuelled by an exhilaration which he dared not express, although its cause was obvious to Carr.

"I suspect that the rumour mill has begun to turn its wheels, George," he said. "I see no reason to remain silent about it. You will all be interviewed by the police in due course. Mr Erskine died last night in the reading room upstairs."

George lowered his head, a concession to decency in the wake of death, but it was momentary only. He looked back into Carr's eyes almost immediately. "Was he murdered, sir?"

"I'm afraid so." Carr made no comment about the twist of excitement in the young man's voice. He was not experienced enough in the ways of life, thought Carr, to view murder as anything other than a thrill. He would come to learn the truth in time, the inevitability of which was itself a cause for sadness.

"I can't say I'm sorry, sir, if you'll forgive me," murmured George, "although I'd say it to nobody but you. He showed me up, in front of everyone, the other day, sir, and not for the first time. He was a beast for it."

Carr smiled gently. "I know about that, George."

"It doesn't mean I -"

"Of course not," assured Carr. "I doubt anybody will think anything of the sort either. I don't want to speak to you about that incident, George. I wanted to ask you about something else entirely."

George squinted. "Are you some sort of detective?"

Carr shook his head, his cheeks flushing slightly. "Certainly not. I wouldn't dare to presume to be anything of any kind. This is all a matter for the police, and you must co-operate when they speak to you. Do you understand?"

"Yes, sir."

"For example, if the police ask you whether Colonel Wharton and Mr Faraday came into this bar last night, you must tell them the truth."

George was nodding. "They both did, sir. The colonel first. He looked proper upset about something. Then, a bit later, Mr Faraday joined him. He didn't look much better himself."

Carr smiled amiably, but his dark eyes hardened with interest. "I see. Well, if the police ask you what had upset them so badly, you must tell them."

George shrugged. "I wouldn't know, sir."

"Neither Colonel Wharton nor Mr Faraday explained their behaviour to you?"

"No. But they wouldn't, would they?"

"What time was this, George, can you recall?"

The youth made a show of trying to do so. "Nine o'clock, just after."

"How long was it, would you say, between the colonel coming into the bar and Mr Faraday joining him?"

There was the same display of recollection. "Only a few minutes, no more. The colonel had barely started on his drink when Mr Faraday arrived."

"Did it seem to you to be a pre-arranged meeting, George?"

There was a shake of the head, the slim features adamant in their reply.

"Not a chance of it, I'd say."

Carr gave a bow of gratitude. "Now, remember, George, you must tell the police everything which you have said to me. It is your duty, and it takes precedence over your duty to the club. Do not allow anybody to persuade you otherwise."

He dismissed the young man and sat down for a moment in one of the leather chairs which furnished the bar. Absently, he stroked his knee. It was not aching, even in a psychosomatic fashion, but he may not have noticed even if it had been. His thoughts were so intense, his brain seized with such a profound concentration that his other senses seemed to have been paralysed by it. A forefinger and thumb pulled at the Imperial beard, and the lips beneath it were pursed in meditation.

Wharton and Faraday had both been in states of nervousness, according to George. Wharton's anxiety might well have arisen from his discovery, moments before, that his Webley had been stolen. It was not an unreasonable explanation. If he was innocent of the murder, the theft of the gun would have been a sufficient cause for concern; if he were guilty of it, the aftermath itself would explain Wharton's unease. There was no evidence at all that the revolver had been stolen, Carr reminded himself, beyond Wharton's own word, and it would not be the first time a criminal had attempted to conceal his own crime under the cover of a theft which he had staged himself.

But what of Faraday? As with Wharton, if Faraday had murdered Erskine then he would naturally be disturbed by the fact. It was not credible to assume that the taking of another person's life left no adverse effect on the perpetrator of such a crime. Committing the most terrible sin of all took a certain psychology of mind, but it did not presuppose an absence of emotion. In Carr's experience, the opposite was generally the case: murder was driven by the very strongest of emotions and, once they had been ignited into action, it must surely take a period of time for them to regress. Was Faraday in this period when he entered the bar? In frustration, Carr slammed his cane on the floor and forced himself out of the chair. If Faraday was the killer, he must have had a motive and, as far as Carr could tell, there was none.

And yet, there was one curious point concerning Faraday which had struck

Carr as soon as it had occurred. It had seemed strange to him at the time and, in the wake of George's evidence of distress, it now appeared crucial. If nothing else, it was a direct connection between Faraday and the murder of Jacob Erskine, and it was possible, if not probable, that further investigation of it might well uncover that motive for Faraday to murder Erskine which, at present, frustratingly eluded Everett Carr.

Chapter Sixteen

I t was immediately obvious that Leonard Faraday had been crying. His attempts to hide the fact were so obvious that Carr did not pursue the point, but there could be no mistake about the bloodied whites of the eyes and the rawness of their lids. The wrinkled handkerchief, clutched in one of the trembling hands, erased any doubt. Carr had apologised for intruding and had voluntarily withdrawn from Faraday's office, but the secretary had called him back.

"A friendly face is most welcome, Carr, if you don't mind," he said.

Carr closed the door and helped himself to a seat. "These are very trying times."

"Strange, isn't it?" Faraday was trying to smile. "We read detective stories insatiably, and we even devour reports of murder in the newspapers. But nothing prepares you for the brutal reality of it happening on your own doorstep."

"By thy great mercy defend us from all perils and dangers of this night," quoted Everett Carr. "Such perils and dangers are always more terrifying in reality than in fiction, dear boy."

"The police have arrived, I understand," Faraday said. "They have not yet questioned me, but I suppose it is only a matter of time."

Carr nodded. "At the moment, the inspector is with Hector Wharton."

"They don't suspect him, surely?"

"The murder was committed with his revolver," argued Carr.

"Everybody knew about that gun. It is hardly conclusive proof."

Carr conceded the point with a smile. "By definition, you include yourself?"

Faraday's fingers curled into fists, and his eyes crystallised with an emotion which was as much fear as it was outrage. "I didn't kill Erskine. I had no reason to."

"None at all?"

"Of course not. What are you suggesting?"

Carr shook his head, dismissing the question. "I have been wondering about something, Faraday, and I rather thought you might be able to help me."

Faraday was immediately suspicious. His lips pursed, and his eyes began to dance, like those of an animal cornered by a hunter. "Wondering about what?"

Carr examined the silver handle of his cane. "The money found on Erskine's body. I think it struck you as strongly as the murder itself."

Faraday forced a laugh. "I don't think so. You make it sound as if I view murder as being less important than afternoon tea."

Carr smiled benignly. "Forgive me, my friend, I mean you no disrespect. But perhaps you could explain your words when you saw the body."

Faraday frowned, but it was not so much from confusion as, in Carr's estimate, from fear. "I don't know what you mean."

Slowly, quietly, Carr repeated the words. *"My God, the money.* That was what you said."

Faraday thought back to the previous afternoon. He had gone to his office after lunch, disappointed that Vincent Overdale had not been able to join him for the meal, so that he had barely tasted the chateaubriand or the green salad which he had ordered. He had entered the office and had seen at once that the door to the safe was open. He recalled now the sensation of nauseating panic which had risen inside him, and he could see himself running uselessly to the safe, as if he could prevent what had happened simply by slamming shut the door. It had been a foolish, irrational reaction, and it had been so instinctive that he had been unable to control or suppress it. He had not felt foolish, though. He had felt nothing but fear. He had looked inside the safe, already knowing what he would discover, but this instinctive knowledge had not prevented or lessened the sense of shock. The safe had not been empty, but it might well have been. The papers which he kept inside, and which had remained untouched, meant next to nothing when set against the disappearance of the envelope of money which he had placed in the safe on the previous morning.

Faraday retained his composure in front of Carr, whilst these memories tormented him. He smiled back at Carr and could only trust that his expression was as casual as he hoped. "Did I say that?"

"You did."

Faraday laughed unconvincingly. "What a stupid thing to say. I can't explain it, other than to say that it was a reaction to the shock of the whole situation. I didn't expect to see a dead body, let alone one buried in money. Whatever I said must have been an instinctive response."

It might have been a reasonable explanation, were it not offered to Carr with a sincerity which was so intense that it was barely credible. "You joined Wharton for a drink last night, I believe."

The change in topic was a welcome one. "Yes, a little after nine o'clock."

Carr conceded the point. "Did it strike you that Colonel Wharton was disturbed by something? Anxious, perhaps, or distressed?"

Faraday considered the question carefully before nodding his head slowly. "Yes, I think I would agree with that."

"Can you think of any reason why he would be ill at ease?"

"The argument with Erskine earlier that day, perhaps."

Carr's eyebrows raised. "You heard about that?"

"You know how gossip spreads in this place, Carr." Faraday's expression altered, as if something had dawned on him suddenly, like a sudden shaft of sunlight in a darkened room. "Are you suggesting that might be a reason to kill Erskine? I'm bound to say that I cannot accept Wharton as the murderer."

"I am sure that none of us can imagine any member of the club being a killer," argued Carr, "and yet it appears that one of us most certainly is."

Faraday removed his spectacles and ran a hand down his face. "It's a nightmare, all of it."

"What would you say if I told you that a witness has suggested that you were also distressed when you entered the bar?"

Carr watched as the spectacles were replaced, the eyes behind them hardened with caution. "I would say that someone was mistaken."

"There was nothing on your mind last night?"

Faraday's mind flashed back to the theft of the money. "Nothing."

"What had you been doing before you went to the bar?"

"Working in here, on various club matters." He gave no suggestion that he was prepared to elaborate on what those matters had been. A second thought seemed to consume him, and his attention was deflected accordingly. "As a matter of fact, that reminds me of something. I took a break from my work and walked around the office, to stretch my legs, and I happened to look out of the window. You will see that it looks out onto the rear courtyard of the club."

"Indeed," said Carr. He looked out of the window and down into the paved square of the courtyard, the high brick wall surrounding it broken by the double gates in an archway on the far side, which led out onto the main street.

Faraday had joined him at the window. "I saw someone crossing the courtyard. They were leaving the club, by the look of it, but when they got to the gates, they loitered for a few moments, before disappearing through them."

"Did you recognise who it was?"

"No."

"Could you say if it was a man or a woman?" He watched as Faraday gave a regretful shake of the head. "What time was this?"

"A little before eight, perhaps."

Carr frowned. If Faraday was suggesting that this person, whoever it had been, was involved in the murder, the timing was inappropriate. And yet, if the person concerned had legitimate business in the club, why enter or leave through the back entrance? Carr smiled benignly at Faraday, but his thoughts were dark, and the primary idea in his mind was whether this story of a mysterious visitor was a concoction of Faraday's, designed to deflect Carr's attention from his previous line of questioning.

Before he could say anything, however, Faraday was indulging himself in a further request for confidence. "I say, Carr, there's something else. Can I trust you with it?"

Carr put his hand to his breast. "Of course."

"It didn't seem important at the time, but it might be now, given what has happened."

"I would be pleased to advise you, Faraday, if I can be of assistance."

"Well, as I say, I left this room just before nine o'clock and went down to the bar. As you know, to do so, I had to pass the main entrance." He watched Carr nod in agreement. "Cyril Parsons was supposed to be on duty last night, but when I passed the entrance hall, I chanced to look at the front doors, and I couldn't see him."

Carr's fingers tightened instinctively around the silver handle of his cane. "Did you investigate?"

Faraday nodded. "Only briefly, I must confess. I walked past the cloakroom and opened the front doors, but there was no sign of the man."

"You didn't go to look for him?"

A shake of the head left the matter in no doubt. "I merely thought I would advise Wharton about it and let him deal with the matter. He is looking for a reason to dismiss Parsons, as you may have heard, and I thought this would give him the excuse he needed. I suppose that in itself might be a motive for Parsons to kill Erskine."

Carr found it difficult to argue. There was no direct evidence of Parsons' guilt, but nor was there of anybody else's, and there seemed to be as much circumstantial evidence against him as there was against others. Certainly, Parsons had cause to want Erskine dead. Wharton had explained about the illicit gambling sessions, organised by Erskine, in which Parsons had been involved. And Carr himself had overheard an argument between the two of them only a couple of nights previously, in which it had been clear that Parsons owed Erskine money. It was no stretch of the imagination to assume that the money related to gambling debts left unpaid. Men had killed for lesser reasons, certainly, and Carr had sentenced such men to hang on account of them. There was the money, too. Was it a sign that Parsons had satisfied his debt, but then watched Erskine count out the notes in a final insult of mistrust and shot him in the chest in retaliation at it?

"Did you know that Parsons was decorated in the war?" asked Faraday. "He saved a number of his battalion during one of the bloodier Yprès campaigns. He held off German troops whilst his fellow officers made their way to safety. He was commended for it. Military Cross, no less."

Carr was fascinated by this record of Cyril Parsons' military bravery, not least because Parsons was hardly distinguished by his displays of gallantry, respect, or decency. His actions in the war and the decorations he had received on account of his valour seemed at odds with the man Carr had known. Nevertheless, courage in the face of war did not preclude a man from being a murderer. Perhaps, after all, it might turn a man into one.

Faraday was still talking. "My point, Carr, is that Parsons was able to save the lives of those men because he was proficient with a gun. In fact, as I understand it, he was one of the best marksmen in the regiment."

Carr's dark eyes seemed to blacken further, as he recalled Parsons himself say as much to Erskine. It had struck Carr as a threat against the dead man and Faraday's revelation of Parsons' prowess with a gun seemed to confirm it. Parsons not only had a reason to kill Erskine but also, it seemed, the skill to do so.

"Listen to me, my friend," Carr said, his voice not only insistent, but intense. "You must tell this to the police, but repeat it to nobody else. Do you understand? If you are careless with this information, it might prove very dangerous. For you and for Parsons."

There was something authoritative in Carr's expression which Faraday found impossible to defy. "If you say so, Carr. Do you think Parsons killed Erskine?"

Carr remained impassive. "There is much to be learned, Faraday, and speculation can be destructive."

He said no more, preferring to allow his warning to settle into Faraday's consciousness. Slowly, Carr rose to his feet and walked towards the door. Once he had closed it behind him, Faraday leaned back in his chair. His stare glazed, the blue eyes almost vacant behind the lenses of the spectacles, and the lips curled into a vague, barely discernible smile of triumphant relief.

Chapter Seventeen

Hector Wharton was not surprised that the police had wasted no time in contacting Margaret Erskine. He had hoped that he would be able to inform her of the death of her husband personally but, on reflection, he realised that it was a forlorn hope. He should have had no doubt that official procedure would take precedence over more personal considerations. Nevertheless, he could not help but feel a certain regret that Mason and his men had robbed him not only of an opportunity, but also of a duty which he felt it was his alone to perform.

There was no evidence of tears. The Erskine marriage had not been happy, as Wharton knew only too well, but it had endured for a number of years, and Wharton wondered whether it was possible for there to be no sense of loss at all. He supposed there must have been happiness at some point, even in the most fractured marriage, so that the finality of death must be expected to leave some trace of tragedy, but Margaret's face was almost devoid of emotion. Wharton was not sorry to note this absence of grief, and nor was he ashamed at how pleased he was with it.

Margaret had made tea, but it remained untouched. Wharton doubted that neither of them would register the taste of it, nor be refreshed or invigorated by it. It was a bow to convention and nothing more. It had certainly not been a desire for refreshment which had prompted her to undertake the task. There was something about the stoicism in the pale cheeks, and the distant eyes which impressed him deeply, and her courage in the face of such adversity seemed to reveal a depth of character which, to his shame, he realised that he had underestimated previously or, worse, never detected.

Looking at her, Wharton seemed to love her more than he had ever done before.

"The police have questioned me about my whereabouts," Margaret said.

"What did you tell them?"

"That I was at home all night."

"You made no mention of our plans?" He watched her shake her head. "Good."

She shook her head. "Have we made a terrible mistake, Hector?"

"No." His reply was adamant. "Jacob left us with no choice, Margaret. Remember that. He can't hurt you anymore."

She had either not heard him or had not considered his reply worthy of comment. "I can't stop thinking about what must have gone through his mind when he saw the gun pointing at him. Did he have time to feel any fear or pain, or was it all so quick that he wouldn't have had time to register anything?"

"He most likely felt nothing." Wharton tried to be sensitive as well as factual. "It would have been over in a flash."

Her eyes were wild. "How can you know that?"

"I've shot men before now, Margaret. In the war."

"Oh, yes, of course. You're an expert."

The insult was unwarranted but possibly unintended, so he did not retaliate against it. In the silence which followed it, Wharton realised suddenly that the absence of tears was not because Margaret was feeling no emotion but that she had been suppressing it with more skill than he had credited her with. What the emotion was, he did not feel able to say. It might have been grief, and Wharton was aware that it was an emotion which could manifest itself in many different forms, each of them as surprising as the others. Equally, it might have been a perverse sort of relief. There was no reason why relief should not manifest itself as unpredictably as grief.

"It was my gun," he confessed.

He had expected an immediate reaction, but it did not come. It seemed as if her mind had to take its time in accepting not only that the words had been said, but that they had been heard correctly. Slowly, she turned her head to face him, the movement so careful that it appeared as if she thought any sudden shift in her poise would shatter her senses. "Your gun…?"

He saw at once the idea which had formed in her mind, and he recognised immediately how dangerous it was. "I didn't kill him, Margaret."

Her words came out in short, rasping sobs, her eyes widening with terror as their meaning registered with her. "You said Jacob was the problem and we could solve it. What we planned, everything we said… and all the time you intended to… Oh, God!"

"I didn't kill him," Wharton reiterated, with more urgency.

"You wanted him dead." Her terror was palpable now, her body shaking with it. "You wanted him gone because of me. In spite of everything, you wanted him…" The words would not come.

"Now, listen here," he said, "you're talking nonsense. Not only that, you're talking dangerously. Damn, Margaret, you could get me hanged if you talk like this. I did not murder Jacob. My gun was stolen. Anybody could have taken it from my drawer. Including you," he whispered as the fact occurred to him with a startling, unnerving abruptness.

"What?"

He was pacing the room now, his hands clasping and unclasping. "I told you about the gun a few weeks ago. You knew where I kept it."

She was snarling with outrage. "You're being horrible, spiteful."

He laughed cruelly. "Years of suffering, Margaret. Motive enough, I'd say, if we're going to accuse each other like this. How long before you broke under Jacob's abuse?"

She stood up swiftly, her arm arcing out, the palm of her hand striking his cheek with such force that they both recoiled in simultaneous pain. The movement was so quick, so fluid, that Wharton had been unable either to anticipate or prevent it. After the violence of it, the silence and stillness which followed seemed suffocating. In the depth of it, their mutual hysteria seemed to evaporate. She stood, shocked, her hands clasped to her lips and her breath held in her lungs by fear. By contrast, Wharton was breathing heavily, his brow damp with sweat, as if suddenly exhausted by the confrontation. Gradually, his breathing slowed and a smile drifted gently over his lips. He moved towards her, taking her in his arms, and kissing her forehead. She allowed herself to take refuge in his embrace, and she began to weep silently into his breast.

"We mustn't fight, not now," he said. "Not after everything we've done."

She pushed herself away from him and turned her back on him. It was not a dismissive gesture, rather an assertion of her own private space. When she looked back at him once more, her previous stoicism was in the process of reaffirming itself. Her hands were not quite steady as she lit a cigarette, but they were no longer the hands of a frightened woman.

"Where were you last night, Hector?" she asked.

He bristled at her suspicions, angry that his belief in her was not reciprocated. He supposed that love did not require an unconditional acceptance that a lover's words were always truthful.

"I was in my office at the club," he stated as dispassionately as he could. "I went to the bar and happened to meet Faraday there. I stayed with him until Everett Carr broke the news of what had happened." He allowed a moment to pass. "Just as I told the police, Margaret."

She watched him, his eyes fixed on hers, as if daring her to question him further. She drew on the cigarette and allowed the smoke to break her glare. "I believe you."

Wharton was not so blinded by his love for her that he was unable to detect the lie. "I had better go. Leave you in peace. I shall see myself out."

It was only after she was left alone and the tears were falling freely that she realised how badly she had treated him. She had allowed her suspicions of him to twist her feelings, to manipulate how she reacted to his attempts to console her. Had she really believed that he was guilty of murder? It had been her instinctive reaction to the news of Jacob's death, certainly, and somehow, even from a distance of thought, she could not entirely dismiss the idea that it had been Hector Wharton who had shot the man who stood between them. The thought both terrified and saddened her and, because of it, the silent sobbing intensified into violent howling of agony, and it seemed to her that it would never come to an end.

Chapter Eighteen

And yet, her tears had stopped by the time Everett Carr called to see her. She had not expected a visit from him, and she supposed that her expression of surprise might have camouflaged any trace of her previous upset. Certainly, as she spoke to him on the threshold, he displayed no indication that he had detected any evidence of sobbing. If he was surprised by her lack of tears, though, he did not declare it. Instead, he smiled warmly at her and requested entry, which she granted. She took his hat and gloves, but he retained his cane. It was only after he had done so that she recalled that he was lame. It seemed foolish of her to forget the fact, given it was so clearly a defining physical characteristic of him, but she reminded herself that she did not know him particularly well. Having acknowledged this fact, his presence in her house seemed all the more curious. Despite his genial and affable manner, and the kindness of his smile beneath the extravagant moustache and beard, Margaret Erskine felt a sudden sensation of discomfort in Carr's company, one which might even be mistaken for fear.

He declined the offer of coffee but accepted the one to sit. He lowered himself into a chair, sighing at the effort, and stretching the injured leg out in front of him. "It's a rather chilly day, and it is always worse in the cold."

Margaret watched him stroke the joint and its surrounding areas. "Forgive me, Mr Carr, but how did you injure your leg?"

She saw immediately that the question had either offended or unsettled him. His eyes, so dark that she found them strangely alluring, flickered erratically before settling on her, and the smile faded temporarily from his mouth. She made an attempt to withdraw the question with apologies, but he assured her that such recrimination was unnecessary.

"It is not a topic on which I tend to dwell, that is all, dear lady," he said. "Since you ask, it was a bullet wound."

To say any more might have been indiscreet, not to say tactless, and Carr hoped that his tone of voice, neither rude nor encouraging, might have suggested as much. Margaret stared once more at his broken knee and smiled at him, an indication that she was willing to oblige.

"I am sorry about what has happened," said Carr. "To lose a loved one is difficult enough, but to do so in such circumstances is beyond horror."

"Thank you, Mr Carr. Did you know Jacob well?"

Carr inclined his head. "I could not say that. We were members of the same club, and I knew him to speak to, but I could not admit to a close friendship."

She smiled, a shade of regret darkening her features. "I can't say that we had many friends at all. Jacob was not an easy man to like."

Carr made no reply. It was not the sort of comment which a bereaved woman might be expected to make, and it seemed somehow incongruous for her to say it. Carr recalled that he had said words not so dissimilar only a few days previously, but to hear them come from the man's widow struck him as a startling confession. Margaret seemed to recognise it, and she lowered her head, not so much in shame as in resignation.

"Perhaps I shock you, Mr Carr," she said. "It's true, nevertheless."

"I have no wish to distress you," Carr replied with care, "but the truth is what we must have now. The truth is sometimes so difficult to tell, but murder demands it. If there is a reason you can think of for someone wishing to harm your husband, you must inform the police. They have been here, I suppose?"

She nodded. "Earlier this morning. A detective sergeant, making a preliminary enquiry only, he said. An inspector will be coming to see me later, I believe."

Carr smiled. "I know Inspector Mason personally, and you may trust him. If you are prepared to take the word of a stranger, that is."

She could not help but return his smile. There was something ingratiating about his manner, something about the eyes which demanded trust and promised comfort, despite their darkness, and the affable, gentle smile likewise suggested both discretion and consolation.

"Is it true that you were once a judge?" she asked.

He bowed his head. "It seems a lifetime ago, but it is true. Why do you ask?"

"I suppose you have a deep knowledge of murder. Why people do it, the sort of people who commit it."

Carr frowned. "I'm not sure I understand you, dear lady."

"I wondered… whether you might be able to say what sort of person did this to my husband?"

Carr was silent for a few moments. "Anybody can kill, in the right circumstances. We are too complex to be so easily categorised."

"Do you really believe that?"

"Oh, yes. I have seen as many depressed wives hang as I have violent criminals. I have known religious men, heathens, the educated, the wealthy, and the dispossessed all be guilty of murder."

"What a grisly thought."

Carr nodded agreement. "But true, nonetheless. People kill for all sorts of reasons. The question which must be asked first is why one particular person was killed. It is the victim who must be the starting point."

Margaret was already nodding. "Which means it is all going to be about Jacob, about what he was, who he was, what he did. That is what frightens me, Mr Carr."

"Frightens you?"

She looked at him with eyes which were as defiant as they were anguished. She was about to say something more, Carr was certain of it, but a thought must have occurred to her which convinced her that silence was a better option. The eyes retained something of their pain, but the voice contradicted them with its efforts to suggest composure. "I mean the prying into our lives, which I suppose will be necessary for the police. Poking around into every aspect of our marriage, into all our private affairs."

"It will be necessary, dear lady, but Mason is discreet. I would imagine that, for the present, he will concentrate mainly on the most basic enquiries. Where people were when the tragedy occurred, for example."

If Margaret recognised the trap, she was not afraid to walk into it. "I was at home, all night. I didn't leave the house."

Carr smiled warmly. "If that is the truth, dear lady, that is all you need say to the police."

"I have already said it to a detective sergeant." She held his gaze and returned his smile.

Carr looked down to his clasped fingers around the handle of his cane. "Is there anybody you can think of who might wish to harm your husband?"

How was she to respond? It was hardly possible for her to say that, between them, she and Hector Wharton had just cause to want Jacob dead. No more was it within her present frame of mind to be able to confide in this kind but somehow disconcerting man how Jacob had treated her. Margaret was aware of her own betrayal in suspecting Hector Wharton, but she was not about to allow any third person to be equally conscious of it.

"I can't think of anybody," she said.

"You never saw him quarrel with someone, perhaps?"

"No."

"Have you ever met anybody from the Icarus Club?"

Her mind, twisted by guilt, detected a malicious intent behind the question, one designed to trap her. Was it possible that her relationship with Wharton had already been discovered? She doubted he would have confessed it himself, even under duress, but she could have no certainty about it until she had the opportunity to ask him directly. A denial would be unwise, but Margaret had an intuition that caution might be sensible.

"I know Colonel Wharton," she said. "And I have met Leonard Faraday, but I don't know him very well."

"Anybody else?" Carr watched her try to recollect, and he waited for the attempt to be concluded with a shake of the head. He returned it with one of his most ingratiating smiles. "Do you receive many callers to the house, Mrs Erskine?"

And it was then that the memory returned to her with a brutal force. It had been only last week, a matter of days before Jacob had died, that she had seen the man. It had been one of her nights of insomnia, a common aftermath following one of Jacob's bouts of tyranny, when the ache in her ribs and the pain in her stomach would deprive her of sleep as much as the shame and hatred in her mind. She had gone downstairs, her motive uncertain beyond the fact that anywhere in the house was preferable to the confines of her bed. She might have wanted cocoa, warm milk, or some much more effective drink, or she might simply have wanted to distance herself from Jacob. Whatever her motive, she had been unable to remain in her bed. She had been careful not to wake him, as to have done so would have been to invite further violence, so she had made her way down the stairs with slow and deliberate steps, each one carrying its own danger of discovery.

Once downstairs, the allure of alcohol had overtaken her. She had made her way to the living room and indulged her wakefulness in a glass of whisky. It was never a drink to hold any special appeal for her, and it had done nothing to convert her on that night, but anything else would have seemed wholly inadequate. She had sat alone in the darkness for some time, her thoughts barely registering in her mind, although it wasn't clear whether it was an effect of the alcohol or a subconscious refusal to allow their destructive nature to affect her.

It had been as she was crossing the hallway that she had heard the noise. A slight interruption into the silence of night, so unexpected that it might have been a product of her imagination, but she had not thought so. She had stayed motionless in the hallway, her senses alert, but her intentions undecided. Whether or not she had expected a further noise, she had been unable to say, but it had come and, this time, Margaret had been sure. She had moved swiftly yet silently to the door of Jacob's study, certain that the noises had emanated from there. Looking back now, she was not able to say from where she had summoned the courage to pull open the door, but she had done so. She had thought to switch on the light immediately afterwards but, in the event, it had not been necessary. Telling the story to Carr, she was aware that its climax had occurred swiftly but, in retrospect, her memory forced them to play out at an unnaturally slow speed.

"I couldn't tell who it was," she said, "but they must have seen the door open, even in the darkness, and fled."

Carr had listened to the story with a growing intensity. Now, his eyes were alive with curiosity, and his moustache and beard quivered as his lips pursed in concentration. "Could you tell if it was a man or a woman?"

Margaret shook her head. "Whoever it had been was dressed in black, a scarf around the lower part of the face, and a cap pulled low over the eyes."

"Did you approach the window?" He watched her shake her head. "But the intruder had seen you?"

"Whoever it was had been trying to force the window. He had a weapon with him, which he was trying to slide under the catch when, as I opened the door, he stopped. He was motionless for a matter of seconds, then he ran back across the lawn and over the garden wall. Surely that means he had seen me."

Carr's eyes remained fixed on her. "Or, at least, perhaps, that he had detected some sort of movement in the room. Can you think of any reason why someone would want to break into this house? Or, more particularly, into the study?"

From the way she looked back at him, it was as if she had never given consideration to the question before. The focus of her eyes seemed to shift in confusion and her lips began to form half-realised and silent words. After some thought, she provided as honest an answer as she was able to give. "We are not without money, Mr Carr, as you can see. I suppose a burglar might think that was sufficient reason to break in."

Carr rose slowly from his chair and began to stretch the pain out of his leg. She had missed his point entirely. It had seemed to Carr that an attempt to gain access to the property would have been more discreet if carried out through the rear of the house. The window to the study opened onto the front steps of the house, which themselves looked out onto the main thoroughfare of the residential square in which the house stood. An intruder would surely have run a greater risk of discovery by forcing the study windows, rather than those of the kitchen or dining room. To Carr's mind, capricious and quixotic as it was, the idea suggested not so much a careless rashness on the part of the intruder, but a definite destination in the plans of his mind.

"I wonder if I might be permitted to have a quick glance around the study," he asked.

"Why should you want to do that?" She asked the question without displaying any indication of offence.

"I am curious, dear lady, that is all. One day it will kill me, if the proverb is to be believed."

She gave a slight bow of her head and rose from her seat. Carr, his calm exterior disguising the turmoil of speculation and conjecture within him, followed her out of the room and down the hallway. Margaret had paused at the door to the study and, as he approached, she opened it and allowed him to enter.

The room seemed to encapsulate the spirit of Jacob Erskine. It was ostentatious rather than elegant, well-furnished, but with a lack of refined taste. The paintings on the walls were lurid rather than attractive, save for a rather elegant oil painting of an attractive village church. The books on the shelves were designed to impress rather than to be read, and both the desk and chair seemed to be too large for Erskine, bought for their imposing size than for any practical function. Carr judged the room to be nothing less than tasteless, but he was cautious enough not to betray any negative reaction to it. He walked slowly around it, making his way to the window, through which he stared out into the small green park of the square opposite. The clasp showed no particular sign of being forced. It was true that some of the paintwork had been scratched away, evidence perhaps of a knife against the frame, but beyond such defects there was little more to be gleaned.

"Did you mention the intruder to your husband?" Carr asked.

"Yes, of course," replied Margaret.

"How did he react?"

"He was angry, naturally, but he decided that we should do nothing about it. Nothing was stolen, after all. The man didn't even gain entry."

Carr's eyes drifted around the room once more, and they came to rest on the desk. It was tidy, well-organised, the pens and paper set out so that they would always be readily to hand. There was a series of ledgers and notebooks neatly stacked to one side of the desk, and Carr pointed to them.

"Do you know what these contain?" he asked.

Margaret shook her head. "This was Jacob's private study. I was never allowed in here."

Carr stared at her. Even now, as if to prove the truth of her words, she remained on the threshold of the room as if waiting for an invitation to enter. "Would you be offended if I looked inside these ledgers? Or perhaps in the drawers of the desk?"

She was not about to comply immediately. He was aware that his request would have seemed strange to her, and that he had no right to ask it, but he doubted she would be able to refuse. To do so might appear to be an attempt to keep some secret concealed. He held her gaze, his smile as harmless as before, but she was not about to be so easily dissolved in her resolution.

"Is there a reason for you to do that?" she asked.

"None at all." Candour was Carr's deadliest weapon. "And you would be quite right to refuse. And yet, I can see no harm in it, can you? The police will do so without seeking permission, and they will not replace anything as neatly as they found it, whereas I shall be careful to do so."

Margaret contemplated his words carefully and, on reflection, she shrugged her shoulders in agreement. "The room was never mine when he was alive. I see no reason why I should be precious about it now that he is dead. Any secrets in here are Jacob's, not mine." She turned her back on him, and he watched her walk away. Perhaps there would be tears now, in the wake of this reference to the distance between them which had existed in their marriage.

Carr remained motionless for a moment, allowing her words to settle into the silence, before slowly sitting down at the desk. He pulled open the drawers, only mildly surprised to find that they were not locked. Margaret had been forbidden entry to the room, and Erskine's apparent disregard for security in the room was perhaps a sign of the arrogance of a man who is not accustomed to having his word disobeyed. Inside the drawers were similar ledgers and notebooks to those on the desk itself. There were spare pens and bottles of ink, neatly placed beside each other, the pens tied together by a length of string. There were numerous folders containing official documents: medical bills, bank statements, used chequebooks. Something about the folders' contents disturbed him, but he could not for the moment say what it was. He disregarded it, concentrating on more tangible matters. There was a discarded draft of a letter to the Icarus Club, declaring Erskine's intention to usurp Hector Wharton as club chairman, but it was incomplete, as if the venom behind it had not been toxic enough to suit his purpose.

Carr was on the point of abandoning his examination of the desk when one particular set of leather notebooks caught his attention. They were scarlet in colour, a stark contrast to the black which Erskine so obviously favoured. This radical change in habit intrigued Carr, and he pulled the notebooks from the drawer and spread them out on the desk. As he flicked through the pages, he was confronted by a series of letters and figures set out in three columns. The first of the columns contained pairs of letters, some of which were repeated over and over; the second column clearly set out sums of money; the third contained what were unquestionably dates. Payments, of course, and the dates upon which they were made. And might the pairs of letters not be the initials of the people who had made those payments? Carr pulled out the folders which contained those official documents, conscious now of what it was which had disturbed him earlier. The accounts were all Erskine's alone, with no mention of Margaret, and when Carr compared the dates and sums of various deposits with the scarlet notebooks, he was less than surprised to find that they were identical. The story, squalid and disreputable that it was, seemed clear. The notebooks were details of debts to be paid and the dates upon which they were discharged; the statements confirmed receipt of the money. The payments had come from the same people, assuming that the letters were initials, and they had been made on a regular basis but, interestingly, with increasing value.

Carr replaced the notebook with the others and closed the desk drawer. To take what was so obviously crucial evidence would be not only inappropriate but criminal. He would advise Inspector Mason of his discovery and allow the inspector to perform his duty. He rose from the desk and made sure that everything was left exactly as he had found it. Satisfied to that extent, but far from at ease generally, Carr walked out of the room. As he closed the door of the study behind him, he had the unerring sense that he was shutting out the fetid but unmistakable stench of blackmail.

Chapter Nineteen

Faraday and Overdale lunched away from the Icarus Club. The restaurant they chose was one where they were known, and they were guaranteed discretion and privacy. In the wake of current events, the club could hardly be said to provide either. Both ordered simple meals, neither of them feeling particularly hungry, but Overdale ordered an additional cocktail to accompany the small carafe of wine, which Faraday had considered appropriate refreshment. The older man glared disapprovingly at the chilled glass of the cocktail, its transparent fluid so like water that it appeared entirely innocuous, but the smell of it betraying its power and strength.

"Must you drink so much in the afternoon?" asked Faraday.

"I like it." To prove the point, Overdale drained the glass in a single, avaricious gulp and immediately ordered another. "Besides, I'm in shock."

"As am I," said Faraday coarsely, "but I'm not getting tight when the morning is barely over."

"Perhaps you should, Leonard. It might stop you acting like such a stick."

It was peevish rather than insulting, and Faraday could hardly feel offended by it. He was less hurt than saddened. This essence of a spoilt child, the spiteful petulance which Overdale could display on occasion, was an aberration in an otherwise perfect specimen, like a hairline crack in a marble statue, and it was Faraday's inability to alter it which upset him. As Overdale drank the second Martini, sipping it lovingly this time, Faraday poured himself a small glass of the chilled, white wine.

"I wanted to apologise for last night," he said. "It was my fault entirely."

"Yes, it was."

Faraday had hoped for, but not expected, a similar concession of culpability, and the fact that Overdale did not oblige him was as depressing as it was anticipated so that Faraday was left without any definitive emotional response to it. He wanted to feel sorrow, but his expectation left him feeling only numb.

"What did you do after I left you?" asked Faraday.

Overdale shrugged. "I stayed in the games room, drank heavily, and then I went home. What did you expect me to do?"

Faraday looked down at the two cocktail glasses and the wine, both of which Overdale was greedily enjoying. It could only have been a matter of hours between his alcoholic indulgencies. "Should you be drinking so heavily now, then?"

"Yes." The word was an impudent syllable.

"What about your health?"

Overdale laughed, a raucous and snarling cackle so loud and intrusive that several other patrons looked across in disapproval. "I'll worry about my health when I'm old and rotting. Now is the time to feel alive."

"And do you feel alive?"

"Incredibly so."

"You're on a road to destruction, Vincent."

Overdale's eye flashed with anger. Here, once again, was the recrimination, the attempts to rule him, to dictate how his life was lived. It was in moments such as these that he despised Leonard Faraday, moments when the kindness and gentle loving of the older man were forgotten, replaced only by this image of dictatorial oppression. Instinctively, Overdale grabbed his butter knife and held it like a weapon. It could never do any harm, but the action, its swiftness, as well as what it represented, took away Faraday's breath.

"Calm down," he said. "I'm not being a tyrant or a prude. I'm trying to protect you."

"I don't need looking after, Leonard. I just want to have some fun."

Faraday nodded, not in any concession of defeat but in an anxious desire to avoid a repetition of the argument the previous night. It had been typically ignominious, and without restraint, neither man retaining much of his dignity, but Faraday suspected that it was he who regretted it the most. It was questionable whether Vincent Overdale recalled very much about it. His existence was largely of the moment. Faraday, however, had no such ability to erase the past, and the details of the argument were still vivid and raw in his memory.

It had been a little after dinner. Faraday had dined alone, Overdale having rejected an invitation to join him due to a prior agreement. The suggestion of a drink before dinner instead had been made, although Faraday anticipated that it would be rejected, so that its acceptance had delighted him, to an extent that its culmination in recrimination and insult had been all the more tragic. It had been the usual topic which had sparked the flame of dispute.

"Where are you dining?" Faraday had asked.

It would have been forgivable to assume that it was an innocent, even innocuous, enquiry but it had angered Overdale. "Why must you ask me things like that? What does it matter where I eat or don't eat?"

"I am asking out of interest."

"You are prying."

Overdale's eyes had bulged with indignation, but there was something unnatural about their glare, as if their annoyance were fuelled by a deep-rooted paranoia. The sweat on his temples had glistened, and his breathing had become erratic. The sudden darkness of his mood was as charged as his previous euphoria and charm. The cause had been only too evident to Faraday.

"I thought—hoped—that you had turned your back on that way of life," he had said.

"On what way of life?"

"Where do you get it? Who plies you with the filthy stuff?"

It had been the first time that such a direct question had been asked. Overdale, clearly unprepared for it, had struggled to reply. He had gasped for air, disguising it with sharp, mirthless laughs, and the sweating had intensified. "What I do and how I do it are none of your business."

Faraday had ignored the evasion. "And how do you afford it? Your allowance from the father you barely speak to anymore can hardly support your way of living."

"Have I ever asked you for money, Leonard?"

"No."

"Then, until I do, and until you have the undoubted pleasure of denying me, my finances are my own business."

"I could never deny you anything," Faraday had whispered. "And I think you know that."

The tenderness had thawed some of Overdale's hostility. He had placed a hand on Faraday's cheek. "You mustn't worry about me."

This time, the anger had been Faraday's. He had slapped the smooth, flawless hand away and struggled to keep his voice within the bounds of discretion. "How can I do otherwise when I know the sort of people you are involved with? Don't you think I know what you do on those evenings when I don't see you? It makes me sick to think of it."

"You're suffocating me," Overdale had roared. "Can't you see that?"

Faraday had not seemed to hear him. "Did you lie to me about owing money to Jacob Erskine?"

"No."

"I don't believe you." He had gripped him by the shoulders. "You were heard arguing with him about money."

Overdale had shaken himself free of the threatening embrace. "You're mad. And I'm not lying."

"What's going on between you and Erskine?"

"Nothing."

"Tell me the truth." The demand had been accompanied by tears forming in Faraday's eyes. "What's happening with Erskine?"

"Nothing, nothing, nothing." The repetition of the denial had increased in volume and intensity, just as it had decreased in meaning and honesty.

Faraday, knowing and recognising the lie, had struck Overdale sharply across the face. It had been unexpected to both of them, and the shock which had followed it was mutual. Faraday, instantly repentant, had reached out to the younger man who, in turn, had recoiled. For a moment, they had stared at each other in a kind of tableau of impotent absurdity, neither knowing how to react nor what to say. At last, Overdale had begun to laugh. It was a shrill, unbalanced, and paranoid cackle, a sound almost wild in its hysteria, perhaps closer to a scream of madness than any display of humour. It was as if the irrational foolishness of their frozen forms had suddenly become apparent to him. In contrast, Faraday had felt humiliated both by the slap and the consequent hilarity. It had been as if the manic laughter was a direct mockery of his own attempt to assert himself. Faraday had walked away, heading straight for his office, and he had not seen Overdale again that night.

Now, sitting in that small restaurant, the memory of that ridicule was suddenly fresh once more in Faraday's consciousness. He tried to bury it, to concentrate his attention on the more immediate concern which plagued his thoughts.

"So, you weren't at the Icarus Club when Erskine was killed?"

Overdale rolled his eyes. "No, I've told you already."

Faraday nodded, abandoning the point for another line of enquiry. "There's something I must ask you, Vincent, and I will have to take the risk that it will hurt you."

Overdale frowned. "Hurt me?"

"It's about Erskine's death."

Overdale's brows darkened further until, at last, the eyebrows raised in horror. "My God, Leonard. Did you kill him? Was it you?"

The allegation was so unexpected that Faraday had difficulty in finding his breath in order to respond. "Of course not."

"You thought something was going on between Erskine and me, that I owed him money, so you killed him."

"I didn't."

Overdale began to laugh, a childish giggle of wonderment. "It would be so romantic if you had. To sacrifice your life in order to protect your lover."

"Keep your voice down, for God's sake," hissed Faraday. He leaned forward and kept his voice so low that Overdale had to strain to hear it. "Did you steal fifty pounds from my safe, Vincent?"

Overdale smiled once more and let out a guttural, dismissive laugh, one designed to emphasise innocence and show that any suggestion of guilt was worthy only of ridicule. "No."

"No more lies, please."

Overdale maintained his show of innocence. "I couldn't steal from you, Leonard."

Faraday removed his spectacles and began to clean them. "Last night, after we argued, I went back to my office. The safe door was open, and I looked inside. Vincent, the money was gone."

"And you think I stole it?"

Faraday did not reply directly. "I was there soon after the body was discovered, Vincent. Whoever murdered Jacob Erskine threw a significant quantity of money at his body. He was covered in banknotes."

However bizarre the revelation seemed to Overdale, he did not allow it to shift his focus. "It wasn't me, Leonard."

"When you came to see me in my office a couple of days ago, you saw me with that money. Your lifestyle and all this talk of you owing Erskine money makes it very easy for me to draw conclusions."

"Wrong conclusions."

Faraday's reply was heavy with suppressed mania. "How can I believe that? You lie to me on a daily basis, Vincent, so why should you be telling me the truth now?"

He was struck suddenly with a severe awareness of his own hypocrisy. His suspicions of Vincent Overdale had tormented him for several days, increasing from the moment he had discovered the theft from his safe and witnessed the money found on the murdered man. He had been unable to prevent his instinctive reference to the money, which Everett Carr had overheard, and he had told Carr a direct lie about the night of the murder. He had claimed not to have been upset or disturbed when he met Wharton in the bar, despite Carr's suggestion that someone had testified to the contrary. Of course, he had been unsettled, having discovered the theft from his office and realised its implications. Whether Carr had been convinced by his lie, Faraday could not say, but it was not a thought upon which he dared to dwell too long.

Overdale, unaware of these thoughts, had composed himself. "I am not lying to you, Leonard. I didn't steal your money, and I didn't kill Erskine. I have my faults, I admit, but I'm not a thief. And I'm certainly not a murderer."

There was something desperate in his voice which Faraday could not define properly. It might have been a desire for acceptance, a plea to be believed, or it might have been a resistance against the slur of being accused of either offence by someone he thought had loved him. Overdale shook his head, and Faraday felt as if a blade had been inserted between his ribs and into his heart. Now, Overdale's expression was one of pained innocence, his eyes lowered in betrayed sadness, and his lips pursed in regret, as if offering to be kissed as recompense. Faraday felt as if he could do just that, to try to erase the accusation from his lips by tasting those of the young man he had slighted. His own mother, in the distant mists of his youthful memories, had done something similar, kissing away his nightmares and fears with a succession of gentle, tender kisses of protection. A similar instinct now rose within Faraday, but he knew that to act upon it would be not only indiscreet and unwise, but very possibly unwelcome.

"I'm sorry, Vincent," he said, his voice softened by guilt and remorse. "I had no right to say any of that, not last night and not today. It's the horror of what has happened. Murder twists your thoughts, makes you see the worst in every situation, and suspect lies where there is only truth. I should have known better. Please, forgive me."

Overdale nodded and, unobtrusively, stroked Faraday's fingers with his own. It was surreptitious enough not to be noticed but, despite the brevity and subtlety of the gesture, it seemed to sing to Leonard Faraday with the loudest of choral voices. His fears, his suspicions, his angry bitterness at Overdale's lies seemed to evaporate in that single physical declaration of affection. He gazed at the younger man and smiled warmly, lowering his hands into his lap, as if to protect the place Overdale had touched from the ravages of the open air, as though it was some precious artefact too brittle and delicate to be exposed to sunlight.

"Let's have another drink," he said. "And respectability be damned. After all, isn't now the time to be alive?"

Overdale smiled and then laughed, the noise sounding hollow and distant in his own ears. They did not speak whilst they waited for the drinks to arrive. When they did, Faraday raised his glass in a silent toast and drank happily. Overdale sipped at his own drink, his lips stretched into a smile which almost matched that of his lover's, although it lacked any of its warmth. Nor did it hold any of its devotion or love. There was a quality about it which would have seemed to a casual observer to be closer to relief than genuine happiness, as if it were the smile of a cheat who had successfully averted some sort of personal crisis.

Chapter Twenty

After his visit to Margaret Erskine, Carr had returned to the Icarus Club. The police presence had not lessened in his absence, but Mason was nowhere to be found. Carr was not surprised by the inspector's absence. There was all manner of duties he would need to perform in these initial stages of a murder investigation: routine interviews, attendance at a post-mortem examination, initial collating of evidence. Carr could hardly expect Mason to be available to discuss any small discovery which Carr had made, nor any theory which he had formed on account of it. Nevertheless, the suggestion that Jacob Erskine had been a blackmailer was one which Mason would have to know. A brief word with a detective sergeant that Carr needed to speak to Mason urgently was sufficient for Carr to consider himself relieved of any obligation on the point. Until such time as he could speak to Mason personally, he could do no more. He consulted his watch and decided that not only was it late enough in the day to justify a small glass of pre-luncheon wine, but also that he deserved it.

He made his way to his preferred bar and discovered that Marcus Trevelyan and Ronald Edgerton also shared his desire for a drink before their meal. They beckoned him over, and Carr accepted the invitation, gesturing to the ever-reliable George for an order of drinks. The three members waited for the drinks to arrive before speaking.

"Damned terrible business," said Edgerton. "I can't pretend I liked Erskine, but one doesn't wish murder on anybody."

Carr smiled. "Did you not say to me that you could have killed Erskine yourself and not feel a pang of guilt about it?"

The barrister frowned. "Did I?"

There was a gentle incline of Carr's head. "Only a few days ago."

"I don't remember saying anything of the kind." Edgerton snorted. "If I did, it's a turn of phrase only, Your Honour. I doubt I'm the first person to say it without actually meaning it."

Trevelyan chuckled grimly. "It wouldn't do to go around saying something like that, Edgerton. You never know when your words might be used against you."

Carr feigned laughter too, but his eyes were fixed on Edgerton's face. "I hope you have a sound alibi, dear boy."

Edgerton roared in perverse delight. "Can't say I have. I was at home, working. Poring over briefs and witness testimony. You know how it is, Your Honour. I didn't leave the house, nobody saw me, nobody was with me. I haven't got a ghost of an alibi."

"You seem rather proud of the fact," said Carr.

"Not at all, but there's no sense in worrying about what one can't change. And, in my experience, fabricating an alibi seldom works out well. Wouldn't you say so?"

"It is certainly not advisable." Carr sipped the excellent Chateau d'Yquem.

Trevelyan lit a cigarette and leaned back in his chair. "I am rather more fortunate than you, Edgerton. You see, I *do* have an alibi."

Carr turned to face him, smiling. "Is that so?"

Trevelyan nodded. "I was at the *Duck and Drake*, from about eight until a little before eleven. Plenty of people saw me there, and I chatted to old Petrie behind the bar."

Edgerton laughed. "Once that old scoundrel gets going, Your Honour, it's difficult to stop him, if you take my meaning."

Trevelyan gave a short, amiable laugh. "Quite so, but he means no harm. Once I had managed to escape old Petrie, I did a fiendish crossword, had a couple of drinks, then went home to Sonia."

"I take it you also know this public house, Edgerton," said Carr.

The barrister nodded eagerly. "Of course, a splendid place. Quite a few members of the club go there, as a matter of fact."

"I would be happy to take you, Mr Carr," offered Trevelyan, "if you would like to see what the fuss is all about."

Carr smiled. Public houses had never featured particularly prominently in his own life, and he could see no reason why they should begin to do so as he approached the dusk of his existence. But he was not so detached from the world that he could not understand that a landlord would come to recognise and ingratiate himself with regular customers. That a number of his fellow members of the Icarus Club frequented such a place so regularly came as a mild surprise to him, he was forced to confess, but it was perhaps more indicative of his own character than theirs.

"Rumour has it that the body was covered in money," Trevelyan was saying. "Is that correct, Mr Carr? You found the body, so you ought to know."

"It is true, yes," muttered Carr.

"I don't pretend to be able to understand it."

Carr examined his fingernails. "Does nothing occur to you?"

Trevelyan leaned forward, his eyes suddenly filled with a mixture of wonder and intrigue. Edgerton's eyes flickered between the two of them. For himself, Carr looked at neither of them, his concentration fixated on his fingernails, and, when he spoke, it was in a voice which was so carefully pitched that its softness seemed to enhance the seriousness of the words.

"Would either of you think Erskine capable of blackmail?"

Neither Trevelyan nor Edgerton moved, but they glanced at each other as if in some sort of silent collusion. Carr remained motionless, his face impassive, save for the slow movement of his eyes, which rose and glanced from one man to the other.

"Blackmail?" Edgerton hissed.

Carr inclined his head. "It seems to me to be a means of explaining the money."

Trevelyan leaned back in his chair. "I can well imagine Erskine being a blackmailer. It's the sort of underhand, dirty thing he would do."

Edgerton was shaking his head. "He would never do it. Erskine was too bombastic, too full of his own importance, to engage in something so insidious. Remember how he confronted Hector Wharton over chairmanship of this place? He had his fights out in the open, not hiding in the shadows."

Carr shrugged his shoulders. "The money must be explained. If not blackmail, what other reason might there be?"

"It might have been his own money," said Trevelyan. "He might have been counting it when he was shot."

Edgerton seemed to find the explanation persuasive. "That seems more likely."

Carr agreed. "The impact of a gunshot might be powerful enough to scatter the bank notes, certainly."

Trevelyan frowned. "You don't seem convinced, Mr Carr."

Carr shook his head vaguely. "I confess that I do wonder whether the reading room would be a suitable place to count a substantial sum of money. Anybody could have interrupted him at any time. And, for that matter," he added, as the thought occurred to him, "why would he count it at that particular moment?"

"I'm not sure I see the point," said Trevelyan.

"Does the fact that he had the money about his person at all not suggest that he had only come into possession of it that evening?"

Both men considered the point, but it was Edgerton who replied. "I don't see that it is of any importance either way."

Carr shrugged with a broad smile. "Perhaps not."

The intrusion into their discussion was as loud as it was unexpected. The door was thrown open and slammed shut once more. The three men turned to face the explosion and found Hector Wharton looming over them. His fists were clenched, and his face wild with feral anger. His lips were stretched back across his teeth, and his nostrils flared as the air surged through them noisily. He glared malevolently at Trevelyan and Edgerton, as if their presences were inconvenient, but his malice was primarily directed towards Carr. The anger was so evident, so intense, that the danger of Wharton collapsing under its weight was a serious and very real one.

"What the hell do you think you're doing, Carr?" he roared.

Carr was unperturbed, and his stillness under the ferocity of the storm was both impressive and disconcerting. "I do not follow you, colonel."

"Sticking your nose where it doesn't belong, is what I mean."

Carr smiled, but it was not out of humour. "Perhaps we should discuss matters in private, colonel."

"I don't care who hears what I have to say." As if to prove it, Wharton's voice increased in volume. "Why don't you let the police perform their duty and mind your own business?"

Carr nodded his head slowly and with purpose. "You have spoken to Mrs Erskine, I see."

"Indeed, I have. And she told me about you snooping."

"She was perfectly happy to talk to me." Carr inclined his head. "I am surprised how warmly you feel about it."

Wharton seethed for a moment, his breath rasping between his clenched teeth. "You have no right to interfere in a police investigation, Carr."

"Perhaps you are afraid of something, colonel," said Carr, ignoring the accusation of interference. "It was your gun which was used, after all."

"I didn't murder Jacob Erskine," declared Wharton.

"You had the opportunity to do so." Carr smiled gently. "And you had the means. Did you also have the motive? Ah yes," he added, after a moment's pretence of thought, "Erskine was threatening to oust you as chairman of the club."

"That's hardly a motive for murder," sneered Wharton.

Carr's smile broadened, just as his eyes darkened. "Perhaps you have a more fundamental motive, one which you wish to keep very private, and one which would explain your current behaviour."

"What motive?"

Carr began to stroke the silver handle of his cane. "Is there a particular reason you felt it necessary to speak to Mrs Erskine this morning?"

The implication was barely veiled, and it had not been intended to be. Wharton took a step forward. Trevelyan rose from his chair, readying himself to restrain the colonel, and Edgerton made a similar, but less decisive, movement. Only Carr remained motionless, as if untroubled by any threat of violence against him. His eyes were locked on Wharton, a gentle smile flickering over his lips, but there was no humour in that dark, impassive glare.

"I am not interfering, colonel," he said, "but I do give you a warning. A case can be made against you. You have no alibi, the murder weapon is known to be yours, and I daresay you have more of a motive than is immediately present. I would suggest that you are in a very precarious position."

"My relationship with Mrs Erskine is entirely appropriate," insisted Wharton. "We are close friends. And nothing more." This final declaration was spoken with a definite malice.

Carr shrugged. "As you wish. But be assured, colonel, that if the police discover something which you have attempted to conceal, it will be unpleasant for you. And, possibly, for other people."

Wharton's eyes narrowed slightly, as if something in Carr's warning had penetrated through the mist of his rage. He made no effort to speak further, not immediately, but his fists clenched and opened in rapid succession, and the broad shoulders heaved with furious indecision. Carr watched him, suddenly conscious that he could feel nothing but sympathy for him. A realisation that he was a strong suspect for the murder would have been difficult enough on its own, taken in conjunction with the suggestion that his relationship with the dead man's wife strengthened that suspicion must have been something approaching torture. Whether Wharton was in love with Margaret Erskine or not, Carr could not say with certainty, but it seemed to him to be a strong possibility.

Wharton's fury subsided, in part at least, and his glare now, whilst still confrontational, had a trace of sadness within it. Carr, in deference to it, lowered his own eyes.

"I did not kill Jacob Erskine," Wharton repeated. "And damn anybody who says otherwise."

He walked away with more dignity than Carr would have thought possible. He had opened the door before Carr called his name once more. Turning round, Wharton moved stiffly, as if preparing himself for a further confrontation. Carr pulled himself out of his chair, wincing slightly, and stepped aside from the table at which they had been sitting. He faced Wharton, leaning heavily on his cane.

"I wonder if you would give us the benefit of your opinion on a certain point," he said cordially.

"What point?"

Carr straightened himself. "Would you say Jacob Erskine was capable of blackmail?"

Wharton was unable to prevent an expression of surprise from crawling over his face. He looked from Carr to Trevelyan and Edgerton. Their expressions were expectant, fascinated, but Carr's was patiently resolute. Wharton contemplated the question for some moments, and Carr did not make any effort to hasten a reply.

"I would say he was entirely capable of it," Wharton said, finally. "Erskine preyed upon the misery of others. I should say that blackmail would be second nature to him."

It was said with such certainty that there seemed no further room for debate. Carr bowed in polite gratitude, and Wharton, waiting for no further questions to be asked, stepped out of the bar and disappeared down the corridor.

Chapter Twenty-One

Inspector Mason had disliked Cyril Parsons almost immediately. He was not in the habit of forming instinctive judgments of that kind, but there was something about the doorman's hostile attitude and sneering expression which demanded animosity. He had refused an offer to sit, preferring to stand to attention, his hands clasped behind his back and his eyes fixed on a spot above Mason's head. There was an insolence about his glare, as if the summons to a police interview had been an irritant to him, a waste of what he evidently took to be his valuable time. If this pretence of defiance was supposed to intimidate Mason, it was a failure, and he made no attempt to disguise the fact. Similarly, Parsons was unaffected by Mason's ambivalence, which itself was of neither interest nor importance to him.

"I understand you enjoy a bit of a flutter, Mr Parsons," said Mason.

"No law against it."

It was a defensive response, which might not be surprising in itself, but it seemed to Mason that it was unnecessarily belligerent. "Tell me about the card sessions with Jacob Erskine."

"Nothing to tell. Just a couple of hands and a few drinks, a bit of fun."

"Against club rules, as I understand it."

Parsons smiled unpleasantly. "That didn't seem to trouble those members who took part."

"The members are permitted to gamble on the premises. It's staff who aren't, so only you would get into bother for it. Am I right?"

"Wharton felt the need to say something to me, yes, but it was fuss over nothing."

"As I understand it, Colonel Wharton told you he would reprimand Mr Erskine about these gambling parties also." Mason watched Parsons nod his head in confirmation. "Would you be surprised to learn that he did nothing of the sort?"

"Wharton's always been a hypocrite. They all are."

"Meaning what?"

Parsons laughed spitefully. "They come in here, privileged and protected, not knowing the first thing about the world. They spend all day drinking, smoking, lounging around, and achieving nothing. And yet, we're supposed to say they are the peak of society."

There was something about his tone of voice which troubled Mason: not quite malice and not entirely envy, but a subtle blend of the two. He could not be certain whether Parsons despised the members because of their privilege or because he could never attain it himself. Whichever it was, for him to be in servitude to the members of the club would surely be a distasteful reminder of his own lack of status.

"If you loathe them so much, why do you work here?"

Parsons shrugged. "I have to eat."

And drink, thought Mason. The smell of alcohol, though not overpowering, was unmistakable on the man's breath. "Did you owe Erskine any money as a result of these gambling sessions?"

Parsons shrugged. "What if I did?"

Mason sat back in his chair. "A significant amount of money was found on the body. As if whoever killed Erskine threw it in his face before they shot him."

"It wasn't me."

"Where were you between half past eight and ten o'clock last night?"

"On duty."

Only later, when the detective sergeant in question handed him the note written by Everett Carr, would Mason realise that he had been told a lie. For now, he allowed Parsons' response to pass him by. "You knew that Colonel Wharton possessed a gun, I believe."

"Saw him cleaning it the other day, but it was no secret anyway."

"Did you know where he kept it?"

Parsons shrugged. "In his desk. The drawer was open when he was cleaning it."

"You were at Yprès." Mason posed it not as a question but as a statement of fact.

Parsons nodded, but the clenching of his jaw suggested that it was a subject which he had little or no inclination to discuss. Looking at him now, Mason could see no trace of the man he must have been when he saved the lives of his battalion. There was none of the determination it must have taken, none of the spirit of sacrifice which must have been within him at the time, and none of the courage which must have fuelled the action. Now, there seemed to be nothing but disdain, as if the memory of his actions was as disagreeable as the conflict which had necessitated them.

"I believe you were handy with a gun," said Mason. "A crack-shot."

Parsons was non-committal. "I could handle myself, right enough. But knowing my way round a gun doesn't mean I shot Erskine."

Mason conceded the point with a smile. "You were highly decorated for your heroism at Yprès."

"I don't talk about it."

It was understandable, perhaps. Mason assumed that others might view such bravery as heroism, but he supposed that Parsons himself would be unable to think about the incident outside the context of the war itself. To him, no doubt, it would be a recollection stained with the mud of the battlefield, any cheers of heroism silenced by the screams of the dying and the roaring of guns. It would be a reminder not of Parsons' own selflessness but of fear and death.

"Strange, isn't it?" said Mason. "The war is something best forgotten, but none of us can do it."

"You served yourself?"

Mason nodded. "I did my duty, sir. It'll never leave us. We might not think about it too much over time, but it will still be there."

"It's always there," hissed Parsons. "You don't really know a man until you see the fear in his eyes before he dies. You don't realise how fragile we are until you see how easily blood and bones can be blown apart. You've no idea how useless you are until one of your best friends has begged you to help him, but all you can do is hold him tighter in your arms, because you know, full well, he is beyond any help."

He had begun to shake, sweat forming on his upper lip. Mason wondered how badly the man needed a drink now, how soothing a measure of whisky would be, and how often Parsons was compelled to soften the edges of his memory with it. Mason might not have liked the man, but he could empathise with him and, although Parsons would find it condescending, he could sympathise with Parsons' feeling of being haunted by the ghosts of the past. Parsons may have been rewarded for his bravery, but it had come with its own breed of misery. If his courage had impressed his superiors and the public, it had been nothing less than a private curse to him.

"Do you ever ask yourself what it was for?" asked Parsons without warning. "All those men dead, too many to count, and what are we left with?"

Mason was unsure how to respond. "I try just to live my life, Mr Parsons."

"Live your life? What life is it? Nobody treats us as equals. We're here to serve. We won the war for them, and now we're their servants. Look at this place. A pompous club filled with pompous men, who have to name their bloody club after a myth, so they don't become too high and mighty. What's this place got to do with the reality of the world? And your job, inspector. How many murders do you investigate where men like these look after themselves before co-operating with you? They don't think people like you and me matter. They let me open doors for them, and they close those same doors in your face. They barely acknowledge my existence, and they lie to you. Is that what we fought the war for? To be treated like that, to allow their privilege to continue without interruption?"

It was a complaint which had come easily to him, and Mason wondered how many times he had recited it, or something like it. How often had a fellow drunk been forced to listen to it in the dark corner of some dingy pub in Whitechapel? Mason was being presumptuous as well as prejudiced, and he was aware of it. He was treating Parsons with as much contempt as the members of the Icarus Club treated him. And yet, the recital had been so swiftly delivered that it could not possibly have been the first time Parsons had delivered it. It was not something for which he ought to be judged, but it was a glimpse into the bitter turmoil which clearly infected Parsons' integrity.

"Life is what we make it, Mr Parsons," said Mason. "We should not allow the war to define us."

Parsons stared at the inspector with volatile eyes. "How can it do anything *but* define us?"

Mason was suddenly disinclined to continue the conversation. "Can you think of anyone who might have killed Erskine?"

"Half the club and the other half would thank them for it."

"You didn't like him?"

"I don't like any of them."

Mason sniffed. "Did you write a note to Erskine on the day he was killed?"

"A note?"

"We found a burned scrap of paper, part of a note. It had been signed with what might have been a single letter P."

"Might have been?" sneered Parsons. "You think I wrote it?"

Mason shrugged. "I'm merely asking the question."

"Then I'll merely answer it." Parsons leaned forward. "I didn't write any note and I didn't kill Erskine."

There seemed little more to say. Mason fell silent, his mind concentrating on Parsons. The doorman made no attempt to break the silence or to encourage further questions. Mason contemplated the sneering face with its broken veins and bitter twists. Parsons was more than capable of using Wharton's revolver, and his lie about gambling debts had been obvious. And yet, Parsons' demons seemed to monopolise his existence, and Mason wondered whether any comparatively petty argument with Erskine would have been able to usurp the prominence of those haunted memories.

He asked a number of additional, routine questions before dismissing Parsons. The doorman did not go so far as to salute, but there was a military formality about his exit from the room. Mason watched him leave, his brows creased in concentration, and he found himself wondering about Parsons and his ghosts long after the door had closed behind him.

Chapter Twenty-Two

Although he was not entirely averse to them, Carr was not a frequent visitor to public houses. The noise of the conversation and the smell of equally stale beer and tobacco had always seemed to him to be rather too suffocating to be appealing. He preferred the more private confines of the club, where the words of his companions could be heard easily and without the competition of other, more rowdy conversations; equally, a solitary glass of wine in his own town apartment had always seemed preferable to him than the raucous atmosphere of a public bar. Nevertheless, his interest had been piqued by Marcus Trevelyan, to the extent that he had accepted his young friend's invitation to join him for a visit. So it was that, on entering the *Duck and Drake*, Carr found that his apprehensions were, to some extent, assuaged. The bar was crowded, but not overwhelming, the voices raised in good humour, but avoiding the particular bawdy harshness which had tainted his earliest experiences. The smell of beer had not yet permeated the air, presumably because it was too early in the lunchtime session, but there was the anticipation of it in the foaming glasses held in the varying types of hands. As a public house, the *Duck and Drake* was typical of its kind. Its structure was the usual mixture of varnished, panelled walls and frosted glass, the upholstery on the stools and chairs the sort of vulgar pattern which strives too hard for elegance, and the lights low enough to suggest intimacy whilst still bright enough to allow the glasses over the bar to glitter with the promise of their unique breed of enjoyment.

Behind the bar, there stood the man whom Carr took to be Mr Petrie, the landlord. His ruddy cheeks, broad smile, and the bright and amused eyes were sufficient to declare his identity, just as much as the white apron around his waist and the proficiency with which he prepared drinks without being asked for them. Standing beside Petrie was a tall, slim woman, brightly decorated with an excess of rouge on her thin cheeks, a colour matched by the vivid crimson of her hair. It was so bright that Carr could not be sure whether it was natural or not; if it were, it was the most vibrant red which he had ever seen. She was not conventionally pretty, but there was a vivaciousness about her manner which was more alluring than any physical trait. She was laughing uncontrollably with a customer, whose smile suggested that he felt his charm was working well for him, but who was so taken by his own assessment of himself that he was blinded to the fact that it was the girl who was in control of the situation.

As they approached the bar, Petrie welcomed them warmly. "Mr Trevelyan, nice to see you again. What can I get you, sir?"

"A pint of the best, please, Petrie," replied Trevelyan. "May I introduce a friend of mine—Mr Carr."

Petrie did not shake Carr's hand, but inclined his head in greeting. "Very welcome you are, sir. What will you have?"

"A brandy, if I may, with a splash of soda," said Carr. He ordered with a smile, so polite that his internal but supercilious assessment of the quality of the merchandise in the *Duck and Drake* was undetectable. He sipped the brandy, finding to his surprise, and to the discredit of his prejudices, that it was excellent. He smiled back at Petrie. "Have you run this place for long?"

"Getting on for ten years." He pointed to the woman with red hair. "Elsie, there, has been by my side for five of them. A cracking little worker, she is. Half the men in here are in love with her and, because of it, half of them don't want to go home to their wives."

Trevelyan laughed, his fingers twisting his own wedding ring. "I can well believe it!"

Carr's smile widened. "It appears to be a thriving business, I must say."

"We're very proud of our little place, sir." Petrie's words, and their delivery, were sufficient to demonstrate the truth of the remark. He called over to the girl called Elsie, who smiled back at him, stroked the face of the now disappointed customer, and skipped across to join them. "I was just saying to this gentleman, Elsie," continued Petrie, "how proud we are of this place."

Elsie grinned and leaned towards Carr. "A lovely place, don't you think, sir?"

Carr thought it one of the less disreputable public houses he had experienced, and he smiled broadly, bowing his head in a show of acquiescence. "It must take a lot of hard work and dedication." Petrie nodded. "You'd be surprised how few people realise it, sir. How many trips away do you suppose we have had in the last few years? One, sir, one. And that was only a week by the sea, six months ago."

"You must have treasured the time for relaxation," observed Carr.

Elsie gave a short, lewd giggle. "There wasn't much relaxation."

Petrie glared at her, his expression suddenly as puritanical as it was embarrassed. "Now, Elise, no more."

"You're so fussy, Eddie." She leaned her head into Petrie's shoulder, and she looked up into his eyes, her thin fingers stroking the older man's heavy, doubled chin. Initially, it seemed a curiously inappropriate, incongruous gesture, and its surprise intensified when she raised herself onto her toes and kissed Petrie on the cheek.

Trevelyan was smiling when he turned to face Carr. "It was their honeymoon."

Carr, taken aback, mumbled some words of congratulation. "Is it difficult, working together as well as being married?"

"Not as long as he behaves himself," said Elsie, with a shrill laugh rippling her voice.

"I could still have it annulled on the grounds of insanity," muttered Petrie, with a smile.

"I'm not mad, silly," was Elsie's defence.

"I meant me," leered Petrie. He was smiling at Carr now, his arm snaking around Elsie's waist. "I'd be lost without her, sir."

Carr smiled warmly, a short, rasping laugh escaping from his lips. "I can see why Mr Trevelyan, here, enjoys your hospitality so much."

"A valued customer is Mr Trevelyan. Always chooses his usual spot over there." Petrie indicated a small table in a dark corner of the pub, under the window. At present, it was occupied by a nondescript man, sitting alone, with a cloth cap pushed on the back of his domed head and an ill-fated game of patience set out on the wooden table in front of him. A half-drunk pint of ale was to his right, and he now drew heavily upon it, throwing down his remaining cards in frustration.

Elsie was grinning at Trevelyan. "Having trouble with his crossword last night, if I'm any judge. Staring out of the window one minute, head in his hands the next."

Trevelyan winked at her. "Solved it in the end, though."

Petrie was nodding. "So engrossed he was. He didn't even see Mr Parsons come in."

Carr's fingers tightened around his glass. His eyes hardened, and the smile disappeared behind the moustache and beard, the lips tightening into a thin line of determination. "Mr Parsons?" Trevelyan, likewise, was staring furiously at the publican. "I didn't see him, that's for sure. Was it definitely him, Petrie?"

"I'm certain, sir."

Carr watched Petrie closely. "What time was that, would you say?"

Petrie shrugged his shoulders indistinctly. "A little before nine, perhaps. He stayed until just before we closed."

The importance of the declaration was obvious. It was confirmation of Leonard Faraday's testimony that Parsons was not at his post when Faraday made his way from his own office to the bar. Nevertheless, thought Carr, if Parsons had killed Erskine sometime after half past eight, he would have had time to get to the *Duck and Drake* for a little before nine o'clock.

Carr looked at Trevelyan. "You didn't see Parsons at all, my boy?"

There was a shake of the head. "I would have said. He was supposed to be on duty, in any event."

Carr's eyes narrowed. "Just so. Why would he abandon his post on that night in particular?"

"Perhaps it was not an uncommon occurrence," suggested Trevelyan, "and we just don't know about it."

If Carr had any further comment to make on the question, he kept it to himself. He looked back to Petrie. "Is Mr Parsons a regular customer?"

Elsie sniffed. "Rather too regular."

There was little more which needed to be said. Carr needed no evidence of Parsons' predilection for alcohol, any more than he needed confirmation of his belligerent personality. He could imagine that, given the appropriate circumstances, a mixture of the two might be toxic, and he could infer from Elsie Petrie's comment that Parsons might have caused some trouble on more than one occasion in the past.

"Where did Mr Parsons sit?" asked Carr, looking back to the landlord and his wife.

Petrie spoke for them both, but Elsie did not contradict him. "At the bar, where you are now, sir. He drank whisky as if Prohibition was about to land on this side of the ocean before the night was out."

Carr smiled in appreciation of the point. Whether Parsons had come into the public house and drank whisky so greedily on account of the addiction which Carr had long suspected, or whether it was because that addiction had been fuelled by the horror of murder, Carr could not say.

"Did you point me out to Parsons?" asked Trevelyan.

Petrie nodded. "He didn't seem interested. No offence, sir."

"What did he say?"

Petrie rolled his tongue around his mouth, glancing furtively at Elsie. Her expression, encouraging to the point of sanctimony, suggested that an honest reply was best and that no blushes should be spared in the name of truth. "Forgive my language, sir, if I quote Mr Parsons directly, but he said he didn't care if any one of the sneering bastards from the bloody club was in here or not."

Trevelyan, far from offended, chuckled mildly to himself. "That, at least, is in character."

Petrie was obviously disconcerted. "Mr Parsons was particularly bitter last night. *'They're all bloody hypocrites,'* he says. *'Every damned one of them. They come in here to see how the rest of us slum it, while they sit in their bloody club lording it over each other. Bastards, the lot of them. And all of them have something to hide.'"*

Carr's spine crackled with excitement, but his manner was nonchalant. "He said that?"

"As God's my witness, sir."

"Did he explain what he meant?"

Petrie shook his head. "And I didn't like to ask, neither. The thing about Mr Parsons is, when he gets a certain look in his eye, you don't like to provoke him. If you see what I mean, sir."

Carr saw only too clearly. He politely declined the offer of a second drink, but left sufficient money for Trevelyan and the Petries to indulge themselves. With the assurance of a further visit to the *Duck and Drake*, Carr stepped back out into the early afternoon air. It was brisk and fresh, the autumnal sun providing a memory of the summer now passed, whilst the chill breeze pre-empted the winter to come. In other circumstances, Carr would have considered it a beautiful time of day, one with cause to celebrate life, existence, and opportunity. However, when he stepped out into the street to make his way back to the Icarus Club, Carr had the inescapable sensation that any beauty in that clear afternoon was corrupted by the stale taste of deception and the foul stench of death. Most pervasive of all, it seemed, was Cyril Parsons' assessment of the members of the club, which reverberated persistently in Carr's mind.

All of them have something to hide...

Chapter Twenty-Three

From the window of the primary bar of the Icarus Club, Patrick Crane watched Everett Carr cross the street and enter the club. It appeared as if he had been to the *Duck and Drake*, which seemed curious, as it was hardly an establishment which might be said to attract a man like Carr. Crane supposed that Carr had a positive reason for visiting the pub. Crane knew him only in the context of the club, not being a particular friend of his outside the confines of the place, but he was sufficiently aware of his personality to suspect that Carr was not a man who did anything without a definite purpose.

By the time Carr entered the bar, Crane was seated once more, sipping the glass of wine which he had ordered, and there was no indication that he had been watching from the window at all. Crane watched Carr order a whisky and sit down painfully in a corner of the room. He was alone, and the position of the chair which he had chosen suggested that he wished to remain so. In other circumstances, Crane might have respected the wish, but he did not feel able to do so now. Even if he had, the overwhelming and selfish need to cleanse his conscience might have prevented him from respecting Carr's obvious but unspoken desire for privacy.

If Carr was annoyed by the intrusion, he did not show it. Crane apologised, but accepted the invitation to sit. He removed his spectacles and began to polish them with such vigour that Carr suspected an obvious tactic to delay starting the conversation. It was evident to Carr that Crane was disturbed by something, and his demeanour seemed to demand an enquiry. But Carr had long since learned caution, and he knew that it was better to remain silent in such situations and allow the secret to reveal itself.

"I wonder whether the club will ever survive this nightmare," said Crane. "Police all over the place, suspicion, interrogation. I doubt the club will ever be the same again."

"The memory of murder can be long and painful, certainly," said Carr.

Crane nodded, but it was doubtful that he had heard the words. "It makes you wonder about us, doesn't it? We sit in here day after day, evening after evening, talking, drinking, playing cards. You can forget what the world is really like. Murder has changed all that. It has shattered our peace."

It had been said in a solemn, haunted tone of voice. Carr had not been surprised by it, but the melodramatic philosophy was still somehow both impressive and shocking. Carr leaned back in his chair, stretching out his shattered leg, and slowly brushed his moustache with the tip of his forefinger.

"What has happened is certainly dreadful," he said. "Its effects will be profound, but not permanent."

Crane glanced at him, but whether he found any solace in that cautious but kindly gaze was impossible to tell. "The police have questioned me, of course. Asked for an account of my movements."

"It is routine." Carr smiled. "As long as you told them the truth, you will have no need to worry."

Carr's words did not appear to have their desired effect. If anything, it seemed to unsettle Crane, rather than placate him. His eyes widened behind the lenses of the spectacles, and the bottom lip curled under the upper teeth. The wine in his glass trembled under the shaking of his hand and, cautiously, he placed it down on the table between them. He clasped his hands together and buried them in his lap, as if to conceal any physical manifestation of his unease. Carr leaned forward and lowered his voice.

"You did tell the truth to the police?" he asked.

Crane nodded. "About myself, yes."

"I'm not sure I understand." Carr's eyes were now heavy with interrogation, like those of an expectant priest, and Crane was aware in that moment that any attempt to maintain his silence would be futile. He reminded himself that he wanted to confide in Carr, but the desire and the execution of it were different matters, the one much easier to admit than the other was to perform.

"I was here, at the club, on the night of the murder," said Crane. "I intended to spend the night, and I had taken one of the rooms for that purpose. I had finished dressing for dinner, and I was on my way to dine. You will appreciate, Mr Carr, that my way from the bedrooms to the dining room would have necessitated me coming down from the landing above the reading room corridor."

Carr's attention was now seized. "What time was this?"

"A little after half past eight."

"Did you look into the reading room?"

"No."

"You did not see Erskine?"

"No."

There was a twist in Crane's voice which was unmistakable. Carr began to smile gently. "But you did see somebody?"

Crane closed his eyes, as if hearing the words had physically injured him. When he replied, the single syllable was little more than a hoarse whisper. "Yes."

"You did not tell the police who it was?" Carr watched Crane shake his head. "Why not?"

"I can't explain it."

And that, at least, was the truth. At the time, under Mason's cool authority, Patrick Crane had withheld what he knew was important information. It had not been an act of will, he was sure of that. The lie had not been premeditated. When Mason had asked if he had seen anyone in or around the reading room as he passed it, something in the moment, perhaps an inflection in the inspector's voice or a sudden impression of fear on his own part, had compelled him to answer falsely. It had been irrational, almost instinctive, but once it had been told, the lie could not be retracted. As soon as the interview had been concluded, Crane had regretted the dishonesty. His mother's voice, domineering and judgmental, had infected his conscience, expressing his own disappointment in himself as if it were hers. Now, on the verge of confessing his lie, he felt no sense of redemption or forgiveness, either his own or his mother's.

"Perhaps I thought that it would cause more trouble than it solved," he said. "What I saw might have had a simple, innocent explanation. It was an impulse, I suppose. A sudden lapse in judgment."

Whatever the cause of it seemed irrelevant to Carr. The lie itself mattered less than what it concealed. "Who did you see, Mr Crane?"

But still, it seemed Crane was not ready to say. "As soon as I lied, I knew I would have to make amends for it. And, somehow, I knew I would have to tell you before I told the police, Mr Carr."

"Why?"

"Because I need you to tell me what to do about it. You see," Crane's voice lowered to barely a whisper, "I saw a friend of yours coming out of the reading room."

Carr felt his stomach tighten, a wave of nervous anxiety passing over him like a cloud in front of the sun. "A friend of mine?"

Crane looked at him now, his eyes widened with fear, and his skin blanched with concern. "I saw Ronald Edgerton."

For a long moment, Carr did not respond; he said nothing, and his expression did not alter. It was as if the revelation had frozen him in some sort of catatonic seizure. The two of them sat in statuesque silence, facing each other, the truth of Crane's confession hanging in the air between them. At last, slowly, Carr's fingers tightened around the silver handle of his cane.

"You are positive?" he whispered.

"Absolutely. I saw him."

"Did he see you?"

Crane shook his head. "No. I was on the landing above him, as I say, and he did not look up."

"Was he going into the reading room or leaving it?"

"Leaving it. He marched away along the corridor. And he was angry. So angry."

"Did you hear any shot?"

"No."

Several conclusions forced themselves into Carr's mind, but he paid them no immediate attention. "Did you overhear anything being said? Any argument at all?"

Crane shook his head. "No, but it was clear to me that there had been some sort of quarrel. Edgerton's expression was self-explanatory."

"Did you see where he went?" asked Carr.

"No, he disappeared from view."

"When you came down the stairs, there was no sign of him?"

"No."

"And you didn't go into the reading room?"

"I swear."

Whether Carr believed him or not was impossible to say. It would have been easy for Crane to have entered the reading room, having witnessed Edgerton walking away from it, and murder Erskine. He could have lied to the police intentionally, having already determined that he would confess to Carr, in an effort to make himself seem like a repentant but credible witness. It would be a shrewd psychological alibi. On a more practical basis, if Crane's present testimony was to be believed, Roger Edgerton had lied about his whereabouts on the night of Erskine's murder.

"You didn't happen to write a note to Jacob Erskine at some point last night, did you?" asked Carr.

"A note? No." Crane shook his head.

"Did you like him?"

Crane shook his head. "I cannot say I did. Does that incriminate me?"

"Not at all. Unless you had cause to kill him."

"He was going to ruin me." The reply was almost automatic, curiously disembodied, as if it had spoken itself without any command or intention from Crane himself. "I have told the police as much, so it is no secret. I doubt it was a secret anyway."

Even so, Carr had been unaware of it. "How did he propose to do that?"

"I was Erskine's solicitor, Mr Carr. He was suing me for professional negligence. I'd been careless in a land dispute, which meant he lost a significant sum of money. My practice would never have survived his claim against me." Crane smiled, but it was fuelled more by acceptance of defeat than by humour.

Carr did not return the smile. He doubted that Crane's confession to a forceful motive for murder deserved any reaction which might be mistaken for amusement. He could imagine how such a motive would have struck Inspector Mason, especially when coupled with an absence of any alibi, and Carr was compelled to confess that Crane's position seemed dangerously precarious. More forcefully than before, Carr was attracted to the idea that Patrick Crane had written the note to Erskine, requesting a meeting, but the sight of Edgerton had been a momentary disruption to Crane's pre-arranged plan to murder the man who was on the point of ruining him. Certainly, Carr was sure, Mason's mind would have speculated along those terms.

But none of it was evidence, and Carr could manipulate his thoughts to accuse Edgerton just as easily as Crane. He had apparently argued with Erskine within the period of time during which the murder was committed, and, more tellingly, he had been in the room in which the murder had occurred. It was not difficult to infer an adverse relationship between Edgerton and the dead man, at the root of which might be a hidden motive for murder.

"Have you ever heard Mr Edgerton argue with Erskine before?" Carr asked.

Crane shook his head. "Nothing so violent."

"But you have overheard something?"

"I would have thought that Mr Erskine was capable of having a disagreement with almost anybody, Mr Carr. Wouldn't you?"

Carr was not about to confirm or deny his views on the statement. "Would you have ever thought Erskine capable of blackmail?"

The question did not disturb or unsettle Crane. He raised his eyebrows and leaned back in his chair, sipping his wine and thinking silently for a moment. "It wouldn't surprise me to learn that he was, I must confess. He was certainly a bully and, I fear, much worse."

Carr inclined his head, and his voice, when it came, suggested that he might have misheard or misunderstood the word. "Worse?"

Crane peered at him over the rims of his spectacles, the eyes haunted, like those of a cornered animal. His voice was the nervous whisper of a child who might have said too much, but for whom silence was no longer an option. "You know Sonia Trevelyan."

Carr nodded. "A charming girl."

"Erskine…" For a moment, it was the only word which Crane could say. "I saw them together once. He was monstrous, the way he approached her, his intentions only too clear in his face."

"He surely didn't assault her?"

Crane shook his head vehemently. "If he had, perhaps I would have found the courage to intervene. But, somehow, the insidiousness of his conduct was more terrifying than any physical attack. Mrs Trevelyan must have felt it too. She just froze, completely rigid, as if a spider was crawling across her skin."

"When was this?"

"A couple of weeks ago."

"Erskine is a married man," Carr felt obliged to say.

Crane was insistent in his reply. "What does that matter to men like him?"

The response was not violent, but it had been said with intense feeling. Carr watched the younger man as he sipped greedily on his drink, as if the onslaught of alcohol would stop the trembling of his hand and quieten the internal discord which was so obvious from his expression. "Forgive me, Mr Crane, but you are fond of Mrs Trevelyan?"

Crane tried not to look into the kindly, avuncular face and the juxtaposing dark eyes, but it was impossible to resist its draw. "I think she is a very remarkable woman."

"Indeed, she is," agreed Carr. He could forgive the evasion of the reply. To admit love to a stranger was as difficult as doing so to the object of that love. The existence of Marcus Trevelyan would make the position even more difficult for Crane. "Have you told anybody else about this scene between Mrs Trevelyan and Erskine?"

"The police, you mean? No, I didn't. It's only just come back to me."

"Have you told Marcus about it?"

There was a shake of the head. "I wouldn't want him to think I was spying on his wife."

Carr smiled. "You weren't, of course."

"I was just passing. They were in the park opposite the club."

"Did anybody else witness it, as far as you are aware?"

"I couldn't say." Crane leaned forward. "Should I tell the police?"

Carr gave it a rudimentary consideration. "No. You have told me, and I shall take responsibility."

Crane's expression of concern deepened. "What I have told you about Sonia – does it give her a motive for murder?"

Carr shook his head. "The killer has to be a member of the club in order to have gained access to the reading room." He paused as a sudden thought occurred to him. "Or one of the staff."

"Of course, I should have thought of that," said Crane.

"And that is why Inspector Mason must know about Ronald Edgerton. It is important evidence."

With a nod of his compliance, Crane took his leave. Carr remained seated, his fingers idly stroking the shattered bones of his knee. Crane's evidence had been important in more ways than the nervous young man might have realised. He had informed Carr not only of Edgerton's opportunity to kill Erskine, but also that Crane himself had a reason to commit the murder. Erskine's negligence suit against Crane's firm aside, if Crane was as much in love with Sonia Trevelyan as Carr now suspected, Erskine's insidious approach to her might provide Crane with a secondary, more personal motive for murder.

With a gentle purr of interest, Everett Carr sipped his wine just as the clock struck the half hour.

Chapter Twenty-Four

C arr had known that Ronald Edgerton would be in the club. His habits were so regular as to be predictable, and Carr was aware that the barrister preferred the social atmosphere of the Icarus Club than the professional confines of his Chambers or the barren solitude of his own home. Edgerton, a bachelor, had never been in a relationship which might be considered serious, not in all the time Carr had known him, and there was no reason to suppose that the circumstances had altered. Carr doubted now that any love affair would be taken seriously, or even be welcome, so settled in his self-possessed habits had Edgerton become. And yet, Carr supposed a man could be unmarried and content with the position, but still require the companionship of his peers. Edgerton might be at ease with his lack of love, but it did not mean that he was necessarily content in his own company. His proclivity for alcohol, if nothing else, would run the risk of continued solitude turning into something not only distasteful, but dangerously self-destructive.

Edgerton, typically, was sitting with a whisky and a cigar. He had not yet dressed for dinner, although his suit was nevertheless immaculate, even if his tendency to excess made it seem strained rather than tailored. His face was crimson, with the usual sheen of imminent perspiration, and the dark moustache curled under the thick, bulbous nose. The fingers were large, with an impression of clumsiness which was belied by the dexterity with which he handled his legal papers when in Court. He wore a gold ring on the little finger of his right hand, the band deep-set into the excess flesh, and the ruby which was set into it glowed brightly against the particular pink of the skin.

"Might I join you for a few moments, Edgerton?" asked Carr.

"Please do, Your Honour." Carr refused the offer of a drink, but Edgerton ordered a second, finishing the first with an unpalatable enthusiasm. "The place is in total disarray. Police lurking in every corner, questions being asked in a tone of voice which can barely disguise its suspicion, accusing glances everywhere."

Carr smiled. "You talk like a man with a guilty conscience."

"I come here for some escape from the outside world, to have a bit of peace. How can one do that with these flatfoots bustling about and peering into every corner?"

"I should have thought you would be more prepared for this sort of thing, dear boy. Our profession has surely given us an insight into how police enquiries are conducted."

Edgerton laughed. "Yes, but we only see the end result, don't we? We're not privy to the actual quizzing and snooping, thank goodness. Seeing this chap, Mason, and his cohorts lumbering about, it's no surprise the defence can pull the rug out from under so many prosecutions."

Carr found the criticism distasteful, and he felt unable to allow it to pass without some retaliation. "Inspector Mason is a very competent officer, dear boy, and his record speaks for itself."

"Well, if you say so."

"Perhaps you are afraid of what he might discover."

Edgerton had been about to take a gulp of his whisky, but Carr's words gave him pause. Now, the deep-set, porcine eyes flickered with suspicion under the lowered lids. "What are you talking about?"

Carr kept his eyes fixed on Edgerton, but the smile which crept across his lips was assured. "Have you told the police where you were when Erskine was murdered?"

"I've had my dose of interrogation, yes." It was a reply not unlike the petulant response of a child confronted by a misdemeanour for which he was not yet prepared to confess.

"And did you tell them what you told me? That you were at home, working."

"Naturally." Edgerton's voice now was defiant.

"I see." Carr's smile broadened, but his eyes did not reflect the humour. "I rather hoped you would have told them the truth."

For a brief moment, there was silence. With a movement which was both definite and mildly threatening, Edgerton slowly placed his glass on the table between them. He considered Carr intensely, his jaw clenched, as if he was fearful of allowing any incriminating words to escape from his lips. Carr stared down at the silver handle of his cane and then, sharply, flicked his glare back to the barrister. Edgerton, momentarily disturbed by the intensity of Carr's eyes, sat back in his chair.

"I don't know what you mean, Your Honour."

Carr gently stroked the Imperial beard. "What did you and Erskine argue about last night?"

"We didn't argue." He summoned as much credibility as he could muster. "I was not at the club last night."

Carr ignored the dishonesty. "What did you argue about?"

"I wasn't here," came the insistent reply.

"You were seen." Carr's voice had raised slightly, as if challenging Edgerton to maintain his pretence. "An independent witness saw you marching out of the reading room at a time when it's known Erskine was in there."

"That's a lie," hissed Edgerton.

Carr did not have to provide any words to the contrary. His dark eyes and the impassive expression were sufficient. "I think you may expect a further visit from Inspector Mason."

Edgerton snorted an impudent laugh, then picked up the whisky and threw some of it down his throat. After a long moment of contemplation, he let out a sign of resignation. "I don't suppose I'll find out who saw me."

"That is a matter for Mason."

"You're not going to tell me?" He watched Carr shake his head slowly. "Well, whoever he is could easily have gone into the reading room after I had left it. So, I hope he isn't so sanctimonious that he doesn't realise he had as much opportunity to kill Erskine as I had."

"Did you have any reason to kill him?"

Edgerton shook his head. "I didn't like him, but then not many of us did. Disliking a man isn't a reason to murder him."

"What did you argue about?" Carr's need to repeat the question was becoming tiresome to him.

"It isn't relevant."

Carr paused before asking his next, possibly dangerous question. "Was he blackmailing you?"

The natural flames in Edgerton's cheeks intensified. "What makes you think that?"

Carr shrugged. "I have reason to think that Erskine was a blackmailer, as I've told you before. A significant amount of money was found on his body, and you were seen leaving the scene of the murder at a time when it could have been committed. I wonder if those three points are connected."

Edgerton's vacillation now transitioned into hostility. "It's no business of yours to wonder anything, Your Honour, if you'll pardon me saying so."

Carr accepted the criticism. "I have a natural curiosity, dear boy. And, you see, it *is* curious, the body being covered in money."

"Rumour has it that it was stolen from Leonard Faraday's safe."

Carr was not surprised that the fact of the theft had become common knowledge, albeit as unsubstantiated gossip. He could hardly have expected something so crucial to remain secret for long in such a closed community as the Icarus Club and, for his part, Mason would be no less surprised. It was as inevitable as it was unhelpful.

"That has yet to be established, as far as I am aware," Carr said, "although it seems unlikely to me."

"And why's that?" Edgerton was unable to resist the question.

"It seems implausible that someone would steal money from the secretary's office only to leave it on a corpse in a room only a short distance down the corridor."

"It makes as much sense as suggesting I was being blackmailed by Erskine."

Edgerton was regaining some of his composure, but Carr's response was piercing. "I don't agree."

"How dare you?" roared Edgerton.

Carr remained calm, his voice level but insistent. "It makes perfect sense to me to say that Erskine was blackmailing you. A thief does not take money and dispose of it in such a public fashion, but a victim of blackmail may well throw money into his tormenter's face in indignation, particularly if he was already agitated by a prior argument."

Edgerton rose from his chair with a violent snarl. "You've got no right to make such accusations. I thought we were friends, Your Honour, but I see how wrong I was."

Carr remained motionless, his eyes averted from Edgerton. "A man has died. No matter how disliked he was, he had a right to his own life. When somebody denies him that right, they offend all our senses of humanity. The truth has to come out, and it is our duty to assist it to do so."

"That's what the police are for."

Carr bowed his head in acknowledgment of the fact. "Satisfying my own curiosity need not hinder the police and their own enquiries. Might I suggest that only those with something to hide would be offended by any trivial questions I might ask."

Despite his fury, Edgerton smiled. "You're a snake, Your Honour. In your own fashion, you're as devious as any killer. I hope your cleverness doesn't put you in any danger."

Whether it was intended as a direct threat was uncertain. There was no explicit venom in its delivery, which was amused rather than menacing, but somehow its dismissive pleasantry came with its own breed of danger. If Carr was perturbed by it, he did not demonstrate the fact. Instead, he looked up to Edgerton with eyes whose darkness displayed his lack of concern.

"I have nothing to fear," he said. "Only the killer of Jacob Erskine has any cause to be afraid. Any word of caution against danger should be directed to him."

Edgerton frowned, as if trying to fathom whether it had been an accusation or a direct warning to himself. Carr was not willing to explain further. He simply smiled, and the eyes now warmed, but he said nothing else. Edgerton offered a curt word of farewell, turned on his heel, and left.

Alone, Carr considered the interview. It had been less than satisfactory. He had failed to ascertain the cause of the argument between Edgerton and Erskine, although he had obtained confirmation that Edgerton had lied about his whereabouts on the night of the murder. Furthermore, Carr was certain that Edgerton had lied about being blackmailed, and that, in itself, would perhaps explain the argument and the money. It was little more than supposition, but it struck Carr as being persuasive. What reason Erskine had to blackmail Edgerton remained shrouded in mystery, but Carr had an idea about how he might uncover it. He mused over the plan which was forming in his mind for a little while longer before finally settling on a course of action with which he was satisfied. He consulted his watch, noting that it was time to go. Slowly, he raised himself out of his chair and made his way to the door.

Chapter Twenty-Five

I t had been several weeks since Carr had last seen Sonia Trevelyan and if the intervening period had blurred the memory of her beauty, then it was brought immediately back into focus when she opened the door to him. She had dressed for dinner already, the gown an elegant creation of dove grey silk, which complimented rather than emphasised the paleness of her skin. Her angular, almost feline features were framed by the short, black hair, which itself was so dark that it reminded Carr of a raven's wings. Her eyes were bright and welcoming, the shading above them a subtle enhancement to their shape and colour. Her lips were a vibrant scarlet, and they stretched into a smile when she saw him as he took her hand in his and placed a gentle kiss on its back.

She led him into the parlour and offered him a glass of sherry. The room was expensively furnished, but it avoided any suggestion of ostentation. The overall impression was one of tasteful elegance, and Carr suspected that the primary influence on the decoration had been Sonia, although Marcus was not without his own sense of style. There were paintings on the walls, reproductions of notable works, and several carved, abstract statues were placed strategically around the room. A Columbia gramophone stood on a low table beside the drinks' cabinet and, at a volume low enough to be heard without being intrusive, Mahler's *Adagietto* could be heard.

"May I say how much I approve of your taste in music, my dear," said Carr. "Mahler is a particular favourite of my own."

Sonia smiled awkwardly. "I'm afraid Marcus is the musician. I cannot pretend to be an expert."

Carr's eyes drifted to the ceiling in recollection. *"In which way I love you, my sunbeam, I cannot tell you with words. Only my longing, my love, and my bliss can I with anguish declare."*

"I'm sorry?"

Carr smiled back at her. "The *Adagietto* is said to be a love letter to Mahler's wife. That poem was left for her to accompany it."

"It is beautiful."

Carr lowered his eyes and stroked his knee. "My wife thought so, too."

"I didn't know you were married."

She seemed so pleased to hear it that he felt dishonourable in telling her the truth. "She died."

Sonia, at once, felt both foolish and embarrassed. "I'm sorry, Mr Carr."

He waved away the apology. "If you will forgive the advice of an old man, dear lady, relish every day of your marriage. It is a gift from God, and you should treasure it whilst you can."

"Do you think marriage is so sacred, Mr Carr?" Her voice was earnest, but there was a quality about her eyes which troubled him.

"Do you not?"

"Yes, of course." She laughed casually, but the distance in her eyes intensified.

"Is Marcus out?" he asked.

"He has gone to the Icarus Club. Did you not see him?" She watched Carr shake his head. "He is such a darling. He wasn't going to go until I insisted. He doesn't like to think of me, sitting here at home, alone."

Carr smiled. "He is a very thoughtful man. And a dear friend to me."

"He likes you, too. We both do." She allowed him a shy smile, one which he reciprocated, and she took a moment to summon her courage to ask what it was which troubled her. "You don't often call unannounced, Mr Carr. Marcus is out, I'm afraid, but he is due home for dinner any minute now."

Carr held up his hand in protest. "I did not come to see Marcus, dear lady. It was you I wanted to see."

"Is something wrong?"

He was unsure how to answer for a moment. The question was somehow so childishly naïve that it seemed uncharitable not to give it the negative reply which it so desperately seemed to demand. But she was not a child, and she was intelligent enough to know that murder was disruptive, that it made everything wrong, unbalanced, and chaotic.

"Have the police been to see you and Marcus?" he asked.

She nodded quickly. "It was awful. They treated us as if we were criminals."

It seemed a melodramatic response, but Carr paid it no heed. Instead, he smiled gently and nodded his head. "They can have that effect, but they have their duty to perform."

Sonia shrugged. "Do the police know who killed that man?"

"Not as yet. It is too soon to know anything for certain."

"Marcus says he was a horrible man."

Softly, the voice stained with regret, Carr answered. "He was not a pleasant man. You have some idea of how unkind he was, I believe."

She attempted to give the impression that his words meant nothing to her, but Carr had noticed the slight widening of the eyes and the stiffening of the spine. He was conscious of a sudden and overwhelming sadness, a cold regret that his compulsion to find the truth necessitated her having to relive something which she clearly preferred to forget or ignore.

"I don't know what you mean," she said.

"Forgive me, my dear, but I think you do."

She refused to look away from him, and her glare was as defiant as she could manage. He was impressed by her determination not to succumb to the obvious and natural temptations either to weep or to rage against the memory. Sensing, however, that she was unwilling to co-operate, Carr spoke once again.

"Sonia, my dear, I am here as a friend, not as an interrogator. I was told you had an unpleasant encounter with Jacob Erskine recently, and I wanted to see if you were all right."

"Who told you about that?" Her eyes were suddenly haunted by the memory of the event.

Carr did not consider that her question required an immediate answer. "What happened?" "Mr Erskine frightened me, that's all," she confessed. "It wasn't that he ever actually did anything, but there was something about him which was sinister. The way he would look at me, brush past me and make sure we touched, the smiles he would give me. There was never any doubt about what was in his mind."

"Did you confront him about it?"

"No. I tried to ignore him, ignore all of it. I wanted to pretend it wasn't happening at all."

"I can understand that." Carr sipped some of the sherry. "I am surprised that Marcus was able to suppress any desire to warn off Erskine. He wasn't afraid to do so, surely?"

Sonia shook her head. "He wasn't afraid of Erskine, no."

Carr detected the slight inflexion in her voice. "But he was afraid of something else?"

She nodded. Tears had welled in her eyes, forming obstinate globes which refused at first to break and roll down her cheeks, as if to do so would be a display of weakness. Her expression had hardened, as though she were ashamed of herself on account of the tears or as a defence against the memory which was surfacing in her mind. Carr placed the sherry glass on a small table by the side of his chair and pulled himself to his feet. He limped over to her and sat beside her on the settee. His face was grave, the brows furrowed with concern. He took one of her hands in his and placed an arm around her shoulders. She did not break down completely, and the sobs, when they came, were as delicate as they were silent. Carr allowed them to come, and he did not interrupt them. They lasted for a short time only, and once they had passed, he handed her the sherry, which she had not yet touched, and instructed her to drink it.

"I'm sorry, Mr Carr," she said, her voice fighting to retain some of its natural confidence. "You must think me very foolish."

"Not at all. Erskine's insinuations towards you are clearly distressing."

But she shook her head. "It isn't that, not directly. It's what it reminded me of."

Carr had the familiar sensation of fingers of ice caressing the nape of his neck before gliding ominously down the vertebrae of his spine. His voice, however, was gentle and sympathetic. "And what was that?"

When she looked into his eyes, she seemed to be no more than a frightened child. The eyes were wide, the lips parted and turned downwards in a fledgling scream, and the cheeks like alabaster, blanched with terror and shame. "About how my father loved me."

And now, Carr seemed to understand everything. Her expression, the tears, and the opinion of Erskine as a predatory, older man now all seemed to make sense. He could imagine it all: the step on the stair, so measured and deliberate as to be horrifying, the slow opening of the door carrying its own sense of menace, the falsely soothing words of the worst kind of paternal reassurance, and the stroking of the hair which mocked genuine affection and tenderness. He could picture her in bed, listening, praying that the night would pass without him intruding into her room. With equal repugnance, he could imagine her agony, the shame, the self-accusations as she wondered if it was her fault that his hands were invading her. Marcus had said that Sonia's father had drank himself to death, and Carr could imagine now the stink of him as he whispered his sickening encouragement. He doubted she would remember herself precisely how many nights her father had come to her room, and he supposed that they would merge in her memory into a vile collage of sinister incidents. Carr was outraged, an almost tangible taste of revulsion souring his mouth and stomach, as if someone had poured acid into him and, suddenly, he was reminded of the very real difference between evil and mere wickedness.

"Monstrous." It might have been futile, but it was no less honest for that.

"It is over. Marcus saved me when he took me away from Shropshire to London."

"There are things which even time and distance cannot heal."

She neither agreed nor argued. "I used to dream about him. It was like being haunted by him, as if he was still tormenting me, even after death. I don't anymore. I try not to think about it at all, but sometimes, something will remind me. Something innocent, perhaps, or something…."

"Something like Jacob Erskine?"

She nodded, grateful that he had finished the sentence for her. She looked into his eyes. "I've never talked about it to a stranger before. I'm not sure why I have done now."

Carr smiled tenderly. "Perhaps you have wished to do so for a long time."

"I never felt the need."

"The mind can play tricks on us, nevertheless. Now that you have confided in me, perhaps you will be less troubled than before."

He said it with such kindness that Sonia could not help but smile and, in the moment, believe him. "Who did tell you? About me and that man?"

Carr rose to his feet, not wishing to be in close proximity to her for longer than compassion had demanded. "It was a member of the club. A man called Patrick Crane."

"I see." Sonia's eyes had grown temporarily distant, as if her mind had drifted onto its own course. A faint flicker of a smile drifted across the scarlet lips, but it was nothing more than a ripple on the surface of a calm sea, lasting no longer than the briefest of moments. She finished her sherry and rose from the settee. She gestured with her glass to Carr, but he refused the inference. "Poor Mr Crane was about to be ruined by that awful man."

"Did he tell you that himself?"

"No, Marcus did."

"When was this?"

"A couple of nights ago. We were out to dinner, to a restaurant you had recommended, as a matter of fact."

Carr recalled Marcus Trevelyan saying something of the sort. "And Mr Crane was there too." He watched her nod her head, sipping some of her second glass of sherry. "Did he see you?"

"I don't think so. Does it matter?"

"Who can say?" replied Carr with a smile.

"I wish he hadn't said anything about what he saw," Sonia confessed. She was saddened rather than angry by Crane's indiscretion.

"He was not gossiping, dear lady," Carr assured her. "He was, I think, concerned about you. If I may say so, I think he is rather taken with you."

Her cheeks flushed. "I'm sure you're mistaken."

But Carr shook his head. "He is a shy and awkward young man, but he has goodness and brains. He will make a caring husband."

"I'm already married, Mr Carr," she reminded him. "But I agree that Mr Crane is a considerate and gentle man, from what I have seen of him."

"Then do not think badly of him for voicing his concerns about you," said Carr gently. He took one of her hands in his, kissing the back of it once again. "I must be on my way. I came here only to make sure that you were all right."

She smiled faintly. "I am, I promise you."

"You must forgive an old man's fussing."

The smile broke into a laugh. "It was very kind of you, but you mustn't worry."

Carr's smile remained beneath the moustache and beard, but his eyes had dimmed with sadness. "I have so few people to worry about, my dear."

She felt she should say something in response, but the comment had thrown her with its unexpected candour. Any reply she could conjure seemed to her to be too prosaic and trite to be effective. Instead, and considering silence to be the most suitable response, she smiled back at him and touched his cheek with her hand. Gently, almost nervously, he removed it and placed it back by her side.

Once outside, he walked slowly back to the Icarus Club. His mood was unusually low, and he felt the need for solitary reflection. On impulse, he changed his direction and walked away from the club and towards his own rooms in the Albany. He craved privacy and the security of domesticity. It was his natural repugnance of the revelation of Sonia Trevelyan's childhood which darkened his mood, and he felt no cause to apologise for it. His fondness for her had arisen originally because he had recognised traits of his wife in her and, in his darker moments of mourning, he had found himself wondering whether his own daughter, had he and Miranda been so blessed, might not have been much different to Sonia herself. Was that why his disgust at what she had confided in him was so acute? Or was it simply a natural abhorrence at her revelation?

It might have been both, of course, but Carr's mood was not simply a reaction against what he had learned. There was something else which troubled him, something less emotive, but no less important to him. Sonia had told him many things in their short interview but, as he walked towards Piccadilly, Carr knew that she had said something of enormous importance, a fact which had eluded him in the moment, just as keenly as it did now. It was useless to try to recall it but, whatever it was, Carr felt sure that it was the one strand of thread which would unravel the dark mystery of the murder of Jacob Erskine.

Chapter Twenty-Six

Cyril Parsons loved the atmosphere of pubs. He loved their noises, the rumble of conversation with its indiscernible words, and the frequent interruption of raucous laughter. He loved the industrious tinkling of glasses and the occasional hiss of the soda syphons, but also the varnished wood, the tobacco blending with perfume, and the insistent but not overpowering aroma of alcohol itself. Parsons, not a sociable man by nature, nevertheless felt part of a certain society when he was drinking in a pub. Even sitting alone at the corner of a bar, with one whisky after another, it was as if he belonged to a collective existence at last, part of a communal purpose in which his presence meant something. Since the war, Parsons had felt no true sense of belonging anywhere other than in a public bar and certainly not in the sparsely furnished, cold, and ill-equipped rooms he was forced to call home.

Thoughts such as these, their pessimism and their self-destructive pity, were not uncommon to him, and his drinking did nothing to alleviate or discourage them. On the contrary, they further polluted his natural instincts about himself, increasing rather than diminishing their adverse effect on him and making the world seem as if its scope for amelioration was so narrow as to be impossible. His thoughts were rarely anything other than dark ponderings, his attitude and approach to life never anything other than bitter, and his opinions of others seldom anything other than contemptuous. Even his job, which ought perhaps to have salvaged something of his self-respect, seemed to mock him, with its constant requirement that he act in servitude to the privileged and the elite. He was aware of their condescension towards him, their stifled ridicule, and their whispered derision, but it was nothing compared to their hypocrisy when they would nod at him as he opened doors, wishing him a good evening with a smile of disdain and a silent snigger at his position in life. Saving lives on a battlefield did not entitle him to anything other than servitude, whereas the officers who planned the attacks, from the safe distance of Whitehall, continued to exist in luxury and status. They ate their rarest of roast beef whilst men like Parsons, who had seen the horrors of the consequences of the squabbles of governments, ate scraps of cheap meat and tinned provisions, assuming they ate at all. The division was clear, and it would not be ignored. But here, under the dimmed lights and smoke of the snug, Parsons had an equal standing. There was no mockery, no sneering looks of disdain, and no insincerity. There were only the sounds, the smells, and the drink.

He ordered another whisky and ignored old Petrie's expression of concerned disapproval. Parsons had no intention of causing trouble, and he was not drunk enough yet to be unnecessarily defensive or argumentative. The whisky was delivered and paid for without further comment, and Parsons drank from it greedily. It would be the last one, he promised himself, and he repeated the promise when, far sooner than he had anticipated, he found the glass surprisingly empty again. Every glass was the last one, but always the good intention inevitably was washed away by one more.

"Petrie, get me another." The offensive tone of the demand was not unexpected.

The landlord walked over to the end of the bar, his head shaking resolutely. "I can't do it, Mr Parsons. Enough's enough."

"I'll decide when I've had enough."

"Not in my pub, you won't." Petrie's voice was unassailable, even within the confines of its own politeness.

"One last drink, Petrie, you old bastard. To celebrate."

"Celebrate what?"

Parsons, his eyes slowly bursting into flame with malevolent intent, smiled back at the landlord. "I've done something."

"Oh yes?"

Parsons nodded. "Looked after myself, for once. It's time I got something out of life again."

Petrie sighed. "One last drink, then."

Parsons cackled with triumph and, when the glass arrived, he sipped at the drink, as if in some form of thanks for Petrie's concession. "The rich think they're above people like us, Petrie. They think we're nothing more than shit to be stepped over."

"I'm not sure I agree."

Parsons ignored him. "They don't see us as real people, you see. They think that they own us, that they control us, and that we're here to be used by them. That's all going to change. They're going to learn what it's like for someone to have power over them for a change."

He laughed, and Petrie offered a professionally polite smile. When he read the newspapers the next morning, of course, Petrie would realise that there was nothing amusing about what Parsons had said at all. For now, though, Petrie returned to his duties, only too pleased that one of his more troublesome customers was leaving without incident.

Parsons made his way back to his lodgings on foot. The cold air had sharpened his senses but not altogether dispelled the effects of his drinking. His mouth was dry, the tongue unusually large, and the stale taste of whisky lingered at the back of his throat. He knew that there was a bottle of the stuff beside his bed, just as he knew that what his body craved was water or, at the very least, coffee. Most of all, he knew that he would deny it that need, succumbing once again to an ever greater, more dangerous compulsion.

Parsons was sitting in a dirty, tattered armchair when the knock at the door infiltrated his senses. He was expecting no visitor, and yet the arrival of one seemed somehow to be of no surprise. He rose from the chair and walked uncertainly over to the door. When he pulled it open, the face which greeted him was familiar and not entirely unexpected.

"You're not supposed to be here," said Parsons. "We agreed to meet tomorrow."

"May I come in, nevertheless?"

Parsons acquiesced by stepping aside. He closed the door by letting it loose from his grip, so that the snap of the bolt seemed like the blade of the guillotine plunging to its destiny. Parsons dragged his feet across the bare floorboards and picked up the bottle of whisky, now half-empty, from the floor beside the armchair. "Drink?"

"No, thank you."

"Suit yourself." He poured a liberal measure. He looked around the room, as if seeing its threadbare bleakness and its embarrassingly dilapidated state for the first time. It was as if he had never realised his own hopelessness until that moment. He could not even say that the frugal furnishings and the bleak rooms were his own, since he owned neither. He could afford none of them on his own terms, his personal possessions being little more than his clothes and his bottles. He was suddenly aware that this was the first time anyone had been inside the place he was compelled to call home and, to his drunken surprise, he felt ashamed of it. "I don't suppose you imagined even I would live in a hovel like this."

"I don't care where you live, Parsons."

"Not the Icarus Club, though, is it? Nothing so fine. But it's all I've got. We're not all as lucky as you."

"I don't care, I told you."

"It's all going to change now." Parsons was smiling. "Sure you won't have a drink to toast our agreement?"

"No."

Parsons shrugged and turned his back on his visitor. "I hope you're not going to go back on your word. It wouldn't do you any good. Not when I know about you."

The blow to his head came without any warning, its force sufficient to make him stumble into the armchair, even if it did not take his life. Parsons heard the distant clatter of broken glass, and the aroma of whisky suddenly overtook him. For the first time, it struck him as disgusting, as if impending death, which he felt certain was upon him, had robbed the drink of all its allure. A second blow, more fierce than the first, brought him to his knees, and the pool of whisky at his feet began to turn red. His vision began to quiver, the edges of his consciousness blurring, so that the familiar objects in the room became confused, unrecognisable caricatures of themselves.

And then, without warning, he was face down, his nose breathing in the dampness of the floorboards, and the distant smell of dust on the rug competing with it for dominance. His eyes could no longer focus, rolling pointlessly around in his head, and the jaw slackened in apparent exhaustion. There must have been a third blow to the head but, curiously, he had not felt it, and nor had his ears registered the sickening sound of cracking bone. He seemed to hear once again the voices of the many men whom he had saved on the battlefield and he wondered, stupidly, whether any soldiers would be coming to save him now. Whatever he had imagined death would be, it had been nothing so brutal or so cruel as this.

Finally, inevitably, there was nothing. No more thoughts, no more breaths, and no more movements.

There never would be anything else now: no other regrets, no further whisky, no more bitterness. There would be no need now to drown out the harsh reality of life with beer and whisky and no reason to hide anymore from the perils and the dangers of the nights. There would be none of it, because there was now no longer a man called Cyril Parsons to indulge in them. Now, there was simply the battered, undignified physical remains of him. He would now never be anything more than a memory which, in time, would fade to nothing. There would be few to mourn him. A handful of creditors, a number of bar owners, and the occasional girl for whom he had paid. In the end, none of it had mattered very much, and very little of it would mean a great deal in the future. Even his courage in battle would begin to be diminished by the fact that he had died by murder. He would be remembered now, if at all, not as a soldier who saved his troops, but as a petty, drunken blackmailer, bludgeoned to death in his own corner of private despair.

The poker which had been used to smash in his skull was dropped to the floor and, with almost preternatural silence, Cyril Parsons' killer stepped out of the room and closed the door.

Chapter Twenty-Seven

Carr's overriding emotion was pity.

The wound to the head had been shocking, both in its violence and its effects, and Carr would have been less than human if he had not wondered for a long moment whether Parsons had felt any pain or whether the blows had been so immediate in their devastation that their surprise had overwhelmed any registration of agony. From beneath the soiled vest, its white now long since suffocated by grey, the thick arms were beginning to display that paleness which was so peculiar to death. The eyes, widened by shock or fright, or a combination of both, seemed to stare uselessly into the past, as if watching the murder take place incessantly but with a cold, morbid objectivity. The blood and whisky on the floor told their own version of the story of what had happened on the previous evening, as did the remnants of the shattered glass, which twinkled like macabre stars in the wreckage.

And yet, as he stared down at the body of the man he had known as Cyril Parsons, those aspects of the crime, whilst tragic, did not impress Carr as much as the surroundings themselves. He knew that Parsons had not been rich, but Carr had never suspected that his destitution had been so absolute. The room was beyond unprepossessing, its poverty enhanced not by the scarcity of its furnishings, but by their futility. The bed was little more than a mattress on a wire frame, the single pillow so flat as to be meaningless, its stains matching those on the equally exhausted mattress. A single blanket was curled at the foot of the bed, but its capacity for warmth was negligible. The wardrobe was functional, but nothing more, and Carr doubted whether it would sustain extensive use. The body lay beside an armchair, mottled with age and the upholstery in need of repair, and there was a small wooden chair placed under an equally unsteady table. There was a rudimentary set of shelves on the wall in the corner, containing a couple of cups and some glasses, only two of which were not cracked. The curtains across the mildewed window, which looked out onto a narrow alleyway at the rear of the lodging house, were so old that they were little more than strips of torn fabric, through which shafts of meagre sunlight would, on occasion, remind the room's occupant that there was a better, more beautiful world beyond them, if he was only able to find it. It was so far removed from Carr's own rooms in the Albany, the Icarus Club, or from the world Parsons would have glimpsed every day in his dealings with the club that, for the first time, Carr could understand at least something of the man's bitterness and his loathing of them all.

"What was it all for, in the end?" he asked, more to himself than to any of the officers in the room.

Inspector Mason looked up at him in some surprise. "I'm sorry, sir?"

"This man was a hero in the war, inspector. He saved people's lives, put his own at risk to do so. Was he entitled to no thanks for that?"

"He was awarded the Military Cross, if you recall."

Carr conceded the point with a shrug. "What good is metal and ribbon, if our heroes are permitted to live in such squalor?"

Mason thought back to his interview with Parsons. "He had similar thoughts, Mr Carr. When I spoke to him about Erskine's murder, he questioned what the war had all been about in the end. I don't think he wore his bravery with pride."

Carr nodded his head slowly. "How he must have hated us all."

"Hated you?"

Carr nodded. "Every day, Parsons would wake up in here and make his way to the Icarus Club, to open the doors for people like me, and, every evening, he would come back to this. What would he have made of all that opulence and privilege? I doubt many of us even noticed him, and those who did hardly cared whether or not he was coping with his life."

Again, although he did not say so, Mason was reminded of Parsons' own words on the subject, and how he had confessed that he despised the club and its standards. "Did you like Mr Parsons?"

Carr, suddenly aware of his morbid philosophising, shook his head with a smile. "I did not know him well enough to have an opinion, inspector. Perhaps that is to my discredit. To the club's collective discredit, come to that."

Mason was not sure what to say in reply. Carr's eyes were dimmed, his brows drawn over them so that they seemed darker than usual, and the lips were turned down beneath the heavy moustache and beard. Mason wondered how deeply Carr ought to be affected by the death of the club's doorman, but it was evident that the murder of Parsons seemed to have awoken something in Carr's conscience. On balance, Mason thought it best to arm himself with the safety of facts and procedure.

"There's no doubt about the weapon used," he said, pointing to the poker. "The doctor says that there were three blows, and the final one was inflicted after death."

"Has he given an estimate of the time of death?"

"Last night, between ten o'clock and midnight. Probably nearer the former."

Carr turned his back on the scene. "There is no sign of any intruder?"

"No. Whoever did it, Parsons let him in."

"Into the room, certainly, but what about into the house itself?"

Mason shook his head. "The back door wasn't locked. One of the tenants had gone out and left it on the latch. He did not return until the early hours."

Carr nodded. "The killer had a stroke of luck and took advantage of it."

"And if Parsons let him into this room, then I suppose it must mean he knew him."

Carr nodded. "The killer is a member of the Icarus Club. Two murders in two days, and each victim is associated with the club. That cannot be a coincidence."

"You think Parsons might have found out something?"

Carr shrugged. "We must not run before we can walk."

He limped slowly around the room, the iron ferrule of his cane tapping a slow and mournful rhythm against the wooden floorboards. On a table, stacked up against a vase of dead flowers, there was a collection of envelopes. They had been opened carelessly, the flaps torn rather than sliced with a knife, the contents glanced at but discarded. They were bills, largely unpaid, reminders for payment, various threats of legal proceedings. Parsons had read them, so much was clear, but there was no suggestion either that he heeded the contents or was concerned by them. Never a man to leave any bill or debt unpaid for any period of time, Carr wondered whether it was possible to reach a point where one more threat and one more request for money became meaningless in the wake of so many previous demands. If Parsons had thought he could sink no lower, perhaps he believed nothing else could harm him. A potential danger would mean nothing if there were no genuine consequences following from it.

"He had no money at all," said Carr, the voice laced with sadness. "On the verge of bankruptcy, I would suggest."

Mason had joined him at the table. "And he owed Erskine money. How could he bring himself to gamble, knowing he could not pay for it?"

"Parsons wouldn't be the first man to think he could win his way out of misfortune, and I suspect he was so far into the mire that he was unafraid of sinking further. What does one more debt matter?" Carr turned to face the Inspector. "Parsons was at the *Duck and Drake* public house from around nine o'clock on the night of Erskine's murder, but he could still have killed him, as long as he did it before that time."

"It would have been possible," agreed Mason. "But if he murdered Erskine, why is he now lying dead himself?"

"Retribution for Erskine, perhaps?"

Mason frowned. "Do you think that's possible?"

But Carr did not reply. He had begun to open cupboards and drawers and, from the darkness of one of them, he pulled out a large metal bucket. It was filled with unopened bottles of various types of alcohol, primarily whisky. It was cheap but potentially powerful, the contents no doubt as explosive as the labels were uninspiring. He placed the bucket on the table and pointed to it, as if it were answer enough to Mason's question.

"A hidden supply?" Mason frowned. "Why hide it from himself?"

"I suspect he was hiding it from his landlady. Despite everything, perhaps he had retained some sort of pride." Carr fell silent for a moment, and his eyes drifted to the body of the dead man. A smile, saddened rather than amused, passed across his lips, but what thoughts were passing through his mind, Mason could only guess.

"I don't see where it takes the enquiry, I must confess," said Mason. "What relevance does Parsons' dependency on drink have either to his murder or to Erskine's?"

Carr was staring into the distance. "It matters because it helps us understand him as a man rather than as a suspect or victim, inspector. It gives us an insight into his life as well as his death. We can see what demons plagued him and how he faced them."

It was a melancholy comment as well as a metaphysical one, and Mason was surprised to hear it come from Carr, whose natural temperament was affable and largely optimistic. It seemed inappropriate to speak, and Carr's expression, with the distant glare in his eyes and the pursed lips beneath the luxurious moustache, did not seem to invite any conversation. At last, Carr seemed to be aware once more of his surroundings, and his dark eyes snapped back into focus. "If Parsons was murdered because of something he saw, what could it have been?"

"The murderer, presumably?"

Carr shook his head. "He couldn't have seen the killer if he wasn't on the club premises, my dear inspector."

"Perhaps it wasn't something he saw, but something he realised."

Carr nodded vaguely. "What could he have realised about anybody which would be dangerous?"

Mason admitted his limitations. "I couldn't possibly say, Mr Carr."

"Have you found anything which might suggest that the meeting between the killer and Parsons was pre-arranged?"

Mason shook his head. "No."

"Nothing which might indicate blackmail?"

Again, there was a shake of the head. "I'm afraid not."

"Then any ideas we may have about the motive for this murder are nothing more than speculation." Carr's voice was placid but there seemed to Mason to be some undercurrent of impatience.

Mason, having thoughts of his own, began to tap the end of his pencil against his chin. "That burned note which we found in the fire at the Icarus Club…"

"What about it?"

"Taking it for granted that there is a connection between the note and Erskine's murder, and assuming that Parsons' death means that he didn't kill Erskine, it follows that it is unlikely to be his initial on that note. If that's right, perhaps Parsons knew who *had* sent it. He might even have been asked to deliver it himself. Maybe that was what Parsons knew, which was dangerous to the murderer."

Carr smiled and shook his head. "To my mind, there is no great mystery about who sent it, and if you think carefully enough, inspector, you will realise it too."

Mason fought to keep his frustrations under control. "I confess that my investigation is stalling, Mr Carr. I see no clear line of enquiry. This second murder has unsettled whatever thoughts or suspicions I might have had."

Carr nodded his head slowly. "There is much to learn, I grant you that. We have learned so much that we cannot yet isolate what facts are pertinent and which are distractions. And yet, I'm certain that I have been given the key to this puzzle, inspector, but I cannot grasp it."

"What key?"

"Something said, a point made which is vital to the solution to the mystery." He sighed deeply. "It will come to me, no doubt."

Mason did not seem interested in Carr's vague instincts, and his expression showed that something of a more immediate concern had seized his mind. "Do you suppose that whoever is responsible will kill again?"

It was impossible to predict, but Carr felt no need to say as much. He allowed himself a shrug of the shoulders and an uncertain shake of the head. "I have the impression, inspector, that we are not dealing with a killer who strikes at random. He has a definite purpose. Jacob Erskine and Cyril Parsons were murdered for a specific reason. Once we discover it, we shall know everything, of course, but I don't think we need cloud our thoughts with hysteria."

Mason expected no guarantees, but the cool assertions offered by Carr, even without any definite support of them, carried their own sense of encouragement. He knew Carr well enough to know that he was not prone to offering false hope and, in the absence of any other comfort, he was prepared to accept what Carr had provided.

They exchanged further words and, with a warm farewell, Carr departed. He walked for several painful miles before a taxi appeared. Having hailed it, he sat back into its seat and watched the slum of the suburb transform into the splendour of the city. The difference between the two, separated only by the black snake of the river, was striking. Carr was appalled that he had not been impressed by it before. It sickened him that he had taken for granted his position in life, living in ignorance or unconscious disregard of the alternative existence which might have been his, if chance had not been on his side. Perhaps he had been wrong to assume that only the dark depths of the Thames distanced one from the other, just as he might have been wrong to assume that his life was down to chance. There was something much more insidious which caused the gulf between the two halves of the city, a moral and economic barrier between opportunity and prospect. How many of the Icarus Club members, he wondered, gave any thought to what occurred across the depths of the river? Very few, he supposed. They would be aware of it, as he had been himself, but they would barely acknowledge it. It meant nothing to them, a world beyond their interest and imagination. They had viewed Parsons only as a drunken gambler, unworthy of any emotion from them other than scorn and derision, and they would consider others like him with no greater respect. Now, as the wealth of the city spread out ahead of him, Carr felt more ashamed of himself than he had ever done before.

Cyril Parsons deserved more than their contempt. He had recognised the hypocrisy of the city, its juxtaposition of wealth and squalor, and the instinctive neglect of one by the other. Parsons had not only known it and acknowledged it, but he had lived it. All of which now seemed to Carr to make him more human, more compassionate, and more privileged in his soul than any of the members of the club. Somehow, he saw more integrity in that cheap, sordid room than in all the finery of the Icarus Club.

Nevertheless, it had been Parsons who had died by violence, and it was to his memory that Carr made a silent pledge not only to discover the truth, but also to administer justice.

Chapter Twenty-Eight

C arr was not surprised to find Margaret Erskine in the company of Hector Wharton. If anything, he was grateful for it. Margaret was alarmed but not irritated by his call, and she greeted him with demure politeness, before showing him into the drawing room. Wharton was standing by the mantelpiece, drinking a cup of coffee, his manner distinctly military in its formality. There was something strangely familiar about his presence, as if he already fancied himself as the master of the house. He was altogether too natural in his attitude to his surroundings that Carr found the confidence both unpalatable and inappropriate. If Margaret shared his view, she did not show it. She sat down on the settee and picked up her own cup of coffee. She did not speak and, even if she had the intention of doing so, Wharton was not content to permit it.

"What are you doing here, Carr?" he barked, his voice laced with suspicion.

Carr did not respond directly, but he looked down at Margaret and smiled gently. "How are you, Mrs Erskine?"

She looked up at him, and he had the momentary impression that his kindness had come as a surprise to her. "I'm coping, thank you, Mr Carr. It is difficult, as you can imagine, but Hector has been a great help."

Carr smiled at the colonel, but it belied his internal opinions. It was unfair, no doubt, but he had the impression that Wharton's attentions would be as suffocating as they were solicitous. For his part, Wharton was evidently proud of her words, and the flush of his cheeks and the inflation of his chest proved it. "It is my pleasure, Margaret, you know that."

She held his gaze for long enough to acknowledge that his words were heartfelt. "Would you like some coffee, Mr Carr?"

"Thank you, no. But I will sit, if I may." He waited for her consent and then lowered himself into an armchair, allowing only a small grunt of exertion to escape from his lips.

"You haven't answered my question," observed Wharton. "What are you doing here?"

Margaret sighed. "Honestly, Hector, must you be so confrontational all the time?"

He summoned as much dignity as he could manage. "I don't think people should be pestering you at a time like this."

"Company does me good," she said, with such persistence that Wharton seemed disgruntled by it, as if any company other than his own was an intrusion.

Carr allowed a moment to pass before he spoke. "I'm afraid I have some bad news. Cyril Parsons is dead."

"Dead?" Wharton glared at him. "You mean an accident? Was he drunk?"

Carr stared deliberately at Wharton. "He was murdered, colonel."

It seemed to take some moments for the words to make sense. Wharton frowned in confused disbelief, and Margaret Erskine gasped discreetly, her eyes widening in shock and throwing a glance to the colonel. Carr watched them both carefully, but he could see nothing definite beyond their signs of surprise and shock. Wharton's frown had intensified and, when he spoke, his voice was hardened by some sort of refusal to believe what Carr had said.

"Murdered? What are you talking about?"

"It is true, I'm afraid. Who did it isn't known, but I think we can assume that it was the same person responsible for what happened to your husband." Carr looked over to Margaret in order to express not only his regret but his discomfort in having to raise the tragedy once again. She rewarded him with a brief smile and a flutter of her eyes.

"How did it happen?" asked Wharton.

"He was beaten to death with a poker."

The stark reality of the words was shocking but unavoidable. Margaret gasped once again, more audibly this time, and raised her hand to her mouth, as if desperate to force the sound of horror back down her throat. Wharton, his stoicism corroded by the violence of Parsons' death, walked slowly to the settee and sat beside her.

"Dear Lord," he said, almost to himself. "When did this happen?"

"At around ten o'clock last night, at an estimate," replied Carr. "You should expect a visit from Inspector Mason."

"Why? We had nothing to do with it."

"The killings are connected, colonel," insisted Carr. "The police are bound to want to speak to you."

Margaret was shaking her head. "I can't tell them anything, Hector. I didn't even know the man."

Wharton took her hands in his and squeezed them. "You mustn't fret, my dear. This damned appalling business needs to end. What are the police doing about it all?"

"Their best," said Carr emphatically. "And we must all give them our full co-operation."

Wharton understood the implication. "They will want to know where we were last night, I suppose. Well, I was at home. As was Margaret, I should think."

"I stayed home all night," she confirmed. "I had a headache, so I went to bed early."

Carr smiled at her. "It is the police you must tell, dear lady, not me. I presume nobody can verify what you say?"

"They shouldn't need to," declared Wharton. "Our word should be sufficient."

He was not so naïve, and nor did Carr feel obliged to say as much. He merely broadened his smile and allowed the moment to pass. Wharton rose from the settee once more and helped himself to more coffee. Carr had the impression that, despite the early hour, the colonel would have preferred something stronger. It was a symptom of shock rather than necessity, but Wharton was able to resist it nonetheless. Carr wondered whether his fortitude would have done him as much credit if Margaret Erskine had not been present.

"The theory is that Parsons must have known something about your husband's death," said Carr. "Something which made him a danger to the murderer."

"Something like what?" asked Wharton.

Carr shrugged. "Do you have any ideas yourself, colonel?"

Margaret spoke softly. "Perhaps he saw the killer."

Carr shook his head. "Parsons may not have been on the club premises when your husband was killed."

Wharton snorted. "Where the devil was he?"

"At the *Duck and Drake* public house around the corner."

Wharton showed no sign of sympathy, but there was a disappointed resignation which it was impossible to ignore. "I can't pretend I'm surprised."

Carr nodded his agreement. "You were aware of his dependence on alcohol?"

"I think it was something of an open secret. I wasn't aware that he was in the habit of deserting his post to satisfy it, however."

"There is nothing to suggest that it was a regular occurrence," said Carr.

Wharton frowned. "Surely it must have been."

Carr did not commit to a view one way or the other. "If we assume that Parsons was killed because of something he had learned, it makes sense to concentrate on the first tragedy. A matter of cause and effect, you might say, if that is not too offensive."

The comment had been made to Margaret Erskine, and she shook her head with a faint, forced smile. "I just want to put all of this behind me, Mr Carr."

Carr bowed his head. "It might assist then, Mrs Erskine, if you tell me what was in the note which you wrote to your husband on the night he was killed."

The silence which followed his question was as heavy and oppressive as the quiet before a tempest. Such a silence has its own sense of threat, a foreboding particular to itself, and Carr allowed it to lengthen. He was conscious of Wharton's blazing cheeks and suppressed fury, just as he was aware of Margaret's pale, drawn face, so pale that the dread in her eyes seemed to burn violently against it. Carr, by contrast, remained motionless, his dark eyes staring down at the floor, his lips slightly parted beneath the impressive white moustache and beard.

It was Margaret, perhaps predictably, who was unable to prolong the quiet. "How do you know about that?"

"You're bluffing." Wharton's voice demonstrated a greater degree of conviction than his eyes.

Carr paid him no heed. "A piece of charred paper was found in the grate of the fire next to where your husband was sitting. It was illegible, mostly destroyed, but a single initial P was clearly written, and it was self-evidently part of a signature."

Wharton scoffed. "Surely that would point to Patrick Crane or Parsons himself. It might even have been part of the letter R."

Carr smiled. "Inspector Mason said something similar."

"Well, then! That would suggest Ronald Edgerton, wouldn't it? Either way, Carr, the initial doesn't refer to Margaret."

Carr remained impassive. "Erskine was well known to use diminutives. He called Ronald Edgerton Ronny, for example, much to that gentleman's annoyance." He looked impressively at Margaret. "Peggy, or Peg, is a common alternative for the name Margaret. Did he address you as such, Mrs Erskine?"

Slowly, as if she were being forced to confess to a terrible crime, she nodded her head. Wharton stepped between Carr and Margaret, as if his physical presence might somehow deflect from the truth of the matter. "This is damned speculation. You can't say Margaret wrote that note because of a name her late husband used for her and because the note happened to have been signed by someone with the initial P. It's a pure coincidence."

Carr slowly raised himself from his chair, ignoring the dull ache of his leg, and glared into the colonel's eyes. "You maintain that Patrick Crane or Cyril Parsons must have written that note?"

"Emphatically."

"Why would they need to?"

The question surprised Wharton. "What?"

"Either one of them could have spoken to Erskine directly." Carr's voice was calm, but as cold as the blood in the veins of the dead. "Why would either of them have needed to write a note when they could have confronted Erskine at any time in person at the club? For that matter, why would any member of the club need to write a note to a fellow member? No, the note had to come from outside the club, from someone who was not a member of the club and, just possibly, *not permitted inside it*. A woman, for example, and one with a name beginning with P."

Wharton was about to remonstrate further, but Margaret put a hand on his arm. "Please, Hector. This can do no good."

Carr sat down once more. His voice was gentle, his eyes sympathetic, as if he were capable of offering her the sanctity and security of the confessional. "What was in the note?"

Margaret looked at Wharton, who gave a slight nod of his head, and she held out her hand. He took it and, sitting down beside her, he kissed it gently. Margaret's eyes filled with tears, but there was a suggestion of reprieve in those tears which Carr knew was unmistakable. "I had decided to leave my husband, Mr Carr."

Carr leaned back in his seat. "I see."

"You think me a coward because I couldn't tell him to his face?"

"Not at all." His eyes seemed to offer so much more comfort than his words.

Margaret smiled, both in gratitude and relief. "You are very kind, Mr Carr, but I am a coward. The truth is that I was terrified of my husband."

Carr frowned. "Forgive me, but I don't understand."

"My marriage was a nightmare, Mr Carr. I hated my husband as much as he despised me. A few days ago, I could have shown you the bruises on my back and stomach, which would have convinced you how much Jacob loathed me."

Whatever Carr had expected Margaret Erskine to say, it had not been this. His eyes hardened, and the thin lips parted slowly beneath the ornate moustache. He looked across to Wharton, and he saw the twist of hatred on the man's features. How many times, Carr wondered, had the colonel wanted to confront Erskine in order to demand some form of retribution? Whatever Carr's opinions of the colonel, he had no difficulty in empathising with his obvious and understandable disgust.

"There are deeper scars, more vivid bruises, which I cannot show you," Margaret was saying. "It wasn't only Jacob's fists I feared."

"I'm sorry," said Carr.

Wharton kissed the top of Margaret's head as she rested it on his shoulder. He looked over to Carr. "Margaret would never allow me to confront him about it. You can imagine how useless it made me feel."

"It wasn't your argument to have, Hector," she said wearily, as if it was something she had repeated over and over again and was now, finally, tired of saying.

"How long had it been going on?" asked Carr.

"Longer than I dare admit," Margaret replied. "But I am free of him, at last."

At these words, as if they had been some sort of vindication of his feelings for her, Wharton tightened his embrace of her and kissed her once again, this time for a longer moment. Despite himself, Carr could not help but wonder whether Margaret Erskine had substituted one form of emotional suffocation for another.

"Colonel, you knew about Mrs Erskine's intentions regarding her marriage, I presume?" asked Carr.

"Yes." Wharton's expression had softened, his bluster now incapable of serving any purpose. "I had wanted Margaret to leave Jacob for many months, but she would not. Even his beatings weren't enough to persuade her to break her vows."

"I have always believed in the sanctity of marriage, Mr Carr," Margaret said, her tone vaguely apologetic.

Carr nodded his head slowly. "As have I, dear lady. It is a contract with God, as much as with each other."

"I agree. No matter how bad a marriage is, one has a duty to abide by the vows one took."

"Even at the expense of one's own happiness?"

"Even then."

Carr smiled gently. "And yet you must have had a change of heart. Why was that, I wonder?"

There was a silence, during which Margaret looked first at Carr and then at Wharton. The colonel, his lips tightened and his eyes heavy with disgust, nodded his encouragement. At last, Margaret spoke, although, despite the tears which brimmed in her eyes, her voice remained coldly detached.

"His violence escalated," she said. She slowly began to unbutton the silk blouse which she wore, lowering the garment off her shoulders and turning her back on Carr. He watched her move, his eyes alive first with anticipation and then with fury. The skin on Margaret's back, so pale and delicate, like bone china of the finest quality, was mottled with malignant, vicious bruises, whose colour was made more livid by the white background of her back. Amid the bruises, Carr could see horizontal strokes of broken skin, as if some sort of whip or lash had been used on her.

"It was a belt," she said, as if reading his thoughts. "The buckle has done its work, as you can see."

Carr felt he was compelled to say something, but he could find no words. Instead, it was Wharton who spoke for them both. "The man was a cruel brute."

Margaret's eyes were fixed on Carr. "This particular attack was only the beginning, Mr Carr. It simply made me compliant, you see, so that what followed would be easier for him."

"I see," muttered Carr.

"Jacob had never forced himself on me before. What made him do so that morning, I could not say. But once he had done it, I could not be sure he would not do so again." Margaret buttoned up her blouse once more. "Does that explain my change of heart, Mr Carr?"

He nodded his head. "When did this happen?"

"The morning of Jacob's death." She looked up at Wharton. "I told Hector at once."

The colonel bowed his head. "I wanted to kill the man, Carr, and I don't think you would blame me for that. Margaret had made up her mind to leave him, and she confided in me. We planned her escape together. She was going to write the note to him and then pack a bag and go to my own flat in town. I was to join her there later. Erskine's death changed everything, of course."

Carr nodded, but he did not express his suspicion about the convenience of it all to these two illicit lovers. "During your altercation with Erskine, which Trevelyan and I witnessed, you said that things were going to change for Erskine. You meant this plan of yours?"

Wharton conceded the point. "I lied to Inspector Mason about that, yes."

"Well, you gave him only part of the truth, shall we say?" Carr smiled diplomatically. He turned to Margaret. "You told me that you were at home all evening on the night your husband was killed, Mrs Erskine. That was a lie."

"Yes," she confessed.

"You were at the Icarus Club on the night your husband was killed. You went into the grounds through the rear courtyard and you left the same way. I suppose you gave your note to a servant to pass on to your husband?"

She nodded. "I did."

Carr smiled. "Naturally, you could not give it to the colonel. Any connection between the two of you had to be kept hidden from Erskine if your plan to hide in his flat was to work. And you did all this at around eight o'clock?"

"I would say so."

"Did you see anybody, either when you arrived or as you were leaving?"

"Nobody."

"You're certain?" Carr watched her nod her head. "And yet, I'm afraid you were seen."

The news startled her. "Who by?"

But Carr shook his head. "That does not matter for the moment, Mrs Erskine. In any case, even if you had not been seen, the use of the courtyard would reinforce my earlier suspicion that it was someone who had no right to go into the club through the front entrance who delivered the note.

Notwithstanding club rules on the ineligibility of women for membership, you would not want to be recognised even as the wife of a member."

Wharton stood up and towered over Carr. "You have known about Margaret and me all along, haven't you, Carr?"

"Not at all, colonel," smiled Carr. "I only began to suspect a tenderness between you both after you caused that scene at the club and chastised me for interfering with a police enquiry. That came immediately after I had come to see Mrs Erskine for the first time. You could only have known about it if she had told you. And why else would she confide in you about my visit, if you were not in some way attached to each other? Your gallant, though impetuous, confrontation with me aroused my suspicions."

Margaret sighed heavily. "For God's sake, Hector."

Wharton turned to her, his eyes wide with indignation and his voice trembling with a desire for forgiveness. "I just wanted to protect you."

"I don't need protecting," she said, with a quiet emphasis. "Not anymore."

"Margaret, please…"

But she was no longer listening. She stepped forward and looked down at Carr, watching as he stiffly pulled himself to his feet. "You're a very clever man, Mr Carr. Being such, you must see that, by writing the note, I remove any motive I may have had for murdering Jacob. I was leaving him. He no longer had any hold over me, which means I had no reason to kill him."

Carr smiled. "My dear lady, even with a motive, your guilt would be questionable. Not only would you have been unable to enter the club, but you were seen leaving the courtyard at eight o'clock. At that time, your husband was still alive."

Wharton laughed, a coarse and intrusive bark of relief. "Then that's proof that you couldn't have killed him, Margaret."

Carr's smile evaporated as swiftly as it had appeared. "No, colonel, but you could have."

"What?" The eyes were fierce, and the teeth bared in fury.

Carr remained motionless, his dark eyes impassive, and it was clear that the suppressed rage of the colonel had no effect on him. "The gun used was yours, you had the opportunity, and you had the motive."

"What motive?" scoffed Wharton. "You've just heard that Margaret was leaving Erskine. If she was my motive, I was already getting what I wanted. He stood in the way of us being together, yes, but when Margaret decided to leave him, that obstacle was removed."

"And I was leaving Jacob," argued Margaret in support, "so his wicked treatment of me would be over too, so there is no motive there."

Carr nodded politely, but his voice remained accusatory. "Nevertheless, colonel, I think your motive remains very much intact. Mrs Erskine may have written the note and stated her intentions, but do either of you think Jacob Erskine was a man who would accept that decision without fighting against it?"

"What are you saying?" gasped Margaret.

Carr turned on her. "Would your domineering and oppressive husband have allowed you to leave, dear lady? He had controlled and subjugated you all those years. Why would he now let you go without resistance?"

The pale shock in her cheeks and the wild panic in her eyes were sufficient to demonstrate that the idea had never occurred to her. Having summoned the courage to write that note, she would have been unable to entertain the possibility that her fortitude might be misplaced. It would be more damaging to her than any number of blows from her husband's fists.

"You have no right to say that," she hissed.

Carr inclined his head. "But it is true, dear lady. There was no guarantee that Erskine would comply. Indeed, the fact that he burned the note itself would suggest the contempt with which he viewed Mrs Erskine's decision."

"How dare you?" roared Wharton.

Carr was insistent. "Given the relationship you and he had, colonel, notwithstanding Mrs Erskine, I doubt he would have permitted you any form of happiness. Was that why you were so anxious on that night, because you knew that Mrs Erskine's plan could not possibly work?"

"Absolutely not." Wharton's anger was palpable now.

"Or was your discomfort down to the fact that you felt guilty over the very definite steps you had taken to protect Mrs Erskine from her husband?"

Wharton seethed. "Get out of here."

Carr's tone was emphatic. "The truth must come out, colonel, and it is always better to allow it than struggle against it."

But Wharton was beyond co-operation. His eyes were narrowed in a fierce glare of confrontation, and his voice was laced with poison. "Get out, Carr, and keep your insinuations to yourself."

"Hector, please..." Margaret began to object, but Wharton was adamant.

"Get out, Carr," he insisted, with a calm but definite malice.

Margaret was by his side, her hands clasping his, and her eyes searching his for some evidence of his innocence. "Tell me you did nothing wrong. Hector, promise me."

Wharton glanced down at her, momentarily, before turning his hostility back to Carr. "I don't have to justify myself to this fanciful mountebank. I have nothing to apologise for."

Carr remained defiant. "The police may not be so easy to dismiss as I am, colonel."

"Your warning is noted, Carr," said Wharton. "Good day."

There was little more to say. Carr stood his ground for a short time longer but, finally, he shrugged and uttered a small sigh, his face tainted with regret. He gave a courteous bow to Margaret and walked out of the room. He waited long enough in the hallway to hear the first sounds of sobbing and the colonel's somewhat clumsy words of sympathy. Then, slowly and silently, he pulled open the door and stepped out into the street, his mind tormented by the question of why both Wharton and Margaret had been at such pains to convince him that any motive for murder on their part had been entirely and unequivocally extinguished.

Chapter Twenty-Nine

Patrick Crane had been amazed rather than surprised to receive the invitation to tea. It had been sent to the club and forwarded on to his home, arriving without either warning or explanation. He had met Sonia Trevelyan only once, and he doubted it was an event which had taken root in her memory. There had never been any reason to suppose that she had been as captivated by him as he had been by her, but this sudden request to join her for tea was perhaps cause to think otherwise. And yet, as soon as the thought had occurred to him, he dismissed it. Hope was not something in which he indulged himself. It had been stolen from him too many times in the past for it to be a meaningful construct in his present. And, as a matter of course, hope was taken from him by the voice of his mother.

There had been nothing different on this occasion. He had told her that he was going out and would be a couple of hours. Her eyes, alive with mockery, had taunted him, and it seemed to him that their glare was more painful than any of the words which she spoke. The words were simply what they were and could have no further meaning, but the eyes betrayed her unspoken contempt for him, the disdain which was so profound that perhaps no words were sufficient to convey it.

"Who are you meeting?" Delilah Crane had asked.

"It is none of your business, mother."

"None of my business, he says. Is it none of my business that I am being abandoned, left alone to wither away, whilst the only son I have ignores me? You owe your life to me, Patrick, and it is time the debt was paid."

199

"I am going out, mother," he had declared. "I've told you that I won't be long."

"You're a selfish, spiteful child. It is cruel to leave me alone at my age. It is far better that you stay here and tend to me. You can understand that." It had all been said with a curiously gentle insistence that what she was saying was true and that it could not be debated or denied.

But he had denied it. "You will be all right on your own for a short while, mother."

She had not argued further. Instead, her lips had pouted in a sullen kiss of disgusted disappointment and those grey, hating eyes had frozen. At some point, Crane had known, she would have her revenge. It might not be immediate, but it was no less certain for that. As he turned his back on her, he had been surprised to find that he was not disturbed by the prospect. Whatever the revenge might be, however it might manifest itself, Crane felt that he was somehow well equipped to confront it. Was an invitation to tea so powerful? Had its unprompted arrival meant so much to him that no other matters, no other consequences, were of any importance? He supposed both ideas were true, just as it was certain that his courage was galvanised by the fact that it had been Sonia herself who had instigated the meeting. The opportunity of tea with Sonia Trevelyan was too enticing, too exciting, to be prevented by any of his mother's retributions.

They sat now in her drawing room, the tea brewing, and the conversation so polite and pleasant that they were at odds with the raging tumult of nerves inside him. His words sounded hesitant and uncertain in his own ears, and he hoped he was not making a fool of himself. The mockery of his mother fought for supremacy within his head, but he suppressed it, concentrating on Sonia's own delicate, melodious voice.

"Thank you for coming," she said. "You must have thought it wholly presumptuous."

"Not at all. I am very pleased, honoured perhaps, that you invited me."

She smiled and began to pour the tea. He declined sugar but accepted a little milk and, when she handed him the cup, his eyes met hers. They looked at him with kindness, possibly even fondness, but he dared not allow himself to interpret it as attraction.

"We have met before," she said.

"A month ago," he said. "I'm surprised you remember."

"Don't you?" Her tone of voice suggested not that she was offended if he did not, but that she was frightened of the possibility.

Crane smiled at her. "I remember very well. I hadn't expected you to, I must confess."

"You were very kind to me." Sonia spoke quickly, as if embarrassed by the admission.

He didn't remember displaying any specific kindness. "Was I?"

She smiled softly. "When I spoke to you, you listened. You'd be surprised how many people don't. And you didn't look at me as if I was something you could own."

He was not sure immediately how to respond. It was curious, this expression of his behaviour which, in itself, had come so naturally to him that he had been unaware of it. He was conscious that his next response, whatever it was, was somehow vital to the continuation of the meeting, that if he said the wrong thing, then he would be asked to leave. Worse, he would never be asked to return.

"I am pleased you were happy with my company," he said.

"I was." She said it frankly, without any pretence or disingenuity.

"But you haven't asked me here to tell me this after a month, surely."

Only after it had been said did it strike him as belligerent, and he looked at her in a sharp glance, hoping that she had not taken it as such. She was drinking her tea, taking slow sips, but if she was offended by his words, she did not show it. On the contrary, she laughed, which surprised him. It was a delicate, shrill noise of genuine amusement, so complete that its effect drifted into her dark eyes, illuminating them with a vitality which seemed to constrict the beating of his heart.

"It does rather look that way, doesn't it?" she said, dabbing at her eyes with the corner of a handkerchief. "No, there was something I wanted to talk to you about."

He shifted his weight in his chair, crossing one leg over the other, and placing his cup down on the table in front of him. "That sounds ominous."

"Not really. I spoke to Everett Carr yesterday. He came to see if the police had questioned Marcus." It was not the truth, and she wondered if he was aware of it.

"Have they?"

She nodded. "I suppose they've done the same to you?"

"Of course. As a member of the club, I had to expect it, as did Marcus. Did they question you?"

"Only briefly. I hardly knew the man who was killed." Her eyes fell on him in a deliberate stare. He held it for a long moment, then smiled, lowered his eyes, and examined a fingernail. She understood at once. "It is true then."

"What is?"

"That you saw Jacob Erskine and me."

Crane did not look up at her. So, Carr had confronted Sonia with the fact of what Crane had witnessed. He was surprised that Carr should have been so interested in what Crane had told him that he felt the need to confirm it. Carr was no policeman, and Crane could not understand what right or benefit Carr thought he had in questioning Sonia. Crane found himself experiencing a kind of angry disgust that Carr had questioned the girl who was now pouring more tea for them both. It was as if Carr's actions had been an affront, an injustice to Sonia which Crane felt obliged to settle. Or, he wondered, was it more personal than that: a defensive embarrassment at being confronted with what she might take to be spying on her.

"It was entirely coincidental," Crane said. "I wasn't eavesdropping or anything of the sort."

"I didn't think you were."

And he believed her, not for any tangible reason or because of anything she did to support the words of assurance, but because her eyes and expression almost dared him to contradict her. "I tell myself that I would have intervened if he had done anything to you."

Now, her expression changed. It was subtle, little more than a hardening of the eyes, but not from confrontation but out of surprise, as if his words had never occurred to her. "Would you?"

202

He smiled, timidly but not without charm. "I would like to think so."

"Why?"

The question was so abrupt that it seemed to startle both of them. They were aware suddenly of how inappropriate it was, how unprepared for it either of them had been. Sonia's pale cheeks flushed slightly, as if the question had been asked by someone else, or as if her mind had tricked her into the query, not allowing her to prepare herself for it.

For a moment, neither of them spoke, but Crane knew that the silence had to be filled. "I don't like bullies. Erskine was nothing more than that."

"I hated him."

It was so frank an admission, and so honestly offered, that he felt as if he ought to repay it in kind. "I feel like that about my mother. Sometimes I hate her, too."

If Sonia's earlier question had caught him off guard, this confession of his own stunned him. It was not that he was unaware of his dislike of Delilah Crane, but his use of that stronger word had been something new, something which he must have kept so deep inside himself that his conscious mind could ignore it. But now, it had been said, and it could not be unsaid. It was a beast, long caged, which now came out roaring.

"I've never admitted that to myself before," he said. "How strange to have done so now."

Slowly, she placed her cup on the table and rose from her chair. She walked around the room, her fingers clenched together and twisting around themselves with such intensity that Crane doubted any intrusion from him would be welcome. At last, she came to a halt beside his chair. He thought for a moment that she was going to kneel down beside him, but she remained standing.

"It isn't right," she said. "Hating a parent. It's not how it should be."

He did not look at her. "No. But it is true."

"I know what it feels like, Patrick."

At first, he thought he had misheard her. He twisted in his chair and looked up at her, his eyebrows raised in polite interrogation, his mouth primed to ask her to repeat what she had said, because what he had heard could not be true. When he saw her face, looking down at him with such paleness that it might have been proof of the supernatural, he saw that there had been no mistake. Her eyes were looking at him, but they were not seeing him. Instead, they were somewhere in the past, relieving something which had drained the blood from her cheeks, and which had made her slim frame tremble. Crane rose from his chair and took one of her hands in his. It was quivering but, more startlingly, it was as cold as ice.

"Sonia, what is it?"

For a moment, she did not reply, as if she could not understand why she was confiding in him and that, by doing so, she was being somehow indiscreet. His eyes held hers, however, and there was a kindness in them, like a gentle entreaty for trust, which she could not resist. "I hated my father."

He was shocked by the words, but he was ashamed also by a simultaneous suspicion of them. Was she mocking his own confession of parental hatred, or was this some sort of attempt to feign empathy, a cynical effort to achieve emotional solidarity for reasons of her own? Almost as soon as the thoughts occurred to him, he was embarrassed by them, and Sonia, unaware of his personal paranoia and condemnation, took his silence as a supportive encouragement to continue.

"Does your mother hate you, in the same way you hate her?" she asked.

"I've no doubt that she resents me and possibly despises me. Beyond that, I couldn't say. It wouldn't surprise me, let me say that."

Her eyes were wild now with a distance to them which suggested not only recollection of her past but also her anger and loathing of it. "My father loved me. He said I was his treasure, that he loved me like nobody else could."

She did not need to say more. Crane rose swiftly from his seat, his face contorted with shock, rage, and pity. She looked up at him, his eyes partly obscured by the reflections in the lenses of his spectacles. His lips were a thin line across the lower part of his face, the teeth clenched, and she suspected that those eyes, which were obscured by shadows and light, would be equally hardened by disgust and anger.

"I'm not telling you for sympathy," she said. "I don't want that."

204

"That doesn't stop me feeling it. Or feeling anger and hatred," he added, his cheeks flushing.

She was shaking her head. "I just wanted to explain what you saw with Erskine."

And he did understand. His mind drifted back to his conversation with Everett Carr, his own words reverberating in his mind, as he told Carr that Sonia had frozen when Erskine came near her. Simultaneously, a visual memory of the scene replayed the incident for him, and he saw again how her fingers had balled into fists, how her spine had straightened, and her muscles had spasmed into constricted stillness. *As if a spider had crawled over her skin*, he had said and, in a sense, it had. The memory of her father approaching her with the same look on his face as Erskine, his hands around her, his breath on her, his mass forcing itself onto her: all those memories must have solidified in that moment, like a malignant and consuming spider wrapping its legs and silk around her, as soon as Erskine had appeared beside her. At the time, Crane had thought her only uncomfortable, caught off guard; now, in the wake of her confession, he knew she had been seized by the terror of her own past.

"Why are you telling me this?" he asked.

"So that you'll understand."

"I do understand. If I had done so earlier, I'd have killed Erskine myself." Sonia shook her head slowly. "You mustn't say things like that."

"Not even if they're true?"

"You couldn't kill anybody."

She was staring at him, her eyes misting over with tears, but her fingers had tightened around his hand, as if to emphasise the impossibility of his capacity for murder. And yet, he felt he could not give her the confirmation she sought.

"Yes, I could," he whispered. "In the right circumstances, I think I could have killed both Erskine and your father."

"Why would you say that?"

"I think you know."

She stared at him for a long time, her eyes wide and her lips trembling, and he had the sensation of her summoning the courage to speak. Neither of them would say aloud why he felt capable of killing those two particular men, but they both knew that his motive lay in the fear and terror which they had summoned in Sonia and in the unexplored depths of his own heart.

"I assure you that I know that I can do nothing about it," Crane said, "and I know that I must live with it."

Suddenly, Sonia knew that he was not talking about killing anymore but about loving. She reached up her hand and pressed it gently onto his cheek. He closed his eyes, breathing in her scent and basking in this most innocent of touches, as if savouring the briefest of glimpses into a life which might have been. How many men, she thought, would have attempted to seduce her in this scene of mutual and personal revelations? Laying bare one's soul could so often be the precursor of spontaneous passion, but the fact that he had displayed no suggestion that the thought had occurred to him made her admire him all the more.

"You are so kind," she whispered.

Crane willed himself to speak, but his natural diffidence and his personal, oral decency prevented him from doing so. For once, he thought, his mother was right; any relationship with Sonia Trevelyan was not only forbidden but impossible and, as if to show that she had followed his silent thoughts, she expressed the reason for the futility of his hopes.

"But I have Marcus," Sonia said. "And he loves me deeply."

She smiled at him, almost pityingly, but whether it was pity for him or herself, he could not say. She walked slowly towards him and, impetuously, raised herself on her toes and craned her head, kissing him softly on the cheek. There was an inevitability in her dark eyes now, and Crane knew that the meeting, his time in her company, and his emotional optimism were coming to an end.

"I made my choice years ago, Patrick," she said.

Crane nodded, and he managed a smile. Which of them it was designed to reassure the most, he could not say. "I should go."

"Will you call again?" she asked.

"I would like that," said Crane, knowing only too well that he never would.

206

Chapter Thirty

Reginald Denniston KC had not seen the former Mr Justice Carr, as he had known him professionally for some months. Carr's retirement from the bench had saddened Denniston, although he was not so far without compassion or empathy that he could not understand the cause. The incident which had resulted in Miranda Carr's murder had been as tragic as it had been violent, and it would be a particularly cold heart who could not understand Carr's grief and the guilt arising from his survival of it. And yet, from a purely professional perspective, Denniston could not deny that the system of justice was weaker for the absence of a judge for whom he had the utmost respect.

It had been with a mixture of surprise and pleasure that Denniston had answered the knock on his door and discovered Carr standing in the light of the lamp hanging from the small porch which fronted Denniston's house. He was dressed formally, the white of the silk scarf around his neck contrasting with the black of his overcoat as vividly as the moon against the night sky above them. The moustache and Imperial, so familiar in their eccentricity, were as impressive as ever and the silver mane of hair was subtly visible under the rim of the soft, felt hat. He was smiling widely, a gesture of friendship but also of an apology for the intrusion. Denniston had wasted no time in ushering Carr into the house and, within moments, the two men were sitting in the luxuriously, but tastefully furnished drawing room of Denniston's townhouse. Denniston had offered and poured both himself and Carr a glass of Tokay.

Carr was pleased to see that Denniston had changed very little since he had last seen him. He was tall and lean, his features angular but not unpleasant, and the grey hair which was swept back from the large, intelligent brow gave him a distinctive, almost tangible air of wisdom. His eyes were a startling shade of blue, peering out inquisitively from behind the lenses of the wire-framed spectacles which were perched on the bridge of his long, thin nose. His cheeks were gaunt, but they were subtly tinged with a pink glow, which was natural but now possibly intensified by the wine he had taken with his meal. As if in response to Carr's thoughts about how little the barrister had altered, Denniston spoke in similar terms.

"You are looking well, Your Honour," he said, "if I may say so."

Carr smiled at the barrister's bow to formality by using his former title. Unlike Ronald Edgerton's sarcastic and mocking use of it, Carr knew that Denniston's sense of respect commanded it. "As are you, my boy. I take pleasure in the reports of your cases, I must say. I am pleased by your success. Is a call to the Bench looming?"

Denniston smiled but shook his head. "I enjoy the theatrics of advocacy too much for that. I would envy those who appeared before me. Did you never miss it when you became a judge?"

"I can't, in truth, remember," said Carr softly.

Perhaps it was only partially a lie. It all seemed so far in the past that Carr felt that he could not say with certainty how he had felt when he was appointed. In truth, it was not so long ago, but so much had happened, so many things won and lost, that the precise period which had elapsed had become distorted. Too often now, when he looked back over his professional life, his reaction to it was always more inclined to regret than reminiscence. Now, with Denniston's unwitting reminder of it all, his shattered knee began to ache, and his hand drifted to it, almost subconsciously, and he began to massage it gently. Denniston watched him do so for a moment, his eyes narrowing with a sudden empathy.

"Does it hurt often?" he asked.

"Every day," said Carr. "Even when it does not ache."

Denniston understood, but further comment was clearly inappropriate. "Dare I ask what has prompted you to call on me after so long?"

Carr sipped some of the Tokay and gently purred in appreciation. "I believe you are still a member of Darrow Square Chambers?"

"Indeed, I am."

Carr held his glass to the light and admired the deep red glow of the wine. "You know Ronald Edgerton, then?"

"As fellow members of the set, it is hardly surprising."

"And Jacob Erskine?"

If Carr had expected some sort of a reaction from Denniston, he was not to be disappointed. The faint smile which had crept over Denniston's thin lips now evaporated entirely. His eyes narrowed, and his nostrils flared, as if a sudden and unpleasant stench had asserted itself beneath them. He adjusted the spectacles, although Carr doubted the alteration was necessary. "I'm not sure I understand your point, Your Honour."

"They are not only both members of your Chambers, my boy, but also of my club, the Icarus," said Carr. "You may have read of some unpleasantness there a few days ago."

"I heard about what happened to Erskine, yes." A thought occurred to Denniston. "Is Edgerton a suspect?"

Carr leaned forward slowly. "Is there a particular reason why you might think so?"

Denniston drained his glass and walked over to the decanter to replenish it. "I don't know anything for certain. It is all rumour and gossip."

"What is?"

"Nothing has been proved, and no formal allegations have been made against him, but there is a growing suspicion that Edgerton is engaging in malpractice." Denniston allowed the words and their implications to settle into Carr's mind.

"What sort of malpractice?"

Denniston was reluctant to answer, as if to do so would be to sanction the gossip of which he so obviously disapproved. "He has lost several trials in recent months, cases which really should have resulted in successful verdicts."

"Bribery?"

The barrister nodded. "The rumour is that a sum of money would be paid and Edgerton would underplay some vital piece of evidence or emphasise the importance of some part of the case which had no real significance whilst ignoring something much more crucial. But it is all gossip and speculation, as I say."

"Has Chambers instigated an investigation?"

Denniston inhaled deeply, as if the answer might be dangerous to say out loud. "Not officially. Sir Julius Keane is a cautious man, as you may know, and he is not inclined to take any formal steps without proof."

"And yet he won't obtain such proof without first making those enquiries," smiled Carr.

"Precisely," said Denniston. "Nevertheless, certain senior members of chambers have sanctioned an unofficial enquiry between themselves. The hope is that this informal enquiry will unearth something more tangible than gossip which can be put before Sir Julius."

Carr's spine had begun to freeze. "And Jacob Erskine volunteered to undertake this informal enquiry?"

Denniston nodded slowly. "It doesn't follow that Edgerton killed Erskine on account of it, of course."

Carr conceded the point. "Does Edgerton suspect that he is under investigation?"

"I wouldn't like to say. Erskine is hardly a paragon of discretion, but he's vain enough to be seduced by the power the task would give him. I can well imagine he would strive to keep it secret, so I suppose it is possible that Edgerton has no idea he's under suspicion."

"How likely is it, would you say, that Erskine would have found any proof of malpractice?"

"Erskine was nothing if not tenacious," replied Denniston. "If there was evidence to find, I'm sure he would have done so."

Carr was staring into the flames of the fire in Denniston's grate. "Why would Edgerton purposefully lose trials? He's surely not in need of money."

"Perhaps not," said Denniston, "but some men can never have enough wealth."

"Common greed?"

Denniston shrugged. "If you know him at all well from your experiences of him in your club, Your Honour, you will know that about him, if nothing else."

Carr had always known that Edgerton was bombastic, belligerent, and pompous, but he had never had reason to make an assessment about the man's capacity for greed. In the wake of this new facet of his character, however, Carr found that he had no strong objection to the idea. "If this investigation into him had been successful, Edgerton would have been dismissed from chambers?"

"Without question."

"In your experienced view, Denniston, if that were to happen, what would the likelihood be of another set accepting him as a member?"

Denniston smiled. "You do not need my opinion on that, Your Honour."

"He would be ruined," said Carr, his voice stressing that it was not a question but a statement of undeniable fact.

"Irrevocably, I would suggest."

Carr gently stroked his beard with his forefinger and thumb. "But if Edgerton could be assured that the enquiry into his conduct would be fruitless, not to say suppressed, his position would be secure, would it not?"

"That would require complicity on the part of Erskine, surely." Denniston suddenly saw the direction in which Carr had steered the direction. "Are you suggesting blackmail?"

Carr nodded slowly. "Assuming Erskine was capable of it, is there any reason to suggest that he would not attempt it with Edgerton?"

"I suppose not."

"And it would make Erskine a double threat to Edgerton, would it not?" pondered Carr. "He was in control of Edgerton's future, come what may. Either he would expose him as a fraud and ruin him, or he could protect Edgerton's career at a heavy financial cost."

Denniston sniffed. "Despicable. I wonder sometimes about the state of our profession, sir, and about the people we permit to practice it. Especially those whom we thought we knew."

"Perhaps we can never truly know another person," said Carr. "It is a sobering and disconcerting thought. If Edgerton were to be blackmailed on account of his corruption, how would you say he might deal with that problem?"

Denniston had removed his spectacles and was cleaning them on his handkerchief. Now, deliberately, he replaced them on his nose, and the blue eyes fixed themselves on Everett Carr. "I know what you're asking, Your Honour, and if I may say so, it is not entirely fair of you."

"No doubt," smiled Carr, "but are you able to answer?"

Denniston considered the question carefully. "Edgerton has a temper, certainly, and he is not a man who accepts criticism easily. I'm not sure I would like to be the one who crossed him. I saw him in an argument only the other week, and it was far from pleasant. If it hadn't been broken up, I would not like to think how it might have ended."

Carr pursed his lips and narrowed his eyes. "All of which suggests that you think he is capable of violence, my boy, but perhaps you don't wish to put it in such specific terms."

Denniston was examining a fingernail. When he spoke, his voice was almost portentous, as if he were about to deliver a judgment which could neither be withdrawn nor otherwise challenged. "On the contrary, Your Honour. I think I would say with a degree of certainty that Ronald Edgerton is entirely capable of solving his personal problems by committing murder."

Carr did not reply, save to offer a polite and appreciative smile. He said no more about Edgerton and, instead, initiated a conversation about Denniston's present career. A companionable and pleasant hour passed, during which he relented and enjoyed a further glass of Tokay, and, as the clock chimed the half hour, Carr took his leave, assuring Denniston that he would call again.

Outside, Carr stood motionless on the pavement. The night air had turned cold, and he wrapped his scarf tightly around his throat. A taxi passed him, and he considered hailing it but, in his indecision and distraction of thought, it passed him by. For a moment, he watched the lights of the passing traffic, blurred by the slowly descending fog, and he listened to the hum of their engines, so familiar now, but so different from the more nostalgic horses' hooves of his childhood. Then, with a dismissal of this nostalgic pessimism, Carr began to walk slowly along the street, his head lowered and his pace as deliberate and careful as the thoughts in his head.

Denniston's conclusion had not surprised Carr. Edgerton had always been volatile, his opinions of other people seldom being anything other than disparaging, and, if hatred and spite were fundamental traits in his character, then it was not impossible to imagine him losing control of his actions in the right circumstances. Furthermore, Carr reasoned, this revelation from Denniston showed that Edgerton was not above committing a crime, notwithstanding his professional vocation to uphold the law. Bribery was a far cry from murder, but Carr was too familiar with the darker side of human nature to disregard the possibility of escalation, particularly if the murder was sparked by a need for personal survival. If Erskine had discovered the bribery, however that might have been achieved, Edgerton was exactly the type of person who would kill to protect himself. And it followed that if Cyril Parsons had learned something about Erskine's murder, Edgerton would have no compunction about silencing him.

And yet, there was no evidence. It was Carr's personal speculation, and there was nothing factual to support it. He sighed heavily, although it was nothing to do with the chill of the air nor with the inconvenience of having no umbrella with him when the rain began to fall from the dark night sky.

Chapter Thirty-One

C arr had slept badly so that he felt less than refreshed on the following day. As a consequence, his mood was low for the greater part of the morning. He did not have breakfast, although this was not unusual, as the meal had never particularly appealed to him, and he satisfied himself instead with two cups of strong black coffee. Over the first, he sat in silence at his breakfast table, his eyes fixed on the ashes of the previous night's fire, cold and grey in the grate. Having poured the second cup of coffee, he rose from the table and walked over to the writing bureau, which was set against the far wall of the apartment, under the broad windows which overlooked the Albany below. From one of the drawers, he took out a notebook, from which he tore a sheet of paper and an envelope. Sitting down in the leather Admiral's chair, which was placed in front of the bureau, he quickly wrote a brief but effective note, which he then blotted carefully and placed in the envelope, sealing it with a swift motion across his tongue. Having taken a definite step, his mind was freed from its previous indecision and, to some extent, from its anxiety.

He dressed and walked out of his rooms, taking the envelope with him. He made his way onto Piccadilly but, by the time he had reached Leicester Square, his knee was protesting violently. It was a curse of his feeling of obligation to exercise the damaged joint that he caused it significant discomfort in doing so. He battled on, forcing himself to ignore the increasing agony, but he was compelled at last to summon a passing taxi on the Charing Cross Road. Having given his destination, he settled back into the leather seat of the vehicle and involuntarily let out a sigh of relief as

214

he stretched out his damaged leg. The traffic on the Strand was typically unmanageable, and it struck Carr that it seemed to grow worse with every passing year. He was not an impatient man by nature, but when, as now, he had a definite purpose in mind, he found that any obstacle or delay to the purpose became magnified in its inconvenience. The traffic eased once his driver had successfully navigated Waterloo Bridge, and, at last, Carr was able to step out of the cab into the familiar cobbled maze of the Inner Temple.

To an outsider, perhaps, the stone arches and the red brick buildings might seem indistinguishable but, for Carr, it was like returning to an old family seat. A brief and satisfying sensation of pleasurable reminiscence swept over him. He heard again the bustle and chatter of legal conversation, evidential debate, and adversarial but professional argument, all of which returned to him with such clarity and force that it seemed that it might actually knock him to the ground. In the distance, he could see the dark-clad barristers making their way to and from Court, like black insects buzzing around their natural marshlands, and Carr suddenly seemed to miss the theatrical elegance of his former profession far more keenly than he would have suspected previously. And yet, as his mind grew colder and more incisive, the nostalgia passed and gave way to the reality that such memories were impossible to rekindle. With a sigh, followed by a smile of self-reproach, Everett Carr made his way to Darrow Square and delivered his note.

He had some minor tasks to perform and, once they were concluded, he spent a charming if idle remainder of the morning in the Victoria Embankment Gardens. At last, allowing himself sufficient time to make the appointment he had requested, he walked slowly to Simpson's in the Strand and took his usual table for lunch. Once seated, he ordered a Bordeaux wine and waited for his guest to arrive.

Ronald Edgerton was prompt for the invitation, but evidently unimpressed with it. He sat down opposite Carr, unfolding the napkin provided and barking an order for a glass of wine similar to Carr's. He was trying to give an impression of disinterest, but his eyes were too cautious, and his lips too compressed for the attempt to be entirely successful. The pink of his skin seemed more livid than ever, particularly around the winged collar of his shirt, as if a heat of anxious discomfort had risen up his spine and exploded over the confines of the collar itself. The two men sat in silence until Edgerton's wine had been delivered. Carr had yet to touch his own glass, but he did so now, to meet the perfunctory toast of good health which Edgerton made.

"I had your note, Your Honour," said Edgerton, unnecessarily. "I don't see why you had to meet me here. I would have been at the club this evening in any event. We could have talked there."

"But the beef here is so excellent that I thought it would be a pleasure for us both," replied Carr, smiling cordially. "Besides, I wanted to speak to you as soon as possible, so lunchtime seemed appropriate, and a meeting at the club would have permitted a degree of privacy, which I don't think would be necessarily a benefit."

Edgerton frowned. "And why is that?"

Now, although his smile remained in place, Carr's eyes hardened. "Because there is less chance of you causing a scene in a public place such as this than in the confines of a members' club."

If Edgerton had any doubts that the invitation to lunch was more of a business than a private one, they were dispelled in that moment. He took a mouthful of wine, dabbing furiously at his lips and moustache afterwards. After a moment's pause, he had summoned the courage to look directly into Carr's dark, disapproving eyes.

"Why would I cause a scene?" he asked.

"You were somewhat offended when I suggested that Jacob Erskine was blackmailing you," said Carr. "When I say that I now know it, you are not likely to take it kindly."

Edgerton's nostrils flared, and his breath came out in short, rasping blasts of indignation. His eyes burned with violence, and the redness of his cheeks and neck glowed with more intensity than usual. He gripped the edge of the table and, in a fanciful moment, Carr wondered if he was about to overturn it.

"I deny it." He said it with a defiant confidence.

CHAPTER THIRTY-ONE

Carr was not perturbed. "This is the time for truth, my boy."

"I am telling you the truth," insisted Edgerton.

Carr leaned forward, placing his elbows on the table. "You have the motive to murder Erskine, you have the opportunity, and you have the means. I don't need to tell a man of your profession how serious that makes your situation."

"I did not murder Jacob Erskine."

Carr counted the points of evidence on his fingers. "You knew where Wharton kept his gun. You were heard to be arguing with Erskine in the reading room, and you were seen leaving it. I think the money found on the body was yours—a payment for his silence."

"He was not blackmailing me."

Carr nodded. "So you say, but when I asked you and Marcus Trevelyan if you believed Erskine capable of such a thing, Trevelyan was certain of it, but you were quick to reject the idea. I found your opposition to the idea to be very interesting indeed."

"Is that so?"

"You were deflecting my suspicions from the truth, because you knew what that truth was, and you knew because you were a victim of it."

Edgerton sneered. "If he was blackmailing me, and I had decided to kill him because of it, why would I pay him off?"

"To catch him off his guard. If he were counting the money, he would not see you take Wharton's revolver from your pocket. Furthermore, if you had decided that this would be the last payment you would make, killing him would be the only way of ensuring it. I think you went to pay him for his silence. I think you argued with him, shot him, and marched out of the reading room, having the misfortune to be seen doing so."

Edgerton smiled maliciously. "And this witness who saw me leaving the reading room didn't hear the shot?"

"You used a cushion to muffle it."

"This is all very fascinating, but it falls to pieces on account of the absence of any reason for Erskine to blackmail me."

Carr remained impassive, his smile slowly disappearing and his voice as hard as his glare. "I believe you are losing more than your fair share of trials, my boy."

Edgerton's instinct was to be violent. His eyes glared malevolently at Carr, his lips compressed into a pursed suppression of rage, and his shoulders hunched as if in some preparation to lunge forward in attack. By contrast, Carr remained motionless, the dark eyes demonstrating not only a lack of fear, but also serving as a warning for him to remain seated and composed. As if in compliance, the barrister's hands balled into fists but remained inert on the table and, in an effort to dispel his contained emotion by some movement or other, he shifted his weight in his seat. Then, with a snort, he drank some of the wine, but he did so with such swift greed that he could not possibly have appreciated it.

"I wouldn't have thought you were a man to be persuaded or fooled by gossip, Your Honour."

"As I understand it," smiled Carr, "the rumours were strong enough to convince your senior members to undertake an informal investigation of them."

"Who told you that?" sneered Edgerton. When Carr did not reply, he laughed mirthlessly. "I suppose I'm naïve to assume you'll tell me, Your Honour." The professional address was given now with disdainful spite.

Carr sipped at the Bordeaux and dabbed gently at his lips with the starched napkin. "What matters is the truth, my boy, which is that Jacob Erskine had appointed himself as chief investigator into your professional affairs. Now, either he would work tirelessly to expose you or, if he was indeed the blackmailer I suspect he was, he would offer to protect you if you paid for his silence. Only you know which of those two scenarios is the truth, but whichever it is, Erskine had an unquestionable hold over you. His murder, of course, removed that threat, which could only be a benefit for you."

Edgerton shook his head. "You still have no proof of what you say."

"Why deny it? I have no official standing. What you say to me can matter in no way at all."

Edgerton laughed, this time with some trace of a dark amusement. "You say you have no official status, yet you walk around questioning people as if you were some sort of detective."

"A man I knew has been killed. I am naturally curious. Are you not?"

"No."

Carr's smile broadened. "That is suspicious in itself. People are prone to morbid fascination in all its forms, I find. If a man is not curious about a murder on his own threshold, I would suggest that he is hiding from it."

Edgerton leaned back in his chair now, his fists uncurling and his anger mellowing. "What a strange man you are, Carr. So polite in your condemnation of others."

Carr shook his head ominously. "Erskine kept detailed ledgers of his blackmail, and I have no doubt that a comparison between those ledgers and your own bank account will tell its own story."

Edgerton said nothing more for a moment, but his eyes showed not only his sudden discomfort at the fact but also his scornful admiration at Carr's tactical withdrawal of it until this precise moment. "Very well, the money was mine, but I didn't kill Erskine. I may be many things, but I am no killer."

Carr steepled his fingers and pressed them to his lips. "What happened on the night Erskine was killed?"

Edgerton waited until the second glass of wine had been delivered, and he drank from it in a long, fortifying gulp. "I did go into the reading room at around half past eight. Erskine was already there, sitting in a chair by the fire. He had a piece of paper and an envelope in his hand and, when I entered, he threw it on the fire. He was smiling to himself. A wicked, uncompromising smile."

That smile seemed to Carr to prove one of his theories. No matter what Margaret Erskine had said in that note, and no matter how much she and Hector Wharton believed they were rid of him because of its contents, Erskine's smile, as wicked and uncompromising in Carr's imagination as much as in Edgerton's description, showed the contempt with which he treated it.

"How long had he been blackmailing you?" Carr asked.

"A couple of weeks."

"The money on the body amounted to thirty pounds. Was that the price of Erskine's silence?"

"Initially, but he had increased his demand that night. I refused. I told him that I would not pay him a shilling more, and he could go to the Devil if he wanted anything else out of me."

"Did you throw it in his face?"

"No."

Carr felt a slight shudder of excitement reverberate through him, like a small electric current. "Did Erskine say anything?"

"No. He simply laughed to himself as I walked out."

"Did you see him count the money?"

"No."

"Did you see anybody in the corridor when you walked out of the reading room?"

Edgerton shook his head. "Nobody."

"You didn't see Cyril Parsons, by any chance?"

"No." Edgerton spoke in a tone which suggested some degree of compassion. "I've heard what happened to Parsons, of course. He was not a likeable man, no more than Erskine, but I wouldn't have wished death upon him."

"But you did wish Erskine dead?"

"I've told you, Carr, that I didn't kill him, but I won't pretend I am sorry that somebody did. Parsons is a different matter." A thought occurred to him. "Why are you asking if I saw him, in particular? You suspect he must have seen something significant, something connected with Erskine's death?"

Carr shrugged casually. "It is nothing more than natural inquisitiveness."

"The two deaths must be connected, simply because they are linked by the club, is that it? It would be a neat symmetry, I grant you." Edgerton raised an eyebrow in sardonic disbelief. "You look on murder as a game, do you, Carr? A puzzle to be solved, like a crossword, or these new double-crostic puzzles which we have begun to see in our newspapers and magazines. Except life is less structured than that, isn't it, sir? Too many loose ends, too many coincidences. You know as well as I do that murder is not a game."

Carr's expression maintained its benevolence, but his eyes and voice were laced with hostility. "I see murder as nothing more than it is. A violent, wicked, immoral act, a crime which is unique in its horror and devastation. There is nothing playful about it, nothing of the puzzle. Coincidences occur, of course, but two deaths in two days, each connected to the club, is too much to believe. People do not kill without reason, Edgerton, as well you know, and Parsons was murdered because of something definite. Something he knew, saw, or heard."

Edgerton attempted to betray none of the sense of reproach which he felt at the words, none of the regret of what he knew to have been his malicious, sardonic accusation. In the wake of Carr's reprimand, his comments now seemed petulant and childish. And yet, he offered no apology for them.

"Well," he said, "for the record, I was at home when I understand Parsons was killed. You didn't believe me when I said as much about Erskine's murder, so I suppose I cannot expect you to believe me now. But it is true, and I can say no more."

"It is not for me to believe you or not."

Edgerton shrugged. He glanced at his watch and drained the remainder of his second glass of wine. "I hate to be unsociable, Your Honour, but I think I should go. I seem to have lost all trace of an appetite, and the beef here, as you say, is so good that it would be a shame to waste it."

He had risen from his chair and stepped out from behind the table before Carr spoke once more. "When will you leave Chambers?"

The question came so unexpectedly, without any trace of a warning, that Edgerton visibly flinched at it. "I don't follow you, Your Honour."

Carr clicked his tongue in disappointment and leaned back in his seat. "You must see that it is the honourable thing to do."

"I have no intention of leaving." Edgerton leaned against the table, so that his face was close to Carr's. "They can prove nothing against me."

Carr smiled. "You have enough pride to dare a blackmailer to do his worst so that you can rid yourself of the shame of his influence, but not enough to do what you know is correct by your profession."

"What do you mean?"

"You cannot continue to practice, not after what you have done." Carr stared up at Edgerton. "You've perverted the very nature of the system to which we devote ourselves. How many guilty men have you permitted to walk free for the sake of your own greed? How many lives have gone unavenged because of it? All those families whose loved ones have been murdered or otherwise violated have been deprived justice because you wanted to fill your pockets with silver. You cannot continue as you have been doing."

Edgerton shook his head. "That does not mean I have to abandon my career."

"Your integrity is dead, you must see that. It pains me to say it, because you had some talent in your vocation, but you have no right to continue." Carr's smile had faded at last, so that his expression now was as black as his eyes. "The law is all we have. Once it collapses, once we tear it down, what can we trust?"

But Edgerton was unapologetic. "The bribes are a thing of the past, I can assure you of that. I am suitably ashamed of myself, if that means anything at all, but I won't give up my vocation on account of an infringement of my ethics. Perhaps I do not feel as strongly about it as you do."

Carr's eyes filled with genuine sadness. "Clearly not, my boy, but I cannot permit you to blemish a profession and a social order which I treasure by continuing to allow you to be a part of it."

"What are you saying?"

Carr stared down at the table. "You may have grown to despise the institution which has been so good to us both, but I have not. For all the tragedy I have witnessed and experienced, the rule of law has remained a constant assurance to me. I won't allow you to corrupt it. For that reason, I feel compelled to advise your Head of Chambers of your conduct."

"You wouldn't dare," seethed Edgerton.

Carr shrugged. "Perhaps not, but I certainly could not live with such a matter on my conscience, so I would have to do something about it. I assure you that I wouldn't take any definite steps without giving the situation some serious consideration. Perhaps we should both take some time to consider the position in depth. Just so that we can be sure that we satisfy our respective consciences."

Edgerton glared at the older man for a long moment, his lips curled in animosity, and his eyes widened in a furious disgust. "Are you threatening to blackmail me, Your Honour?"

Carr shook his head defiantly. "I am offering you a chance for redemption, dear boy. And I have no doubt that you will take it."

Edgerton remained motionless for a moment, his eyes drilling into Carr's with a fierce and violent intensity. It seemed for a moment as if he wanted to say more, but nothing came. He began to shake his head, a deep, guttural snarl rising in his throat. He uttered a brief, hostile curse, then walked out of the restaurant, barging past a waiter with a contemptuous and dismissive shove of his arm.

Carr watched him leave and, in the silence which followed, he sat drowning in his own thoughts. It was later, after he had eaten and was replaying the confrontation over again in his head, that Carr saw with sudden clarity the importance of something Edgerton had said. It was as if a forgotten memory had been rekindled into life, and Carr knew that this single piece of information, and its central importance to the mystery, should have been clear to him when he had first encountered it. He let out a small gasp of enlightenment, and a faint snort of fascinated but self-critical laughter escaped from beneath his moustache and Imperial. From a distance, to the waiters who had served him, it looked as if Everett Carr had unlocked the secrets of the universe in the pleasure of his roast beef and in the depths of his half-empty glass of Bordeaux wine.

Chapter Thirty-Two

His dinner concluded, Leonard Faraday had retired to his study with a replenished glass of wine and the intention of reading a novel. It was a pleasure for which he seldom found time these days, the activities of the club taking up an increasing amount of his attention. As a boy, he had delighted in the escapism and education of novels, and it was a passion which had followed him into adulthood, so that his present inability to indulge it as often as he would wish was an irritating frustration. Now, sitting in a velvet-lined armchair beside the small fire in the marble mantel, he opened one of the leather-bound volumes of Dickens and began to allow the words to transport him. Whatever intentions his heart had planned, however, were foiled by his brain. He found that the words registered with his eyes, but his mind could make no sense of them, so that neither story nor character came alive for him. His concentration was elsewhere, captivated by something more personal than the struggles of a fictional Victorian orphan.

The news about Cyril Parsons had infiltrated the club like a disease, and it had seemed to Faraday that the atmosphere of the Icarus Club, already poisoned by the murder of Jacob Erskine, was now irretrievably corrupted. For the first time in a twenty-year membership, Faraday wondered whether he would be able to continue his association with the club to which he had devoted a large portion of his life. He doubted that he would ever be able to disassociate the club and violence, as if every meal, every drink, every conversation would be tainted by it. He had expected murder to cast a long shadow, but he had not anticipated that it would be so oppressively dark.

It was as if he could not see the club clearly anymore, save through the distorted prism of unnatural death.

The police had questioned him, but he had been unable to tell them anything of value. He had been at home, alone, and had known nothing about Parsons' death until he had heard the rumours on the following day. He had not particularly liked Parsons, he had been obliged to confess, but he had no reason to kill him. He had known very little about the man, beyond his military decorations and his gambling habits, the latter being told to him by Hector Wharton in an official capacity. His drinking had been a similarly open secret, Faraday had told Inspector Mason, but he had taken the view that as long as it did not affect his work, it was not for the club to judge. Parsons' abandonment of his post on the night of Erskine's death was something which Faraday had intended to take up with him, but events had naturally overtaken him. Beyond these innocuous responses and trivial confessions, Faraday had said nothing of consequence about Parsons' demise.

What Vincent Overdale had told the police, he could not say. He had not seen Overdale for a couple of days, and he had tried not to feel the ache of the younger man's absence. He had tried to telephone, sent notes, and dispatched telegrams, but he had received no answer, although he had not lowered himself to go to Overdale's house, being only too conscious of the desperation it would suggest. Instead, he had allowed the silence to torment him, forcing his mind to conjure images of infidelity and betrayal, which Faraday knew had only suspicion and paranoia to commend them, although they were no less powerful for that. It occurred to Faraday that the truth was that he did not trust his lover. Not for the first time, he began to question whether his association with Overdale was worth the pain.

And it was pain, Faraday knew that. He could hardly say that it was a relationship which gave him any continuous happiness, after all. Overdale was selfish, capricious, often spiteful, and in other circumstances, in a life other than this one, Faraday doubted that he would find him anything other than detestable. But these were not other circumstances. This was the only life Faraday had, and the truth was that he was in love. In his youth, Faraday had assumed that love was something beautiful, a thing to be cherished and cultivated, like a resplendent orchid in a glass case. He had never imagined that it could be cruel as well as beautiful, that it could allow a man to relinquish all control of himself and go willingly into emotional subjugation. Now, he knew better, and he knew that, no matter how malicious Overdale could be, it did not matter as much as the crumbs of happiness which he threw down at Faraday's feet. In Faraday's heart, twisted as it was by this love of his, those shards of happiness were, like palladium, all the more valuable for their scarcity.

His tears had only just begun to fall when the bell rang. It was so unexpected that the noise of it seemed to deafen and disorientate him, so that it took him a few moments to come to his senses. He was expecting no visitors, and the idea of a speculative caller was so unlikely as to be almost impossible. Faraday rubbed strenuosity at his eyes with the balls of his palms, willing the tears to disappear. He took a bracing mouthful of the wine and pulled himself out of his chair. He walked out of the study and down the hallway to his front door, which he opened cautiously, as if frightened of what he might see on the other side.

It was Everett Carr, smiling apologetically, his dark eyes begging that no offence be taken. He was wearing a dark overcoat over a dinner jacket, a felt hat perched at an angle on his head, and a white silk scarf hanging loosely around his neck. Now, he apologised verbally, both for the unprecedented nature of his call and the time of it. "You no doubt were looking forward to a quiet, undisturbed evening."

"Not at all," said Faraday as affably as he was able. "Do come in."

He led Carr into the study and offered him a drink. Carr accepted and requested a glass of the same wine which Faraday had poured for himself. Carr sipped slowly at it, taking a moment to savour its excellence. It was evident that Faraday was a man who enjoyed his private pleasures, and Carr could empathise with it. The two men sat opposite each other in the matching armchairs, and, for a brief moment, a companionable rather than an awkward silence descended between them.

"Not that I am sorry to see you, Carr," said Faraday, at last, "but perhaps you would explain why you are here."

Carr dabbed at his lips with his handkerchief. "Forgive me, Faraday. You must find my presence here an intrusion. I won't trouble you for long, I assure you, but I do have something important to ask you."

"Very well."

Carr smiled appreciatively, but his eyes had assumed a caution in their darkness. "How much money did Vincent Overdale steal from your safe?"

The emotions which flashed across Faraday's face were as conflicting as they were varied. Fear, panic, mistrust, outrage: they blurred into each other in the fraction of a second, and Carr thought he could distinguish each of them. He continued to smile, now with an even greater degree of apology, and he lowered his glare to his glass, as if looking at Faraday might only increase the discomfort.

"How did you know?" stammered Faraday.

Carr spoke softly. "The words you spoke when you saw Erskine's body. *My God, the money.* You said it almost instinctively, as an impulsive reaction to the sight of the scattered banknotes. Clearly, you saw some significance in the money and recognised it at once. If you had put it on the body, you would not have drawn attention to it or have been surprised to see it at all. That meant somebody else, in your mind, had done so. Given your somewhat emotional, frightened reaction, I surmised that it was somebody close to you, someone of whom you are fond. You and Overdale are, after all, very good friends."

"And how did you know about the safe?"

"The amount of money on the body was not insignificant. You had no opportunity to count it, of course, but you were quick to identify it. If you mistook it for some of your own, therefore, you were obviously in possession of a similar sum. A financially careful man such as yourself would naturally keep it somewhere secure, and I have seen the safe in your office many times."

Faraday smiled like a defeated man accepting his fate. "Is there any point in denying it?"

"If you are inclined to do so, perhaps it will help if I tell you that the money on the body belonged to someone other than you. If Overdale did steal money from you, it was not to give it to Jacob Erskine."

Faraday closed his eyes, basking in the relief provided by Carr's words. Carr could well imagine Faraday's torture of himself with his suspicions of Overdale, just as he could understand the obvious unburdening of that suspicion. He recalled discovering Faraday in tears in his office a few days earlier and it seemed churlish now not to allow Faraday to savour the momentary liberty from his self-inflicted torment. Carr sat silently and waited for Faraday to speak once more.

"It was fifty pounds," Faraday said at last.

"There was only thirty pounds on Erskine's body," said Carr.

"I am so very relieved to hear it," said Faraday. "I was due to hand the fifty pounds to my stockbroker, who had advised me to invest some funds into the Duellona Conglomerate. Vincent interrupted me when I was counting it. I was careless to allow it to happen, no doubt."

"When did you discover it was missing?"

"On the night Erskine was killed."

Carr nodded. Here, then, was the explanation for Faraday's troubled expression when he entered the bar that night, as testified by the estimable and observant George, "You're certain Overdale stole it?"

"As sure as I can be. He denies it, of course." Faraday drank some wine, not only to fortify himself but also to delay the inevitable. "Is Vincent a suspect for Erskine's murder?"

Carr examined a fingernail. "There may be good reason to suspect that he has a strong motive to kill Erskine. You see, the money he stole may not have been found on Erskine's body, but there is still some sort of financial bond between them. You recall me saying that I overheard Overdale and Erskine arguing about money?"

"I remember."

"You said then that Overdale does not play cards, so the argument could not have been about gambling debts."

"That is true."

"Why, then, would the two of them be quarrelling about money?"

CHAPTER THIRTY-TWO

"I don't know."

It was so obviously a lie that Carr could not allow it to pass. "We must have honesty if this dreadful business is to be cleared up, my friend. Jacob Erskine was a blackmailer. Do you not see any connection to be made there?"

Faraday bowed his head. "You think Erskine was blackmailing Vincent?"

Carr nodded. "As do you, is that not so? It would explain why you thought the money found on Erskine's body was yours."

"Yes."

"And yet the money on the body was not taken from your safe. Assuming that Overdale did steal from you, what has he done with your fifty pounds?"

Faraday closed his eyes, as if in some effort to avoid facing the truth he knew he was compelled to tell. "Vincent is addicted to drugs. He has fallen in with a crowd who live only for pleasure, regardless of the consequences."

"And fifty pounds could easily be swallowed up in such a habit," observed Carr.

Faraday shrugged, as if unwilling to commit himself. "I have known about the drugs for some time, and I have been trying to dissuade him from it, but he is stubborn. He thinks I am dictating to him."

"Would Overdale succumb easily to blackmail, do you suppose?"

"Vincent's father is a strict disciplinarian. A tyrant, if truth be told. If he discovered what Vincent was doing, he would disinherit him. Vincent is too fond of money and wealth to allow that to happen."

Carr began to stroke the silver handle of his cane, but his eyes remained fixed on Faraday. "How would Overdale's father react to your relationship with his son?"

Faraday glared at him, his eyes widened with horror and fear. For a moment, he was unable to speak, but words were not necessary to demonstrate the truth of what Carr had said. The scarlet glow of embarrassed shock which crept up the sides of his neck and spread to his cheeks said all that was necessary. His mouth moved, nevertheless, but only in futile, impotent gestures. Carr, out of some degree of sympathy, felt that the silence was both unhelpful and cruel.

"Your feelings are your own affair, my friend," he said. "Whatever the law may say about them, they are no less profound or private for it."

"You don't judge me? Despise me?"

Carr shook his head slowly. "Are you a different man now to the one I have called a friend for so many years? No. Then why would I despise you?"

Tears welled in Faraday's eyes, but he did not acknowledge or dispel them. They rolled swiftly down his cheeks, and gave himself time to find his voice again, knowing that if he spoke too soon, the tightness in his throat would restrict the words. "I have no idea if Vincent feels for me the way I do about him. I have told him I love him many times, but he has never reciprocated."

"Perhaps he finds it harder to say."

Faraday seemed never to have considered the possibility until that moment. "He finds it easy to be cruel."

"The young often do."

"I wonder sometimes how I can stand being near him but, somehow, I know that to be away from him would hurt more than anything he could say or do to me."

Carr smiled sadly. "Being separated from the one you love is a pain like no other."

Faraday nodded slowly. He was discreet enough not to say anything further. To make any comment now would be inappropriate and, in any event, further discussion was prevented by another ring of the bell. Mouthing an apology, Faraday left the room. Carr did not move, his eyes fixed on the flashes of light which flickered on the surface of his wine, his thoughts stretching out long into the past.

"Speak of the Devil and he shall appear, Carr."

Faraday's voice cut through his memories like a knife through flesh. He turned round and found his host standing in the doorway with Vincent Overdale by his side. The young man was pale, his eyes showing as dark circles against the white of their sockets and his thin fingers flexing and unflexing with nervous rapidity. Carr rose to greet him but it was clear that Overdale considered his presence to be an intrusion. Sensing the same, Faraday addressed the subject without decoration.

"No need to be shy, Vincent," he said. "Mr Carr knows everything."

Overdale glared at Carr, but his expression softened when Carr smiled gently and bowed his head. Even in Overdale's agitation, he could see that there was neither malice nor judgment in those dark eyes. "Could I have a drink, Leonard?"

Faraday poured him a glass of wine, at which Overdale gulped immediately, as he walked over to the fireplace. He leaned against it, his elbow resting on the mantel. "May I ask what you are doing here, Mr Carr?"

"Calling on an old friend," said Carr.

"Poking around in private business?"

Faraday sighed. "Vincent, must you?"

"Well, what is he doing here?" snapped Overdale.

Carr walked slowly and painfully towards him. "I am not your enemy, Mr Overdale. I am here as a friend. As I understand matters, your real enemy is dead."

"And you think I killed him?"

Carr inclined his head. "I suspect you had cause to. Did you have the opportunity?"

Overdale's eyes flickered, and the muscles in his face contracted. "I was at home."

Faraday sat down in his chair. "Tell the truth, Vincent."

"I am telling the truth."

"You patently are not," replied Faraday. "For once in your life, do the right thing. For your own sake."

"Don't you dare speak to me like that."

Faraday looked across to Carr. "Vincent and I were together for some of the evening. We had a drink in the club before dinner. I asked him to dine with me, but he refused. We had a drink together, but I'm sorry to say that we argued. I dined alone as a consequence and went back to my office. I didn't see Vincent again that evening."

Overdale, sensing that a contribution was expected of him, fixed his attention on Carr. "I stayed at the club for a while and then went home. I can't swear to the time, I'm sorry to say."

Faraday leaped from his chair with a bitter curse. "You are a liar, Vincent.

A dirty, filthy liar, and I have had enough of it."

The outburst was so unexpected in its violence that the younger man was startled by it. He stammered a mumbled response, but nothing coherent came from his lips. Faraday had marched towards him, standing now between him and Carr, his face only inches from Overdale's, so that when the older man spoke, flecks of spittle mottled Overdale's cheeks.

"How do you suppose I know you're lying, Vincent?"

"How?"

"Because I telephoned your house, that's how. And there was no reply."

"You telephoned me?" Overdale seemed baffled by the admission. "Why?"

"Because I was worried about you. Because I care about you. Damn me for it, but I love you, however difficult you might find that to believe. I had no idea where you were going that night, who you would be with, but I had a good idea what you would be doing. So, tell us the truth, Vincent. Where were you? Did you go to the reading room and murder Erskine? Or are you so riddled with cocaine, opium, or whatever you're killing yourself with to know?"

It seemed to Carr that the confrontation somehow had been inevitable. He had learned enough about the two men to realise that Faraday had felt belittled, demeaned, and rejected, more perhaps than he had ever felt loved, and he must have swallowed too many words of complaint too many times for him now to remain silent. Overdale, seeing for the first time this assertive version of the man whose emotions he had played until this moment, seemed to see Faraday as a man now rather than a commodity. He was surprised to find that he was crying, so silently and gently that he barely registered the fact. His tears seemed to demand a candour which was alien to him.

"I went to a party," he said. "In Soho. A friend of a friend. I don't remember any of it. I so seldom do. I don't know where I was when Erskine was killed. I could have been anywhere."

"There were drugs at this party?" asked Carr.

Faraday grunted and sat back down in his chair. "Of course, there were. That's why he can't remember anything about it."

"Would anybody at the party remember you being there?" asked Carr.

"I don't know," muttered Overdale. "Not for the whole night, I shouldn't think, even if they remember me at all."

Carr frowned, his expression now genuinely curious. "Why do you do it?"

Overdale shrugged, rather peevishly. "It's exciting, fun, makes me feel alive."

"It will kill you," warned Faraday. "And, for once, I don't care if you do think I am lecturing you, suffocating you, and patronising you. I don't care about any of that anymore, because one day you're going to end up dead, and there will be nothing more to be said."

Carr cleared his throat. "What Faraday says is true, Mr Overdale. There will come a time when there will have been one party too many. Eventually, the music and the dancing will stop. You would do well to think about who will be left to remember you. Life is transient and, in a flicker of time, it can be gone."

Overdale now smiled, but its malice was less assured. "As it was for Erskine and Parsons?"

Carr bowed his head. "Precisely."

"I didn't kill either of them." Overdale looked across at his lover. "I wish I had done, Leonard, God help me, but I didn't."

Carr offered no assurance that he believed the boy. "But you did steal fifty pounds from Faraday's safe?"

Overdale considered denying it, but the intensity of Carr's dark glare dissuaded him. "All right, yes, I did. I'm sorry, Leonard."

Faraday ignored the apology. "Did you use it for drugs?"

"I've spent it. What does it matter how?"

Carr was frowning. "Did you attempt to burgle Erskine's house a few days before his murder?"

Overdale's eyes widened. "How do you know about that?"

"His wife disturbed you before you could gain entry," persisted Carr, ignoring the pleas for an explanation. "That was why Erskine did not report the burglary to the police. He was afraid any investigation would expose his own criminality, but he recognised that it gave him yet another hold over you."

"I suppose he must have done," said Overdale.

Carr bowed his head in concession. "Your idea was to break in to find out exactly what Erskine knew about you."

Overdale nodded. "I wanted to see if he had any evidence."

"Of your drug use?"

But this time, the young man shook his head. "No, I wanted to find out what evidence, if any, Erskine had about Leonard. He knew about us, you see. He called it a dirty, unnatural secret. He made us seem so squalid, so filthy. I wanted to protect Leonard."

Faraday looked up at him slowly, his eyes glazing with initial confusion and then with a slow realisation, which he could not bring himself immediately to accept. "You wanted to do what?"

"He had his claws in me, it's true, but perhaps I deserved it. I think I must have believed that. So, if he did ruin me, it was no less than I had coming to me. But you're a good man, Leonard. I couldn't see him destroy you because of me. I wouldn't allow it. But Mr Carr is right – Erskine's wife saw me, and I had to run."

Carr spoke quietly. "In fact, she did not see you. She only saw your silhouette."

"I still failed."

Faraday stood up once again and walked over to Overdale. Kneeling in front of him, he took hold of his hand and, with the other, he gently raised the now lowered head. The tears had returned to those deep blue eyes, and Faraday wiped one of them away with a caress of his thumb. "You wanted to protect me from Erskine?"

Overdale nodded, slowly, as if he were now embarrassed by the gesture. "Was it stupid of me?"

Faraday shook his head, an involuntary laugh bursting from his tightened lips. "No. Far from it."

Carr began to feel that his presence was becoming an embarrassing one. "I have said all I need to say, Faraday, so I shall intrude no more. I shall see myself out. Goodnight."

Despite Carr's words, Faraday walked him to the door. Offering a single word of gratitude, Faraday shook his hand and slowly closed the door behind him. Turning on his heel, Faraday walked back into the study. Although the hallway was dark and the night sky outside was black, it occurred to Leonard Faraday that his world had never been so bright, and the sun which shone on it seemed to have the potential to last forever.

Chapter Thirty-Three

Overdale had helped himself to a second glass of the wine. He was sitting by the fire, where Faraday had left him, and he looked up as the door opened. He had stopped crying, not that the tears had fallen particularly violently, but the lack of hysterics seemed to suggest an honesty in those tears, which made them all the more potent for Faraday.

"This wasn't the evening I had anticipated," said Overdale.

Faraday smiled. He dared not say that it was a far better evening than he could have expected or felt able to deserve. "Carr is certainly a man of surprises."

"I'm not sure who he thinks he is or what he intends to achieve by playing detective."

It was an unnecessary comment, as if Overdale felt that his previous emotive display needed to be balanced by a reminder of his capacity for vindictiveness. Faraday might have been irritated by it were it not for the deeper understanding of Overdale, and his relationship with him, which the evening had demonstrated.

"I owe you an apology, Vincent," he said. "For thinking you might have killed Erskine. I should have known it was beyond possible."

"Are you so sure I didn't do it?"

"Of course."

Overdale smiled and looked back into the fire. "Mr Carr isn't. He suspects me still and perhaps more than before."

Faraday sat in the chair opposite his lover. "If he does, he's a fool."

"But I did steal from you, Leonard, and I lied to you. I've lied about everything."

"You tried to protect me. That matters more than a handful of lies."

Overdale looked into Faraday's eyes, and he saw a confirmation of the truth of it, as well as the deep glow of gratitude, despite the glinting of the flames against the lenses of his spectacles. It seemed to Overdale that he was suddenly aware of a kindness in Faraday, a gentleness which had always been there but which he had previously failed to recognise. It was as if the flames from the fire had illuminated more than the colour in Faraday's eyes and lit up something much more profound within him. Overdale wished, devoutly, that he had seen it earlier than this and, moreover, that he had understood himself as keenly as he did now.

"I'm beyond saving," he said, with a smile, "but you're not. You're too respectable to have a man like Erskine spoil you."

Faraday laughed. "None of us are so flawless, Vincent, not even me."

"I'm riddled with vice," spat Overdale. "It's a miracle you can bear to look at me."

Faraday took hold of his hands, kissing the back of one of them softly. "You're a selfish, irritating, malicious swine, Vincent, which makes what you did all the more special, because you did it for me and me alone. So, you see, there is decency and virtue inside you."

Overdale removed one of his hands from Faraday's grip and stroked his cheek, the fingers delicately brushing the flesh. "You've never given up on me, have you?"

"No." He smiled wanly. "Although I have come close."

Overdale held his gaze, and Faraday knew that there was one more secret to be told. The earnest pleading of Overdale's eyes, his deep breaths, and the expression of fearful expectation were evidence of it. "About the money, Leonard."

"It doesn't matter anymore."

But Overdale was insistent. "It does. It matters more than ever. All my secrets have to come out, Leonard, and you need to know everything about me."

"I do know everything now," said Faraday.

Overdale shook his head. "No, you don't, not yet. There's one more secret I need to confess, Leonard, and it's the worst of all."

And now, the ice had begun to crystallise along Faraday's spine. "Then tell me the worst."

Overdale had begun to tremble. "I didn't steal the money to pay off Erskine, although he was blackmailing me. About the drugs, about us, about everything. But it wasn't really him I was scared of, and I thought I could deal with him myself."

Faraday had a sudden image of Overdale holding Wharton's revolver towards Erskine's breast. "Go on."

"I owe a lot of money to people, dangerous people."

"What people?"

"People in Soho. I did steal your money, Leonard, but it did me no good, not really. Fifty pounds is only a fraction of the debt. You've no idea what they will do if the full sum isn't paid back, and I'm running out of time."

"This is all because of that filth you shove into your body?" Faraday hissed.

There followed a violent nodding of the head and an onslaught of tears. When he spoke, Overdale's words were almost incoherent, gushing out uncontrollably like a river which had burst its banks. "I'm so far out of my depth, Leonard. Threats, against me, against father, even against you. I don't even know if what they say I owe is accurate. It's all so confused in my head."

Faraday put his arms around the shaking, frightened boy. For a moment, they remained like it, a combination of limbs and backs, rocking gently in soothing support. Faraday realised in that moment how small, how frail Overdale was, a shadow of the man whom he had met all those years ago. He had assured Overdale that there was still some decency within him. Now, it seemed as if Faraday was going to be forced to test that belief.

"Tell me how much more you owe," he said. "We will pay them off once and for all and they will leave you alone. I promise you that."

Overdale looked up into his eyes and, perhaps for the first time, it seemed to Faraday that there was a genuine honesty reflected in them.

"My help comes at a price, Vincent," continued Faraday, his voice now stern, all trace of fondness replaced by a seriousness which demanded respect. "We pay them what they want, and then you never go back to them. It ends here. No more drugs, no more lies, no more recklessness. I will help you, but only if you help yourself."

Overdale took a moment to respond. Faraday suspected that his brain was straining under imagined images of the life which was being suggested to him, of the consequences of relinquishing his hedonistic impulses, of an existence based only on its own terms with no artificial stimulation. It may yet have seemed bleak to him, but Overdale seemed to sense that he had no choice in the matter. Without Faraday, he would be lost, abandoned to whatever sinister intentions these nameless, faceless monsters might have in mind. And yet, when he nodded his head in agreement, Faraday was sure that the decision had not been made solely with reference to personal survival.

"I promise you, Leonard. I will change."

Faraday was in no doubt that it was true. He had to believe that Overdale wanted to make changes to his life, that it was not a cynical acceptance of a change which was nothing more than a more palatable option to the alternative, and he was secure in his belief on the point. If he had any doubt about it, however, they would have been dispelled when Overdale spoke once more.

"I love you, Leonard." It was said without any suggestion of sarcasm or deceit. "I have always loved you."

Chapter Thirty-Four

E arly on the following morning, the Reverend Edwin Somerset replaced the receiver of the vicarage telephone and looked at his reflection in the mirror which hung on the wall above the small, wooden table in the vicarage hallway. He saw the sympathetic blue eyes peering back at him over the half-moon spectacles and his wayward hair, grey and wiry, and bunching out over his ears, desperately in need of a long overdue trim. The corners of his mouth, normally upturned in a perpetually vacant smile, were now a reflection of themselves, drawn down in a curious, slightly concerned frown.

The telephone call had brought back the painful memories, of course, although Somerset had thought the whole incident long forgotten. Certainly, he seldom thought about it himself, and he never heard any of his parishioners talk of it. Perhaps it was not that it was forgotten, but simply that people preferred not to remember it. To Somerset, there seemed to be a definite difference between the two. One could remember a tragedy in one's private moments, but not actively encourage the memory by talking about it; and one's private thoughts were a matter only for one's self and God. Nevertheless, it seemed that people were now thinking once more of everything that had happened two decades ago in the village, but it was both surprising and confusing that it had been two strangers who had resurrected the incident.

Following its horror, it had been the children, now orphans, for whom sympathy had naturally been reserved. The mother, Somerset had never known; his understanding was that she had died before the family came to the village. He had tried not to listen to the scaremongering amongst the women in his flock that old Henry Tiverton had murdered his wife, and Somerset was quick to chastise them, however gently, when they began to speculate along such lines. He was not naïve enough to assume that his words of caution would be heeded, but he felt it had been his duty to make a point of attempting to stop it. The family, no doubt, had suffered enough without additional trouble being caused by idle speculation and gossip. If Henry Tiverton was aware of the gossip about whether he had murdered his wife or not, it had never seemed to bother him.

Following Tiverton's fatal accident in his greenhouse, as Somerset had understood matters, a distant uncle had been appointed as guardian. There had been a belief that the uncle was a prominent military man of high rank and not without wealth, if Somerset recalled correctly. He could remember vividly those children being taken away in a closed carriage, driven by a pair of impressive horses, and the sound of the hooves against the main high street of the village came back to him now, in a rhythmic clopping of nostalgia.

It had been Mrs Brogan, the schoolmistress, who had suggested that something had not been right for some time. She had noticed a change in behaviour in class, for example, a sort of guarded hostility, as if any form of authority and discipline had become hideous and adults had become something to be feared rather than respected. Mrs Brogan did not wish to say anything formally, of course, not without definite proof, but she had said enough for the village to wonder. When old Tiverton died, the rumours did not stop; they merely became more surreptitious, as if saying them aloud was somehow disrespectful. Mrs Brogan, in particular, refused to discuss the business again.

Following this morning's telephone call, Somerset had engaged himself with his usual morning duties. The time passed swiftly, as he found it often did when one was busy, so that only a matter of moments seemed to him to have elapsed before he realised it was lunchtime. He ate frugally, a simple meal of bread and cheese, and he rinsed his plate and teacup meticulously. By the early afternoon, Somerset was sitting in his parlour. The clouds had darkened, but it was not raining yet, although he suspected that it would not be long before the windows were mottled with water. A decision made, and his mind troubled by this sudden reminder of the tragic history of Henry Tiverton, the vicar rose from his chair, put on his overcoat and felt hat, and walked out into the churchyard.

Henry Tiverton was buried towards the back of the church. The stone which bore his name and dates was flecked with mildew, the etching of the letters and numbers still legible but partly corroded with age. It struck Somerset as one of the greatest of all human tragedies that, eventually, everybody is forgotten. No matter how loved, how despised, how admired or vilified, eventually death made equals of us all. At some point, every person's existence would be obliterated by mildew and corrosion. It was a pessimistic thought, if not a fatalistically self-indulgent one, and Somerset castigated himself for it. In doing so, he recalled that it had not been an entirely original display of cynicism on his part either. He realised now that he had said something similar to someone only recently and standing by this very grave itself. Slowly, Somerset's mind drifted back over the last week.

He had seen the figure from the windows of the vestry, a motionless, black outline which seemed to rise from the lawns of the cemetery, as if it was one of the souls peering down on what remained of a life long since passed. It was not unusual for people to visit the graves of those they mourned, but Somerset had been intrigued by this particular visitor, not least because it was Henry's grave which was being watched. It had been the late afternoon, a cold and biting wind promising to bring an early frost. When Somerset had spoken, his breath had exploded into the air like the smoke from a series of silent gunshots.

"Good afternoon," he had said. "Are you a member of the family?"

"No." It had been a man's voice, deep and well-educated, with something of a local accent buried somewhere beneath the culture. "I knew Henry well, in the old days."

Somerset had looked at the man. The cheeks had been reddened by the chill of the air, the eyes fixed ahead. He had not flinched, his attention never shifting from the grave in front of him, but Somerset thought he could detect a sort of suppressed amusement beneath their glare. "It was terrible, what happened."

"Yes," the man had said. "Tell me, does anybody else ever come to visit his grave?"

Somerset had shaken his head. "Oh, no, never."

"Not even the children or their guardian?"

"No, sir."

"He was a solider, I believe."

Somerset had nodded. "A colonel, if I remember correctly. Or was he a major? Silly of me, but I can't recall. But no, nobody comes to the grave. You can see from the stone itself how neglected it is. Sad, really, to think that we might all be forgotten forever, once death has taken us. We are all equals under death, are we not?"

"I suppose we are."

It was then that the man had turned to face the vicar fully, and Somerset had remembered that he had seen the man before. "You came here not long after Henry died, I think."

"I did, yes." The man had looked keenly at Somerset, his brown eyes amused but unable to disguise entirely their natural bitterness. Above the scarf around his neck, a cruel smile had stretched out beneath the heavy moustache, stained yellow by a long addiction to tobacco.

Somerset had felt his own expression twist with sadness. "May I ask why, sir?"

"I have my reasons," the man had said. "I am a local boy, after all, and I hoped to find an old acquaintance here. An enemy, perhaps you might say, vicar."

What any of it meant was beyond Somerset's understanding, but this sudden interest in the village's past had troubled him, and it continued to do so. First, there had been the stranger in the cemetery, and now, on this very day, Somerset was expecting a second visitor with still more questions to ask. It all seemed so dangerous to Somerset that, perhaps not unsurprisingly, he found himself praying for guidance and protection.

It was a little after four o'clock when there was a knock at the vicarage door. Somerset answered it with trepidation, unsure what to expect from this unknown caller. He found himself strangely relieved, reassured even, when he saw the kindly looking man standing on the doorstep of the vicarage. He was smiling benevolently beneath an extravagant moustache and Imperial beard. A pair of dark eyes looked keenly at Somerset, their intensity seemingly at odds with the benignity of his smile. He stepped nimbly into the hallway when invited to do so and, when Somerset took his coat, he saw that the man was wearing a suit of black, with a lurid violet necktie and handkerchief standing out against the darkness.

"Thank you so very much for agreeing to see me, Mr Somerset," said the man. "I realise that this must seem very strange to you."

"I must confess it does."

"I shall take up no more of your time than I must," said the man who had introduced himself on the telephone, and now, as Everett Carr.

They spoke together for a little over an hour, first in the vicarage parlour and then, at Mr Carr's request, in the churchyard. They might have been old friends meeting up after a long period of mutual absence. Eventually, Carr stopped walking and looked up at the spire.

"A very beautiful church, vicar," he said.

"Yes, we are very proud of it."

"I have seen it before, but I hadn't expected it to be so beautiful in life."

The comment struck Somerset as strange, but Carr offered no explanation, only giving a small and ingratiating smile, which Somerset had returned. He found this man, Carr, so easy to talk to that he was surprised at how long the conversation had lasted and how easily it had flowed.

Only later, once Carr had left, and Somerset was sitting in his armchair with a final cup of cocoa, did he worry that he had said too much. He had seen no harm in telling this polite, compassionate man about old Henry's death or about how the children had gone to live with their uncle, the colonel. And, for that matter, Somerset had not hesitated to tell Everett Carr about the mysterious stranger who had preceded Carr's visit and with questions of his own. There had seemed to be no harm in it at all, and Somerset might not have been troubled by those later doubts at all, had it not been for the curious expression which had passed over Everett Carr's features as he bade farewell to the vicar.

"I am much indebted to you for your kindness, Mr Somerset," Carr had said, "and I trust you will forgive me for my intrusion."

"Not at all," the vicar had replied. "I am only sorry that we talked only of such tragic events."

And Somerset would have said more, but the words had frozen on his lips at the sight of the sudden alarm which had risen in the dark eyes of his visitor. Those impenetrable eyes had stared ahead, as if seeing matters which were beyond Somerset's perception, but with an intensity which suggested the realisation of a matter of immense importance. Somerset could not recall anything which he had said which could have produced this startling, almost disconcerting effect, but the evidence of it was plainly written in the expression of Everett Carr.

"My apologies, vicar," he had said, as the spell on him had broken almost as quickly as it had been cast, "but I have been somewhat blind. Now, I see everything and, if I may say so, you have been the key to the puzzle all along."

There had been no further explanation and, as the evening darkened into night, Somerset thought less about it. As he went up to bed, Somerset had ceased to think of either Henry Tiverton or Everett Carr. It was a few days later, when he received a courteous and grateful letter from that gentleman, that the Reverend Edwin Somerset understood how important a role he had played in identifying what Mr Carr's letter described as a cunning and ruthless murderer.

Chapter Thirty-Five

T hey had all been summoned to the reading room at the Icarus Club at nine o'clock that evening.

Everett Carr stood at the fireplace, his arms placed behind his back, and he watched as they took their places in the chairs which had been arranged in a crescent in front of him. He surveyed each of them, the smile on his lips suggesting an amiability which his dark eyes did little to encourage. Those eyes fell on each of them in turn, and they returned it with differing emotions, ranging from defiance to intrigue. Wharton sat beside Margaret Erskine, his hand protectively holding hers, although she barely seemed to notice it; Faraday sat apart from Overdale, and Carr wondered whether their mutual confessions on the previous night had taken their toll; the Trevelyans sat beside each other, Marcus mildly amused and Sonia gazing up at Carr in some mystification, for which he offered her a reassuring smile; Edgerton glared at Carr and lit a cigar, the smoke drifting into the face of Patrick Crane, whose attention was too fixed on Sonia Trevelyan to notice. Inspector Mason stood by the door, his expression grave as well as official. It was only when Carr saw them all assembled that he seemed to become aware of the unpleasantness of his task. By exposing the killer, he would be damaging more than one life, a fact of which he was keenly aware, but which he felt obliged to ignore.

"Ladies and gentlemen," he said, after gently clearing his throat, "my apologies for any inconvenience in insisting that you all come here. I hope not to keep you longer than necessary, but what I have to say is very important and, I'm afraid, most unpleasant."

"Are we to take it that you know who killed Erskine and Parsons?" asked Wharton. Carr bowed his head in confirmation. "Then isn't it the duty of the police to inform us? Is this charade really necessary?"

Mason felt it prudent to intervene. "Mr Carr is speaking with the full support and approval of the police, colonel. You need have no worry on that account."

Wharton, less than placated, turned his attention back to Carr. "Very well, Carr, if you must have your moment of theatre, I suppose we have no choice but to indulge you but, please, do get on with it."

Carr smiled benevolently. "I shall do so much quicker without interruption, if I may say so."

He waited a moment for his words to take effect. During this momentary silence, the remainder of the group shifted uncomfortably, and Carr wondered how deeply their own suspicions of each other ran. It must surely be obvious to them all that they had been summoned to the reading room for a reason, and it would be beyond foolish to suppose that they did not have the intelligence to realise that the murderer must be amongst them.

"Last week, as you know," Carr said, "Jacob Erskine was shot in this very room. It is common knowledge that it was Colonel Wharton's revolver which had been used, having been stolen from his office here at the club, just as it is known that the shot had been fired through one of the cushions from the chairs in this room, and you will all have heard about the money which was found on the body. Such was the scene as I discovered it myself on that evening.

"It is not unfair to say, I think, that Erskine was widely disliked. Mrs Erskine will forgive me for saying so, since she herself had no reason to love her husband. Her marriage to him had been violent and abusive. In her fear and isolation, she had developed feelings for Colonel Wharton. I do not think I am speaking out of turn." He watched Margaret shake her head, although he was aware of Wharton's suppressed rage at his words. "Your husband's treatment of you, Mrs Erskine, had become increasingly dangerous. Your life with him was unbearable."

Her tears fell silently. "I didn't kill him."

Carr nodded, smiling kindly at her. "No, but you were here at the club that night, delivering a note to your husband, which told him that you were leaving him for Hector Wharton. Leonard Faraday saw you crossing the courtyard at the back of the club, although he did not recognise you. Erskine, having received and read this note, burned it in this very fire"—Carr indicated the grate with a swipe of his hand—"and I have indicated to you previously that I have grave doubts that he would have permitted you to leave him for Wharton. Be that as it may, his treatment of you alone would have been a solid motive for both you and the colonel to want Erskine dead. And, crucially, neither of you had a provable alibi.

"But, in that, you are not alone. Mr Edgerton, for example, was seen leaving the reading room not long before Erskine was killed. When I confronted him with that fact, he was swift to point out that whoever had seen him would have had a similar opportunity to kill Erskine. It was a valid argument, one which I might have expected any competent barrister to raise in a defence, and its relevance was that it meant that Patrick Crane could not be discounted as a suspect, at least in terms of opportunity, since it had been Mr Crane who had seen Mr Edgerton leaving the reading room and disappearing down the corridor.

"But what of motive? Did either Edgerton or Crane have reason to murder Erskine? Mr Crane was honest enough to tell me that Erskine was bringing a claim for professional negligence against him, one which would ruin him financially if it were successful. In addition, if I may say so, there is a certain tenderness of affection on his part towards Sonia Trevelyan, who herself had been subjected to unwanted sexual advances by Erskine. On that account, a case might be made for Mr Crane having two strong reasons to commit the murder.

"Mr Edgerton was less candid than Mr Crane, but his motive was no less viable. He, too, was in danger of having a guilty professional secret exposed. Erskine had discovered that Edgerton has been suppressing evidence in trials in exchange for money, and, on behalf of their mutual Chambers, he was undertaking an investigation into the matter, although Erskine's actual intentions were rather more sinister. I need not say what damage that would cause Edgerton, nor do I need to explain why it was important that the secret did not come out.

"Equally obvious, from what I have said, is that Erskine was a blackmailer. I suspected as much when I discovered a collection of notebooks and ledgers in his study, which showed a series of numbers and initials, very clearly a record of payments of some sort. Blackmail seemed a likely explanation, and I asked several of you if you could accept the possibility that Erskine was capable of it. I was not surprised that the majority of those I asked agreed with my own notion that Erskine was not only capable of blackmail but was actively involved in it. His treatment of Ronald Edgerton and Vincent Overdale was enough to convince me of it. I am satisfied that a detailed examination of those ledgers and notebooks will reveal the initials of both of those gentlemen, should proof of it be necessary."

Overdale rose from his chair violently. "I didn't kill him. I swear I didn't."

"Sit down, Vincent, for pity's sake," demanded Leonard Faraday.

"Why should I?" His eyes were wild, like those of a petrified animal. "I won't let him set out all my failings for everyone to hear. If it must come out, it will be on my terms. All right, so be it. I am addicted to drugs. That's what I am - a miserable, squalid dope addict. I have been for years. Erskine knew and was blackmailing me. You need have no doubts about what he was, Mr Carr."

"It was you whom Mrs Erskine saw attempting to break into Erskine's private study," declared Carr.

Overdale looked over to the widow and bowed his head, possibly in shame, but certainly in guilt. "But not because of the drugs. It was because of Leonard."

Carr placed his hand on the young man's shoulder and gently urged him to resume his seat. "Your friendship with Mr Faraday is obvious. I doubt it comes as a surprise to any member of the club, regardless of any of our private moralities, but the world beyond these walls may be less forgiving towards it. What is pertinent for our present purposes is that such a relationship is dangerous, not to say illegal. Erskine, certainly, recognised your need for secrecy, and he saw an opportunity to exploit it."

Faraday closed his eyes. When he spoke, it was with a quiet dignity, which surprised him, given that he felt as if he had lost all trace of it. "Vincent and I had as much reason to kill Erskine as anybody else, but I speak for both of us when I say that neither of us did it."

Carr interjected. "But you both had the opportunity to do so. Neither of you has an alibi."

"No," said Faraday, resigning himself to the fact.

Carr was nodding his head. "Nevertheless, that point alone is not perhaps as important as the fact of Erskine's capacity for blackmail. That is the crucial point, *because it is the reason he was murdered.* Jacob Erskine knew a terrible and dangerous secret from the past, one which had to be kept hidden no matter what, even at the cost of Erskine's life."

Wharton leaned forward in his chair. "What secret?"

But Carr only smiled. "We must examine each point in sequence, colonel. Firstly, let us consider the circumstances of Erskine's murder. As I have said, there was a sum of money found on the body. Mr Edgerton had been seen leaving the reading room at a time when it was known that Erskine was in there. With that in mind, and knowing what I did about Erskine's taste for blackmail, it was not too difficult to imagine that Edgerton had given Erskine the money as a payment. It seemed to follow that if Erskine was counting that money when he was killed, the impact of the shot would explain the scattering of the bank notes across his body.

"It was an important point, not least because it distanced the money from the murder. If the money had been handed to Erskine by Edgerton, who had subsequently left the reading room, according to Mr Crane's testimony, the murder must have been committed *after that exchange.* It occurred to me, therefore, that the money was not connected to the murder. Moreover, if the shot had scattered the bank notes, Erskine must still have been counting it when he was killed or, at least, he had not yet secreted it in his wallet and put it in his pocket. *The murder must have been committed, therefore, only a short time after the money had been handed to Erskine.*

"Mr Crane had heard no shot, but he had been in the vicinity of the room as soon as Mr Edgerton had left it. Had he followed Edgerton into the room and shot Erskine? Certainly, he was the only person in the vicinity that I knew about, and by his own confession no less, as Edgerton had already left the scene."

Crane made some effort to protest, but Everett Carr held up a calming hand to silence any such interruption.

"The second point of interest about the scene of the murder," Carr continued, "was the discovery of a small, white feather on the body. It seemed clear that it had come from one of the cushions placed, as a matter of course, on the chairs in this room, and, indeed, one of the chairs was missing its cushion. Colonel Wharton's revolver had been used to commit the murder, and that struck me as a pertinent fact, *because revolvers do not take silencers.* However, a cushion would be an ideal substitute for one and would assuredly deaden the sound of a gunshot. The cushion was subsequently found discarded, and, sure enough, there was a bullet hole in the centre of it. All this seemed perfectly clear, but it raised a question which puzzled me. Why did the killer wish to silence the shot?"

It was Faraday who answered what might have been assumed to be a rhetorical question. "Otherwise, people would have come running, and the killer might have been seen."

Carr held up a finger. "That is not quite right, if you will forgive me, my friend. Yes, the cushion silenced the shot and, without it, people would certainly have investigated the noise. But if the killer wanted to be discreet, if it was vital that he operated in silence, why use a gun at all? Why not a knife, poison, a blunt instrument? You see my dilemma. *The natural and obvious explanation of the cushion made the use of the gun itself nonsensical.*

"And yet, Faraday, in a sense, you are correct. The use of the cushion *did* delay the finding of the body, if only by a few moments, and the killer knew that a delay was necessary. The cushion, then, became vital to the killer's plan, *simply because it was essential that the body was not discovered immediately.*"

"But why use my revolver at all?" asked Wharton.

"To divert suspicion," said Carr. "To confuse, to disorientate. Every member of the club knew about the gun and where to find it. Using it to kill would make suspects of us all and provide yet further camouflage for the murderer."

"Why did he wish to delay the finding of the body?" asked Crane.

Carr looked at him meaningfully. "To gain time. Aside from a natural desire not to be found on the scene, the killer had to be elsewhere as soon as possible."

"Elsewhere?" barked Wharton. "What do you mean?"

"Precisely what I say," replied Carr.

"Where did he have to be?" asked Margaret Erskine.

When Carr replied, his voice was low, heavy with regret and accusation. "The same place he had been before the murder. The same place he had left earlier that evening, unseen, to come here to kill your husband, and the same place he returned to, in order to complete his alibi. I have been at pains to point out that no one had a solid alibi for the time of Erskine's murder, and I have done so in order to illuminate the glaring contradiction which emerges as a result. Namely, that there is one person in this room to whom it does not apply. One person in this room, in fact, had an unshakeable alibi for the time of Jacob Erskine's murder."

He had been walking slowly around the back of their chairs, and now, as he stopped speaking, he paused and placed his hands on the shoulders of the murderer of Jacob Erskine.

"Marcus Trevelyan was in the *Duck and Drake* public house from eight o'clock to a little before eleven," he said. "The landlord, Mr Petrie, and his wife, confirm it."

Trevelyan twisted round in his chair. "Which means I cannot have been here shooting Erskine through a cushion."

Carr's face was impassive. "But that is precisely where you were and what you were doing. You went to the public house and seated yourself at your usual table in the corner. There you occupied yourself with crosswords and solitary thought. Both Mr Petrie and his wife confirm it. And yet, I am convinced that a little before nine o'clock, you left the public house, came here, and shot Erskine."

"Not so." Trevelyan had risen from his chair, prompting Mason to take a step forward in readiness for violence. "Are you saying that Petrie and his wife are lying?"

Carr shook his head. "He is telling the truth but lying at the same time."

"What does that mean?" scoffed Trevelyan.

"It was when Mr Edgerton accused me of treating murder like a crossword puzzle that I recalled Mrs Petrie saying that you were struggling with the particular crossword you were tackling that evening. She said that your head was in your hands. The table you usually use is in the far corner of the public house. In the evening, it must be very dark indeed. Now, with the darkness of the corner of the room and with a head partly covered by hands, neither Mr Petrie nor his wife could have seen your face."

"Which means it was someone else," snapped Mason. "An accomplice."

Carr sighed softly. "I'm afraid so. In a crowded bar, it would be possible for Trevelyan to leave the public house without the landlord noticing, and it would be equally possible for someone else to take his place at the corner table whilst he came back here and murdered Erskine. That was why he needed the delay provided to him by the use of the cushion—to give him time to get back to the public house, resume his seat, and allow his accomplice to disappear before the substitution was discovered. The deception was a risk, and the timing had to be perfect. Trevelyan could not afford to be away from the public house for a second longer than was necessary. If the shot had been heard, he may well have become embroiled in the initial commotion of the finding of the body. It was vital that he was back at the public house at the earliest opportunity. Silencing the shot gave him those extra, precious minutes."

"And this accomplice?" asked Mason. "How would they know when to leave the pub? If you're correct, Mr Carr, it wouldn't do for Trevelyan and any confederate to be seen together, so whoever it is must have known when to leave the table in order to allow Trevelyan to return to his seat."

Carr smiled. "As I said, the timing had to be perfect, but you must remember that Trevelyan is a regular visitor to the *Duck and Drake*. He would have had ample opportunity to time the trip between there and the reading room of the Icarus Club, just as he would have had numerous chances to undertake a dress rehearsal of the scheme. The accomplice would wait for that length of time, or a little longer, and then visit the lavatory. Trevelyan would enter the public house again, hidden by the crowd, and make his own way to the lavatory. After a suitable length of time, Trevelyan would then return to his seat and his accomplice would vanish from the public house, again through the crowds, and nobody would suspect any substitution."

Edgerton shifted in his chair. "And both Crane and I were well away from the reading room by the time Trevelyan came back here at around nine o'clock."

Carr bowed his head in agreement. "Nobody would have questioned Trevelyan walking around the club, given that he is a member. It would only seem strange if someone knew that he should have been in the public house. As long as he didn't mention that, he would arouse no suspicion."

"And this accomplice?" asked Crane, his voice hesitant.

Everett Carr's voice was gentle, but filled with regret. "There is only one person it can be."

Sonia Trevelyan let out a small, stifled cry of anguish, like some strained squeal of confession. As her tears began to fall, Trevelyan's expression intensified in its defiance. "I thought you were a friend of ours, Mr Carr. Clearly, I was wrong."

Carr was unimpressed by the tactic, and his eyes blazed with fury. "No! It is you who have deceived me. Our friendship has been broken by you."

Trevelyan held his gaze, his emotions conflicted, but he said nothing more. Carr's glare softened as he looked back to Sonia Trevelyan. When he spoke, his voice was soothing and gentle. "Will you now tell me the truth, dear lady? There is nothing more to fear."

Crane had risen from his chair, his cheeks flushed with shock. "You can't believe that Sonia has anything to do with murder, Mr Carr."

"It is the truth," said Carr in response, his eyes still fixed on Sonia. "Her features are as dark as Marcus', her hair cut short enough to pass for a man, and they are of similar build and height. Across a crowded public house, with the face hidden, it would be hard to detect the substitution. Remember, Mr Petrie had genuinely seen Trevelyan sitting at the table, so he had no cause to think that any switch had occurred. Mr Petrie saw what he expected to see – and what he was intended to see. To that extent, he told the truth."

Crane was still shaking his head. "I can't believe it."

"Because it isn't true," snapped Trevelyan. "I don't know if this is some sort of device to prompt a confession from the actual killer, Carr, but it is clearly not working."

"It is no device," said Carr. "When I first went to visit her, Sonia herself told me that Trevelyan didn't like her being at home alone. If that were true, why would he sit in the *Duck and Drake* for an entire evening instead of being at home with her? The answer to that question is that she was not at home alone. She was in town, assisting him with his alibi."

"She was not," barked Trevelyan.

Carr ignored the denial and began to pace the room. "We suspected that Cyril Parsons was killed because he had seen something or learned something incriminating. He must have had a reason to abandon his duty on that particular night, and I could not accept that it was on account of his sad addiction to drink. If that compulsion had been the cause of his dereliction of duty, he would have left his post on any number of previous occasions, but he never had.

"I could only make sense of Parsons' conduct on that evening by concluding that he had seen something which intrigued or concerned him. *What he had seen was Sonia going to the public house, and he followed her.* He realised at once that it must have been Sonia whom Mr Petrie had pointed out to him, although he could not have known why she had taken the place of Marcus. He must have had an intuition that it was not for an innocent reason, otherwise, he would not have smiled and talked to Mr Petrie about people at the club having something to hide. That instinct was rewarded when Parsons learned that Erskine had been murdered because he immediately made the connection and realised what had happened. When Mr Petrie told Trevelyan and I that Parsons had been in the pub that night and had talked about members of the club having their secrets, Trevelyan recognised at once the danger which Parsons posed."

"I don't know what you're talking about," said Trevelyan.

Carr, as if sensing that he could make no progress with him, turned his attention to Sonia. "Tell me the truth, my dear. I am right, am I not?"

"Don't answer him, Sonia." Trevelyan's voice was like a whip.

Sonia was crying now, her face contorted with torment, her eyes clenched shut as if that would prevent any of the horror of her situation from affecting her. Her lips moved silently, forming voiceless words of no meaning. Carr took her hands in his and entreated her with his eyes to co-operate.

"When I came to see you," he said softly, "you said that the police had treated you and Marcus like animals. It struck me as odd at the time, because there would have been no cause for the police to treat you in that fashion, not so early in the investigation. I see now that your opinion of the interview was tainted by the secret you were carrying. The police were a threat to you only because your complicity in the crime which they were investigating gave you that impression."

But Sonia was shaking her head, despite the tears which were filling her eyes. "I don't know what you want me to say."

"I want you to tell me the truth," pleaded Carr. "If you do, all will be well, I promise you."

"Leave her alone," barked Trevelyan. "Stop badgering her. She has done nothing wrong, and I won't allow you to bully her."

Carr looked back into Sonia's eyes. Behind the tears, he could see her guilt staring back at him, as vibrant and clear as a summer daybreak. He felt his grip on her hand tighten, as if in retaliation against his inability to protect her. His jaw clenched in frustration, knowing that he would be unable to make her speak even if he had the persuasive powers to attempt it. Slowly, she removed her hands from his and shook her head in apology.

Trevelyan took a step forward and helped her to her feet. "Now, Mr Carr, if you don't mind, I think we've had enough of your games. My wife and I are leaving."

"I think not," purred Carr, his dark eyes fastening once more on Trevelyan and glistening with a fierce determination. "You have no wife, sir, and nor have you ever had one."

For the first time, Trevelyan seemed to betray signs of anxiety. "What are you talking about?"

"You and Sonia Trevelyan are not married," said Everett Carr, his glare burning with triumph. *"The young lady whom we believed to be your wife is, in fact, your sister...."*

Chapter Thirty-Six

For a long moment, there was silence. It was not that nobody could think of anything to say, but rather that no words seemed appropriate or sufficient. The revelation had been so immense that any comment coming in its wake would have seemed futile. Trevelyan glared at Carr, his cheeks now paled by shock, and his eyes widened in alarm. All trace of defiance and belligerence had melted into guarded anxiety. Even Sonia's tears had been cut off in her throat by the shock of Carr's words. Carr looked from one to the other of them, waiting for one of them to speak, but no words came.

Finally, Carr himself spoke. His voice was calm, quiet, but no less powerful for it. "Shall we have the truth now?"

Wharton had risen from his chair. "This is all wrong, Carr. We know they are married. They have been for years."

But Carr was shaking his head. "No, colonel. If you think back carefully, you will realise that they never referred to themselves as being married. Only we ever called this lady by the name Mrs Trevelyan. Nether she nor Marcus ever did themselves. The identical surname and their obvious closeness all suggested marriage, but it was a façade. It is not common practice for men to wear wedding rings, yet Trevelyan not only wears one but frequently draws attention to it by turning it around his finger. Once I had begun to suspect the truth about their relationship, that habit of his seemed to me to be a display of emphasis, as if he were anxious to remind people of the marriage and assert the fact of it. The more I thought about it, the more artificial the situation seemed to appear.

258

"It was when I spoke to Mrs Erskine about marital vows being a contract with God that the truth began to dawn on me. Mrs Erskine devoutly believed in those vows, to the extent that she was willing to suffer abuse and violence rather than break them. By contrast, when I spoke to Sonia Trevelyan about the same subject, her attitude was altogether more complacent. The difference in attitude of the two women was so stark as to be obvious: one point of view came from a genuinely married woman, the other from a woman who had never known the true purity and bond of marriage."

"I cannot believe it," stammered Wharton.

"Because it's a lie," barked Trevelyan.

Carr turned back to him. "When you told me about the death of Sonia's father from drink and your own father's accident with a pair of shears, you were talking about the same man. You made the mistake of saying that Sonia had grown up in a village called Church Benham, and Sonia herself had told me that she had lived in Shropshire before you brought her to London. Tracing the village was not difficult, and the violent death of a drunken man in such a close community is still remembered. Especially by the vicar who buried him.

"I have been there, Marcus, and I have spoken to the Reverend Somerset. He told me about the death of a man called Henry Tiverton, who died in an accident in his greenhouse. He told me about the rumours surrounding the death of Tiverton's wife, about his children, about the schoolmistress noticing a change in their behaviour, and about them being sent away after their father had died. He may not recall their names but he will no doubt remember their faces." He paused purposefully, as if to emphasise the importance of his next words. "Church Benham is not the only place I have visited. I have also been to Somerset House."

"What did you find there?" asked Mason.

"It is what I did not find which matters," replied Carr. "It was as I was preparing to leave Church Benham that the immense significance of Somerset House struck me. I had addressed the vicar by name when I said goodbye to him, you see, and the coincidence of his name struck me almost immediately. I found no trace of a marriage between Marcus and Sonia

Trevelyan in the records at Somerset House and, far more fascinatingly, *I found no record of their births.*

"Officially, therefore, Marcus and Sonia Trevelyan do not exist, but Marcus and Sonia Tiverton, the children of Henry and Martha Tiverton certainly do. I have copies of their birth certificates here." He took two folded documents from his inside pocket and handed them to Mason. "As a name, Tiverton is not too far removed from Trevelyan, and the curious coincidence of the circumstances of Henry Tiverton's life and death speaks plainly. He was a drunkard, and he died in a gardening accident. Marcus Trevelyan told me that Sonia's father had died of drink, and his own father had died in an accident with a pair of gardening shears. It was a subtle sleight of hand, and it was cleverly done, since it was largely true—*except for the fact that the man concerned was the same in each case.* If any doubt remains that these two people are brother and sister, the dates of birth of Tiverton's children are the same as those of Marcus and Sonia Trevelyan."

Now, Sonia's tears came freely. Carr looked down at her with a sympathy which was nothing less than profound. "You hinted to me, Sonia, about everything your father had done to you when you were a child, and you told me explicitly that Marcus had saved you from it."

Crane gasped. "She said something similar to me. I didn't think anything of it at the time."

Carr seemed not to have heard. "What happened, Marcus? Did you find your father bleeding to death, the shears in his hands, stained with his blood? Did you let him die, because of what he was doing to your younger sister?"

"I let him die because he was a sick animal," said Trevelyan. "And sick animals must be put out of their misery."

Carr frowned, as if the realisation of what Trevelyan was insinuating was too heavy for his mind to bear. "It wasn't an accident, was it? You murdered him. That is what Sonia meant when she said you saved her. You performed the ultimate act of brotherly protection by removing your father permanently from your lives. And, of course, that explains why you had to pretend to be a married couple."

"Why?" asked Mason.

"They had to distance themselves as much as possible from the events in Church Benham," replied Carr. "A brother and sister called Marcus and Sonia, especially with a connection to that Shropshire village, would surely have raised some suspicion eventually. Anybody looking for a brother and sister would be less likely to take notice of a married couple. It was an effort to separate themselves from their past, whilst remaining close to each other."

"Is it true, Trevelyan?" demanded Mason. "Did you murder your father?"

"I put him down like the filthy, rabid animal that he was," said Trevelyan. "Are you saying he didn't deserve it?"

"I should have realised it, just as Jacob Erskine had realised it," said Carr. "The cool planning of the murder and the daring nature of your alibi should have suggested some sort of previous experience. If you had killed your father when you were a child, it would explain why the schoolmistress detected a change in your behaviour. Henry Tiverton's murder meant that Sonia felt she was in your debt. When you needed help to carry out your plan to kill Erskine, she had the opportunity to pay it back at last."

Sonia had found her voice. "Marcus had saved me from our father. I had to help him save us both from that other hideous, vile man."

Mason had approached them. "Erskine knew about your past?"

It was Carr who replied. "When Trevelyan talked to me about Church Benham, Erskine was there, sitting behind us. We didn't realise it at the time, but he had overheard everything Trevelyan said. It was too much of a coincidence to presume that his story about a man in that village dying in such specific circumstances as an accident with garden shears was not a reference to a man he had known personally."

"Erskine knew Trevelyan's father?" asked Mason.

"He was at school with him, according to Mr Somerset. Erskine knew that Tiverton had two children, which means that, once he made the connection to Tiverton, he would have known that Marcus and Sonia were not a married couple, but brother and sister. He knew the circumstances of old Tiverton's death, and he may even have suspected the truth of it. In his study, Erskine had a painting of a church. In fact, it was the church in Church Benham. I recognised it as soon as I saw it in reality yesterday. Erskine had gone back there to confirm his suspicions, and the vicar told him exactly what he later told me. Your safety and your family secret were both threatened, Marcus, and Jacob Erskine had to die as a result."

Trevelyan lowered himself into his chair and took hold of his sister's hand. "He wrote a note, telling me he wanted to speak about our father. As soon as I read it, I knew how dangerous he was. I couldn't take any risks."

Carr was nodding. "When I asked you and Edgerton whether you believed Erskine capable of blackmail, you had no hesitation in agreeing with the idea. It is obvious to me now that you had a good reason to be so certain about it. You were a direct victim of it."

Trevelyan smiled malignantly, with no trace of penitence in the defiant eyes which glared back at Everett Carr. "Which makes it two poisonous snakes dealt with."

"You feel no remorse at all?" asked Carr.

Trevelyan's eyes blazed. "What remorse should I feel, Mr Carr? How can I feel guilty about ridding our lives of two men who meant us nothing but harm, who brought nothing but pain and suffering to us?"

"They both had a right to live," said Carr.

"They both forfeited that right when they tried to hurt us," snarled Trevelyan. "All I have ever done is protect Sonia, and that is all I will do now. You have no evidence against her, and I refute entirely that she assisted me. I did it alone. I had no accomplice."

He would have said more, but Sonia pressed a finger softly to his lips and calmed him, as a mother might calm a child. "It's all right, Marcus. They know, and it is all over. At last, it is over."

"I won't let you go to prison, Sonia," he whispered into her ear.

"Nothing can prevent that now," she replied. "What they will do to you is much worse. If you can face that with the same courage with which you faced those evil men, I can face prison with equal bravery. I owe you that." She looked up at Carr, her eyes filled with sadness and a pitiable smile on her lips. She rose and held his hands in hers for a brief moment. "Please don't think badly of us, Mr Carr. You have always been so kind to us, I would hate to think of you condemning us now."

"I can make no promises of that kind," said Carr sadly, his voice little more than a whisper.

She bowed her head. "Perhaps if you understood what it was like, knowing my father was downstairs every night, but never knowing whether he was going to come to your room or not. Perhaps if you could understand that fear, that humiliation, you might be able to forgive us."

Carr smiled sadly at her. "It is not for me to forgive you, dear lady. You must learn to forgive yourself before asking anyone else to do so."

She held his gaze for a moment, failing to notice the small tear which ran down from her eyes. Then, curiously, raising herself on her toes, she kissed him lightly on the cheek. He felt his face redden, and he suddenly felt foolish, as if he was on display in some sort of monstrous sideshow. He wanted to be nowhere near the Icarus Club in that moment, perhaps never again in his life, and her kiss seemed to have demonstrated that, like her, the perfection of the club was now tainted by its own secrets and the deaths which arose from them. None of it made sense to him anymore, as if he was seeing it all through a distorted lens. He took a step away from her and lowered his gaze to the floor.

No more words were said. Mason went about his duty with a cool, detached efficiency and, in a matter of a few uncomplicated moments, the guilty were led away from the innocent. Carr remained motionless, his eyes turned downwards, so that he was only briefly aware of both Marcus and Sonia Trevelyan walking away from him. For a few moments, relentlessly bleak, it was as if Carr was alone in the world, with no company other than his own thoughts. At last, his isolation was interrupted by Patrick Crane.

"What will happen to her?" he asked.

"The law will take its course," Carr replied.

Crane frowned. "I thought once that she might have been able to love me, if circumstances had permitted it, but she was always going to be tied to Marcus, wasn't she?"

Carr nodded slowly. "He had saved her from Henry Tiverton's abuse, and he had protected her ever since. She was bound to him. No matter who else she may have met and could have loved, she belonged to Marcus."

Crane sighed heavily. "She told me about her father, you know. I thought she was confiding in me. She wasn't, was she?" Carr did not reply, so Crane was forced to answer his own question. "She was trying to deflect attention away from Trevelyan by focusing on the similarity in nature between her father and Erskine, so that I would feel sorry for her and not pry any further."

"I fear you may be correct," murmured Carr at last.

"She told me that she had made her choice. I thought she meant marriage, but she didn't. She meant her choice to stay with Trevelyan."

Carr nodded. "Even if it meant living without the opportunity of happiness with someone else."

Crane caught the implication, but he did not respond to it. "Hard not to feel some compassion towards them, I suppose, no matter what they have done."

"What their father did has had lasting consequences, certainly. It corrupted them as children, and they have never been free from it."

Crane nodded, but his expression was grave. "Does it excuse what they did?"

Carr gave a slight shrug of the shoulders. "Such questions are the domain of a philosopher or a priest, my friend. As a matter of law, the answer is more certain. It is done now. We must allow the law to proceed. Perhaps," he added, forcing a smile which he felt was appropriate rather than genuine, "we might indulge ourselves in a drink. It has been an emotional evening."

He received no argument. Together, the small group of people who, for a time, had been under the dark cloak of suspicion slowly made their way out of a room in which the foul but tragic stench of death still seemed to linger.

Chapter Thirty-Seven

It was three days later when Carr returned to the Icarus Club. He had heard nothing from either Marcus or Sonia Trevelyan, although he had hardly expected to do so. He had not seen Mason in the previous few days either, and he assumed that the process of prosecution of the crimes would be underway. Mason and his officers would be much involved with the necessary work.

He found Leonard Faraday and Hector Wharton in the library, sitting together with glasses of wine. Carr declined the offer of a glass, but he accepted the seat between them.

"Ronald Edgerton has resigned from the club," said Faraday. "I believe he has also stood down from the Bar."

"So I have heard," said Carr. "I was sure he would do the right thing in the end."

Wharton was smiling. "You look as if that does not come as too much of a surprise, Carr."

"I doubt he felt he had any choice. Given how he has behaved, his profession would not welcome him for much longer."

"Edgerton doesn't strike me as a man who gives up that easily," said Faraday.

"Perhaps he had some persuasion," said Wharton, his eyes on Carr. If he anticipated any response, he was to be disappointed.

Faraday sipped at his wine. "I heard that Patrick Crane has been to visit Sonia Trevelyan in Holloway."

To this, however, Carr did respond, his eyebrow arching in interest. "Did she agree to that?"

"Yes, I believe so."

Carr seemed relieved by the news. "I am pleased to hear it. When she is released from prison, she will need stability and kindness. Young Crane will be able and willing to offer both."

Wharton clicked his tongue. "I still can't believe any of it. God knows, Erskine was vile enough, but their father seems to have been ten times the villain."

"I think we have given enough thought to Henry Tiverton," said Carr, "and everything his actions have caused."

"I won't argue with that," said Faraday. "Do you suppose the club will survive all this?"

Carr nodded. "I have no doubt of it."

"It is entirely in our hands," answered Wharton. "Personally, I think the sooner we put it all behind us, the better."

Carr found it difficult to argue, but he did not say so. "How is Mrs Erskine?"

Wharton sighed gently. "She is still affected by it all, of course. She didn't love Erskine anymore, but he was a major part of her life for many years. Strange how one can remain attached to a part of life which no longer gives one any pleasure or happiness."

"Some of us are compelled to hope that our circumstances will change," said Carr. "We cling to that belief, even when it has no possibility of being realised. Will you attend Erskine's funeral, colonel?"

Wharton nodded. "For Margaret's sake, naturally."

"And afterwards?"

"Who can say? Marriage, perhaps, after a suitable period." His tone suggested that an acceptance of any such proposal was more than a hope, if not a foregone conclusion. "I owe you something of an apology, Carr. For the way I've spoken to you recently."

Carr dismissed the comment. "Think nothing of it, colonel. All our emotions have been in turmoil."

Wharton lowered his gaze. "Nevertheless, I realise how offensive I was.

Perhaps I've learned something about myself because of everything which has happened. I understand now that I can be overbearing. And possessive," he added quietly. It was not difficult for Carr to trace the influence of Margaret Erskine in the apology.

Faraday was curious. "Was it always your intention to act as detective in this matter?"

"No." Carr shook his head, smiling briefly. "I have no desire to be a detective of any kind."

"That's not the impression you give," smiled Faraday.

Carr was unrepentant. "Sometimes, one is forced to act for the best, even if it is against one's own instincts and desires."

Wharton checked his watch and rose from his seat. "You will excuse me, I am sure. I have some business to attend to. Goodbye for now, Carr. I hope you will remain a regular feature of the Icarus Club. You are a decent fellow."

Carr accepted the hand which was offered, but he made no verbal reply. He watched Wharton walk away and disappear into the corridor. After a moment, he turned in his chair and faced Faraday. "I hope I was not interrupting something between you?"

Faraday smiled. "Wharton felt the need to express his indifference at my friendship with Vincent. I think he felt more comforted by his assurances than I did."

Carr's eyes glittered. "He means well, but he is often incapable of finding the most appropriate words. Still, perhaps we can take it for granted that he has learned something about love and tolerance."

"I suppose I have no right to ask for his respect and acceptance. Men like Vincent and I have to be discreet. More so than we have been during this horror."

Carr stared intently at Faraday. "You are correct in what you say, my dear friend, but you are entitled to happiness. It is not for any others to rob you of that privilege."

"Society is not as tolerant as you, Carr."

"It does not have to be. You need your personal contentment more than you need society's restrictions."

"Wharton is right, Carr. You are a decent fellow." Faraday smiled in such a way as to suggest that the conversation was concluded. "I thought you should know, incidentally, that Vincent has confessed to stealing the money from my safe. It wasn't to pay Erskine his blackmail demand, as you said."

Carr nodded. "Perhaps a more dangerous debt?"

Faraday nodded. "I'm ashamed to say so."

"Was it sufficient?"

"I'm afraid not. I had to give him more money to clear it."

Carr smiled. "Then perhaps it is you who is the most decent fellow of all."

Faraday blushed. "I've sent Vincent away for a time. To Venice, as it happens. I am hoping that it will aid his attempts to change his life."

"And when he returns?"

Faraday shrugged. "We shall see."

"The very fact that he has gone on the trip suggests a willingness in him to change," observed Carr. "He should be given credit for that, at least."

"Of course. I am hopeful, I must confess."

"Perhaps we should toast that optimism," smiled Carr, ordering another glass for Faraday and a small one for himself. They stayed talking together for a little while longer before Carr made his excuses and left. He walked down the staircase into the main foyer and stepped through the ornate doors of the Icarus Club. For a moment, he remained motionless on the steps where Cyril Parsons once stood on duty. The memories of the last week burned in Carr's mind. The realisation that Erskine, Parsons, and Trevelyan would never be seen in the club again now seemed portentously unsettling. Until that moment, Carr had been focused on finding out what had happened, but with the terrible bleakness of the truth unveiled, he was left only with the aftermath of murder. Wharton had hoped that it would be put behind them and, in the initial optimism of the knowledge that the horror was over, it was easy to believe that it could be forgotten. But Carr began to fear that murder was never truly resolved, that there were never any easy answers to those questions which really mattered about why one person harms or defiles another, or what creates in some people the capacity to kill. Perhaps, Carr wondered, there were only certain questions which could be answered and some others whose solutions would never come to light.

Slowly, he tended to his moustache and beard with the small brush he carried in his waistcoat pocket, and he tipped his hat to the new doorman. At last, with a deep and revitalising breath of the autumnal afternoon air, Everett Carr turned on his heel and walked away from those lingering ghosts of murder which he feared might haunt the Icarus Club for many months to come.

About the Author

As a lifelong aficionado and expert on Sherlock Holmes, Matthew Booth is the author of several books and short stories about the famous detective. He wrote a number of scripts for a Holmes radio series produced by Jim French Productions in Seattle, as well as creating his own series about a disgraced former barrister investigating crimes for the same production company.

He is the creator of Everett Carr, an amateur sleuth in the traditional mould, who appears in his debut investigation in the book, *A Talent for Murder*, a traditional whodunit, which offers a contemporary twist on the format.

An expert in crime and supernatural fiction, Matthew has provided a number of academic talks on such subjects as Sherlock Holmes, the works of Agatha Christie, crime fiction, Count Dracula, and the facts and theories concerning the crimes of Jack the Ripper.

He is a member of the Crime Writers' Association and is the editor of its monthly magazine, *Red Herrings*. He lives with his wife in Manchester, England.

SOCIAL MEDIA HANDLES: